the last secret you'll ever keep

also by laurie faria stolarz

Blue Is for Nightmares
White Is for Magic
Silver Is for Secrets
Red Is for Remembrance
Black Is for Beginnings
Bleed
Project 17
Deadly Little Secret
Deadly Little Lies
Deadly Little Games
Deadly Little Voices
Deadly Little Lessons
Welcome to the Dark House
Return to the Dark House
Shutter
Jane Anonymous

laurie faria
stolarz

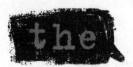the

last

secret

you'll

ever

keep

WEDNESDAY BOOKS
NEW YORK

First published in the United States by Wednesday Books, an imprint of St. Martin's
Publishing Group

www.wednesdaybooks.com

Library of Congress Cataloging-in-Publication Data

Names: Stolarz, Laurie Faria, 1972– author.
Title: The last secret you'll ever keep / Laurie Faria Stolarz.
Other titles: Last secret you will ever keep
Description: First edition. | New York : Wednesday Books, 2021.
Identifiers: LCCN 2020040973 | ISBN 9781250303738 (hardcover) |
    ISBN 9781250303752 (ebook)
Subjects: CYAC: Online chat groups—Fiction. | Kidnapping—Fiction. |
    Impersonation—Fiction. | Survival—Fiction. | Guilt—Fiction. |
    Suspense fiction.
Classification: LCC PZ7.S8757 Las 2021 | DDC [Fic]—dc23
LC record available at https://lccn.loc.gov/2020040973

ISBN 978-1-250-30373-8 (hardcover)
ISBN 978-1-250-30375-2 (ebook)

Our books may be purchased in bulk for promotional, educational, or
business use. Please contact your local bookseller or the Macmillan Corporate and
Premium Sales Department at 1-800-221-7945, extension 5442, or by email at
MacmillanSpecialMarkets@macmillan.com.

First Edition: 2021

10 9 8 7 6 5 4 3 2 1

the last secret you'll ever keep

NOW

1

I've learned some things.

Like that dirt comes in a variety of shades: tan, amber, silver, blue . . . Like that when you claw at it long enough, you'll see these colors and wonder how you never noticed how striking dirt can be, with its pearly flecks of granite and residual bits of mica.

I've learned that the ruddier shades (the reds and the oranges) can conjure up memories of childhood pottery classes—Mommy and me making pinch pots and coil vases—but that the brain only allows such memories for an instant before zapping them away, reminding you where you are.

When you're surrounded by dirt, when it forms the walls around you and the floor beneath your feet, you'll feel the individual granules pushing through your skin, making everything itch, and you'll taste mouthfuls of it, not knowing how it got there: on your tongue, at the back of your throat, and between your teeth.

You'll be so hungry, so depleted of energy, having spent so much time underground. You'll chew the inside of your cheek and search your mouth for food—a lingering popcorn kernel casing or a grain of rice stuck in the crevices of your gums—before curling up into a ball and noticing for the first time how hard dirt can be, like a marble slab, making every bone ache.

You'll smell the dirt too. The scent is different from soil, not nearly as sweet or earthy. Dirt is arid, depleted of moisture, and so it smells like death—a sour, rotten stench.

You'll think a lot about death, racking your brain, trying to remember facts from bio class. How long can one go without water? What happens to the body upon complete dehydration? Is it one of the worst ways to die?

You'll replay the details from the night you got here—over and over again—tormented as to how it happened and what you could've done differently.

Taken another path home?

Called a cab?

Not returned the spare house key to the planter outside?

Because being here is your fault, after all—your stupidity, the result of not following everything you'd learned about safety and defense.

Screaming is a defense, and you'll do a lot of that. You'll also punch the walls, as if you could ever break them down.

Exhausted, you'll find yourself in a fetal position, sucking your thumbs, hoping doing so will produce a mouthful of saliva, the way it did when you were little, all over your pillow. But instead the roof of your mouth will bleed from reaching too far and scraping too hard. Surprisingly, the taste will come as a welcome distraction. You'll tell yourself: There's iron in this blood, and fat in the oil in your hair, as if iron and fat could ever save anyone from a lack of food and water.

Water.

You'll crave it like you've never craved anything, the way lions crave meat, picturing gallon jugs and fresh trout streams. Meanwhile, your mouth will be dry like a desert, like the dirt inside a barren well. And your tongue will feel foreign—too big for your mouth, too swollen to get enough air.

You'll pray for rain to come. And when it finally does, you'll try to catch it in your hands and collect as much as you can before splashing it into your sandpaper mouth, not caring that it's littered with dirt, because you will be too—so damned dirty.

I've felt dirt in my eyes—the scratch, the burn, the constant blur—so perpetual I'd almost forgotten what it was like to see clearly. And I know how it feels inside the ears—so deep you can practically hear it: the sound of dirt.

The crackle of madness.

I've learned about madness too.

Hospital beds.

And doctors' meds.

And "Be a good girl."

"Don't feel so much."

"She's feeling too little."

"I'm not really sure how well she's feeling today."

I've learned to "feel" whatever the people with the name badges say I'm supposed to, because that's what's "sane."

I'm not insane, but I've been diagnosed with some of Insanity's cellmates—Delusional, Depressed, Defiant, and Paranoid—and lost people I thought were my friends.

Thank god for Jane. Saint Jane is what I call her, because she's the one who created the Jane Anonymous website, a place where victims of crime-related trauma can chat with one another and share their experiences.

I discovered the site about a month ago, at the library where I work. The words VICTIMS UNITED screamed at me from a bathroom wall poster:

VICTIMS UNITED

Looking for a safe space to share your honest truth,
without judgment,
regardless of how unpopular that truth might be?
Come chat with us.
We're here for you.
Twenty-four hours a day, seven days a week.
www.JaneAnonymous.com
#JaneAnonymous #VictimToVictor #OnlyTheHonestSurvive

I logged on that very night and have been chatting ever since. The people on the site "listen" without judgment and offer advice and consolation. The site also provides a journaling feature because "Jane Anonymous," the site's creator, firmly believes in writing about one's trauma as a therapeutic means of processing it. Members can write, save, customize, and tag entries, then choose to leave them open (for others to read) or locked up (for privacy).

In her memoir, "Jane" documents her time in captivity and the months after she got out. I'm going to do the same, starting with this entry—not that I need a website to journal, but it's kind of nice knowing there's a whole community of survivors journaling along with me. I've read so many of their stories. Now it's time I wrote mine.

THEN

2

I knew better.

Because my parents had trained me well. A year of cardio kick-boxing, two years of tae kwon do, summer camps for self-defense, a purple belt in Brazilian jiu-jitsu . . .

And that was just the beginning.

As soon as I'd turned double-digits, my parents warned me of the hazards that could happen with a loss of inhibitions. Whenever some poor, pathetic girl got something slipped into her drink at a drunken keg party and wound up as *News at Eleven,* I got an hour-long lecture about personal vigilance and looking out for my friends. Even my thirteenth birthday: while most of the other girls got gift certificates for piercings and highlights, my present included a can of pepper spray and a six-month voucher to work with a personal trainer.

But my parents didn't get it. I would *never* become a cliché. I wasn't anything like those "poor, pathetic girls."

Or so I believed.

But I believed a lot of things back then that have since proven untrue. One of my biggest lessons: There's no such thing as a "poor, pathetic girl."

Unless, of course, you're talking about me.

It started with a party.

The Theta Epsilon sisters were hosting a sorority mixer on the Friday before spring vacation, and my friend Jessie's older sister, the acting sorority president, had given Jessie and me the green light to go.

"Consider this an early graduation gift for the both of us," Jessie said.

Except I still had another year of high school. I'd stayed back in middle school, after the world as I'd known it had gone up in flames. My guidance counselor said that giving myself extra time would translate into less stress and more healing. But repeating my eighth-grade year, not advancing with my friends . . . It just made everything worse.

Jessie flashed me her phone screen; her sister's big, fat YES was typed across it. "You can thank me later."

I thanked her then, on the spot, because I really wanted to go. The high school that Jessie and I attended didn't exactly have the vibrant social scene that you read about in books or see on TV. To out-of-towners, the Tremont Academy name conjured up images of plaid school uniforms and ivy-covered buildings. But to everyone else, we were Emo students—and for good reason. TrEMOnt prided itself on catering to those with "social and emotional challenges." Long story short: There wasn't much socializing that went on outside our therapeutically structured school day, so the green light to this college party . . .

It was a really big deal.

I dressed accordingly, in a sleeveless top, a pair of dark-washed jeans, and the wedges I'd been coveting at Dress Me Up; they'd finally gone on sale.

"You look amazing," Jessie said as we headed up the walkway to the sorority house. "What I wouldn't give to have your killer golden highlights and sun-kissed skin."

"You look great too," I told her. "I love that dress." A short black number, paired with strappy heels.

"Fingers crossed my sister lets us crash here tonight."

"Wait, what do you mean?"

"I mean, wouldn't it be fun to spend a night or three, get a preview of what college life will be like?"

Jessie didn't even give me a chance to respond. Instead, she stepped up to the door, paid the five-dollar cover charge, and led me inside. The Theta Epsilon house looked practically like a mansion with its marble-tiled floors; fancy columns and pillars; and high, vaulted ceilings. Still, despite the size, the place was packed that night.

Jessie and I maneuvered among clusters of people until we got to a makeshift bar: two bookcases pushed together. One of the Epsilon sisters stood behind it, guarding the punch bowl. She ladled us cups full of sparkling purple punch, and Jessie and I made a toast.

"To never looking back." Jessie tapped her cup against mine.

I took a sip. It tasted a little like freedom—like something I wanted to guzzle from a jug, which prompted me to ask the question: "Do you really think your sister will let us crash here tonight?"

At the same moment, Jessie's phone went off. She checked the screen. "Speak of the devil. That's her. She needs my help upstairs. Are you good for a sec? Or do you want to come?"

"I'm good."

"Okay. I'll be right back."

After she went off, I sent my aunt a text: I may stay over at Jessie's sister's tonight. Then I pocketed my phone and waited like a wallflower, taking more of the party in: the dart game in the corner, the drunk girls playing hopscotch (using a lipstick to draw the squares), and a group of boys watching soccer on a big-screen TV. Rule number one on my parents' list of survival tips: *Be aware of your surroundings. Make a mental checklist of all you see.*

But nothing appeared off. So why couldn't I relax? My neck itched. My feet were already aching.

I moved to the staircase and gazed up the steps. The smell of something sweet hung heavy in the air, reminding me of candy canes. I took out my phone and sent Jessie a text: Where are you?

Meanwhile, music pounded—so loud and hard, I could feel it in my ribs; it bounced off the bones of my skull. The lead singer sounded like he was gagging on a chicken bone.

"Looking for someone?" a male voice asked from behind.

I whirled around, startled by how good looking the guy was: tall, with rumpled dark hair; deep blue eyes, framed by artsy black glasses; and just the right amount of facial scruff. I forced myself from gawking by glancing away toward the hopscotch-playing girls. "I'm looking for a friend," I told him, shouting over the music. "She went upstairs."

"Do you need some help finding her?"

My phone vibrated with a text—from Jessie: Im upstairs helping Sarah and her friend with a party game. Be down soon. Or come join. Third door on the right . . . Or left? Lol!

"All okay?" the guy asked.

"It's fine. I mean, she is, rather."

"You sure?" He squinted as though examining me under a scope. "Because I'm pretty much an expert in finding people."

"Oh yeah?" I smiled, unable to bite it back.

He smiled too, gazing at my mouth, making my face heat up. "I'm Garret, by the way." He extended his hand for a shake.

"Terra." I shook his hand.

"And are you in TE?"

It took me a beat to decipher the initials: TE . . . A girl on the staircase had the Greek sorority letters embroidered across her sweatshirt. "Not exactly."

"One of the pledges, then?"

"That depends." I took a sip. *What was a pledge?*

Garret shot me a suspicious grin just as someone bumped him from behind, almost spilling punch all over his shirt. "I think we're in the line of traffic here." He took a step back as though about to turn away, but then motioned to a couple of chairs by a wood-burning stove. "Want to go sit?"

Like a reflex, my body steeled. But I really wanted to talk to him more, so I gave a slight nod.

We sat down, opposite each other, a few feet from the hearth.

"So, how come I haven't seen you around before?" he asked.

"Maybe you haven't been looking."

"Right . . ." He smirked. "I'm pretty sure I would've noticed you." He peeked at my hands.

I couldn't stop scratching. My palms were so itchy. "Do you live on campus?"

"I used to, but now I rent a place with a couple of friends. They're here tonight too." He peered around, searching the throngs of people.

I searched too, still wondering about Jessie. I sent her another text: All still ok???

While I awaited her response, Garret and I continued to talk, everything from favorite places to eat—Taco Tango for him and Fork & Table for me—to the classes he was taking (mostly criminal justice and forensic science courses). He wanted to be a cop. I wanted to talk to him all night.

"I'm really glad I decided to come to this," he said. "I wasn't going to, but my philosophy professor talked me into it."

"Your philosophy professor knows about sorority parties?"

"Not exactly." He grinned some more. "But we had a discussion in class about taking chances, going outside one's comfort zone."

"Your comfort zone doesn't include sorority parties, I assume."

"Not typically. I'm more of a sports-bar kind of guy. Have you taken any of Professor LeDuc's philosophy classes?"

"I can't say I have."

"He talks a lot about conscious choice—how sometimes even the seemingly simplest ones can change the whole trajectory of our lives."

"Sounds pretty intense."

"But it's also kind of true, when you think about it."

"So, if I'd decided to have spaghetti over quesadillas for lunch today, my life would be totally different?"

"Maybe not." His face turned pink. "It's sort of hard to explain, but it made sense when he talked about it in class."

"Well, I have my own philosophy. I think that everyone we meet—from the purest of hearts to the darkest of souls—crosses our path for a reason."

"Talk about intense. Does that philosophy apply to here, now? Meeting me, that is?"

"Definitely," I said, feeling my face pinken too.

"That's pretty deep."

"No philosophy course required."

"So then where do you get your wisdom?"

"Life school." *A.k.a. years of listening to people of all sorts (specialists, strangers, friends, my aunt . . .) telling me the way it is and how I should think.* "I believe we're here to learn lessons—to get closer and more prepared for whatever the big thing is."

"What do *you* think that big thing is?"

"I'm still working on that one."

"So, the teacher who made me sit in the corner in the second grade," he continued. "That dark soul . . . What did I learn from him?"

"The abuse of power, maybe."

"And the sixth-grade bully who kicked me off my bike more times than I could count?"

"Maybe he taught you about compassion."

"And how about right now?" He leaned slightly forward and gazed, once again, at my mouth. "Are you learning anything from me?"

I could smell the spearmint on his breath, and could feel the pounding inside my chest—a deep and rhythmic throbbing that made my pulse race.

My phone pulsed too, vibrating against my thigh. A reminder to take my meds. An icon of a pill bottle rolling its eyes popped up on the screen. I quickly turned it over. How was it possible that two hours had passed?

"Is everything okay?" Garret asked.

"It is. It's just . . . I should probably go find my friend." I stood up just as Jessie stumbled in my direction.

Her eyes looked glassy. She was sucking a lollipop. "I may've had a little too much to drink." She laughed. "But you'll be proud of me: I gave my keys to some girl. In hindsight, I probably should've given them to you, but she said she needed a car, and I really wanted to help. Anyway, I'm sleeping here, in my sister's room."

"Wait, what?" My head fuzzed.

"I'm really sorry." She suckled. "I tried to score you a place to crash, but there are zero spare beds and I've already claimed the futon."

"Hey, wait. *I* can drive you home," Garret offered. "Both of you, actually. Are you guys at the main campus?"

"Try again." Jessie laughed. "We're Emo students."

"Emo?" Garret's face scrunched. He didn't get it.

I wasn't about to explain it.

"Seriously, I don't mind at all," he said.

Part of me was tempted to take him up on the offer. But I knew better; rule number two on my parents' list of survival tips: *Don't go off with anyone you don't know (and only half trust those you do).* "Thank you anyway, but I can call someone," I told him.

"Okay, but I'm right here." He touched my forearm—a gentle squeeze.

I felt it in my thighs. "No, really. I'll be fine," I insisted.

But he insisted too. "I'll wait with you, then. Until someone picks you up."

I wanted to say yes, but I also wanted a moment. The air felt suddenly thick. I couldn't get a solid breath. "I'm going to find a bathroom."

I turned away and headed back through the kitchen. The

bathroom was around the corner. And I really meant to use it—to take my meds, to give myself a pause. But on impulse, I passed it and went out the patio doors.

It felt better outside—calmer, cooler, way less stifling. I told myself, *I'll just take a second to breathe. I'll only need a minute to process.*

But before I knew it, I was out on the street, calling my aunt. It went straight to voice mail, which was really no surprise. My aunt was working until six that morning: the overnight shift. It's her job to stick people with needles, as an IV nurse. But even if I'd wanted to leave her a message, her mailbox was already full.

I called my friend Felix next, a fellow Emo. He'd recently gotten his license.

Felix picked up on the first ring. "Hey, Terra Train. Aren't you the night owl? Calling me after one . . . ? Please tell me you're doing something scandalous and that you can send me a pic."

"Not quite."

"Just the audio, then?"

"Listen, I know it's late, but can you come pick me up?"

"On my magical broomstick? I don't have a car, remember?"

"Can you borrow your stepdad's?"

"Why? Is everything okay?"

"I wouldn't be calling at this hour if it were."

"Where are you?"

"Jordan Road, not far from the college. I was at a party, but Jessie ditched me."

"How many times do I have to tell you not to hang out with that psycho-train? You know she's a compulsive liar, right? All that crap about partying with the royals and her family's private jet . . ."

"Do you think you can come get me?"

"That bad?"

"The worst."

"Okay, um, *maybe*? Give me five minutes, and I'll see what I can do. I'll call you back."

We hung up, and I started walking, trying to focus on the road and not the shortness of my breath or the tearing of my heels in my stupid wedges. I hated them now. I hated Jessie too. And with each step I took away from the party, I hated myself more and more—for ditching Garret, for not saying goodbye. It was too late to go back now.

Cars drove by. Some guy honked his horn. Another guy rolled down his window, stuck his head out, and asked me for my fee.

A VW van slowed down as it passed. I held up my phone and snapped a shot of the license plate, just in case. My parents had taught me that too—rule number three: Always have your phone ready—to make a call, to take a pic . . .

What was taking Felix so long?

I crossed the street and turned a corner onto a quiet, narrow road. Trees lined it on both sides, making it seem even darker. There weren't nearly enough streetlights. A lone one at the end blinked a bunch of times, shining over an old car with a boxy hood.

I moved closer, just as a car door slammed. I stopped short and peered behind me. A prickly sensation crawled over my skin.

Footsteps began in my direction—a scuffing sound, like rubber-soled shoes against the gravel. I reached into my purse, dug into my card case, and felt for the card with the sharpest edge (a trick I'd learned in self-defense class).

A porch light shone a few doors down. I sped up, heading toward it. The person behind me sped up too.

Should I cross the street?

Or call for help?

Or knock on someone's door?

I clenched my phone and woke it up.

"Excuse me?" a male voice called from behind. "I think you may have dropped something."

I started to run, rounding a corner, cutting between two houses and through an open, grassy area.

What was this? A public park? A private field? And what was I doing in a secluded area? Like some stupid cliché.

Tall, massive trees fenced me in on both sides. Should I use my flashlight, or was I safer in the dark, camouflaged by the night?

A stick broke somewhere behind me. I quickened my pace and looked down at my keypad, just as a text came in from Jessie: a drunk emoji, complete with a cockeyed expression, along with a message: Where are you???? My sister said you can crash here too #score

I accidently clicked the message, my fingers trembling, my pulse racing.

And then, out of nowhere . . .

Bam.

Whomp.

I fell to the ground, landing with a hard, heavy smack. My legs splayed open. My card went flying.

"I'm so sorry," some guy said.

My world whirred.

The guy was dressed in black; tiny light reflectors accented his clothes: his pants, his shirt, his hat.

I sat up just as the guy extended a hand to help me up.

"I thought you were going to the right, but then you swerved left," he said. "It's so dark."

And so cold.

Plus, I couldn't stop shaking. Even my teeth chattered.

The guy's eyes narrowed; they were pale blue. His fingers looked exceptionally long, covered by light-reflector gloves. "You really shouldn't be out here alone at this hour."

I scooched away and got up on my own. Where was my card?

His gaze traveled down my legs toward my stupid shoes. "Are you sure you're okay? Do you want me to call someone for you? Or walk you back to the main street?"

Back? How had he known I'd come from the main road? I shook my head and pressed my phone on again.

"Here," he said, shining his flashlight over my Emo ID, just a few inches from his feet (gray running sneakers, the New Balance brand, with a thick white tread). He picked it up and handed it to me.

I hesitated before defying yet another one of my parents' rules—this time about never allowing a stranger to hand me anything. I took the card and secured it in my grip, imagining it like a blade.

"Okay, well, right through there." He nodded toward a path, then pointed his light in the same direction. "Straight ahead . . . It's Maple Street."

I kept focused on his posture. His shoulders were back. His stance was guarded. His feet were set about a foot apart. Predators normally inch forward, commanding space while assessing trust. It appeared he'd actually taken a step back.

Another stick broke from somewhere behind us. His gaze followed.

"Be careful out here," he said before moving on. He started running again.

So did I.

My flashlight shining, I darted for the path, able to see the familiar fluorescent light of the Lightning Gas Station: the golden bolt.

When at last I'd made it, I stood away from the pumps to try phoning my aunt again, on the off chance she might pick up. No dice.

I continued forward. A mini-mart stood up ahead, across the street. I hobbled toward it, tempted to remove my shoes. I'd be faster with bare feet. I started to cross the road just as the VW-van-from-before came screeching around the corner, straight in my direction, stunning me still. Did he see me? Or was it too dark? Did he notice the flashlight beam?

A loud, blaring siren sounded then. The van's horn. The driver wasn't slowing down. He was coming straight for me. The headlights flashed, blinding me, telling me I needed to move.

I lurched forward, diving onto the sidewalk, landing on my forearms, peeling free the top layer of skin. Still, the van continued down the street, screeching around a corner.

I got up and continued to the convenience store, only to discover the CLOSED sign hanging on the door. Meanwhile, blood dripped down the length of my forearms. Dirt tattooed my skin. I sat on a bench, trying to hold it all together. Anxiety walloped inside my heart, cinching my lungs, stealing my breath.

Finally, my phone went off.

Felix: "I'm really sorry, Terra, but I can't find my stepdad's keys. I'm thinking they're in his bedroom, in one of his pockets, probably, but he and my mom are currently occupied—draw your own conclusions—and I can't exactly risk a lifetime of damaging images I won't ever be able to erase. But where are you? I'll take my bike."

I stood up, trying to picture the tension inside my chest like a ball of ice that gets smaller with each breath.

"Terra?"

"Don't worry about it."

"Are you sure? Where are you, even?"

"Not far now. I'll be home soon enough." Two more streets, plus up one hill, then just over a bridge. "I'm about twenty minutes away."

"How about Uber-ing home, just this once?"

"You know I won't."

"It's no different from a cab."

"I don't do cabs either. I'm just going to walk."

"Okay, so pretend I'm walking with you. Talk to me until you get home. How was your night?"

A wheeze escaped from my throat. "I can't right now."

"Talking and walking, I get it. In fact, I get winded just thinking about it. So, how about I tell you about my night?"

"Sure. Sounds good."

"Quite the contrary, not good at all—unless you consider whining, moody, cod-craving pregger-cats endearing."

I'd never been so happy—or willing—to hear about Felix's feline dilemmas (his mother was a breeder of the Persian variety). About fifteen minutes—and three angry cat stories—later, I finally arrived home to my aunt's house. I snagged the key from the planter on the stoop and unlocked the door.

"You there?" Felix asked.

"Here," I said, tossing the key back and locking up behind me. "Better?"

"Much." I let out a breath. "I seriously owe you one."

"How about your vintage Gucci shades? They look way better on me anyway."

"I'll call you tomorrow. Thanks again." I clicked the phone off and peered outside, from behind the curtain, unable to shake the gnawing sensation of being watched.

But the street looked quiet.

And everyone's lights were off.

It's a peaceful night, I told myself. The purply sky was punctuated by the sliver of a yellow moon and a sprinkling of stars. Had my father been by my side, he'd have told me a sky that color meant the following day was sure to be beautiful.

Unfortunately, I'd never find out.

3

I wake up early and go downstairs. My aunt is already up, dressed in her running gear. She places a bowl of oatmeal in front of me, at the kitchen table.

"What are your plans for today?" she asks.

"School stuff," I lie. I'm taking online classes to earn my GED.

"You should get out for a walk. It's a beautiful day." She downs a shot of wheatgrass, straight from the juicer.

I'm actually planning to walk—a five-mile trek through Hayberry Park—but she doesn't need to know that.

"How's school going anyway?" she asks.

The real answer: *I'm failing history, and I got a 58 on my most recent geometry exam.* What I actually say: "It's going pretty well."

"Nice." She nods. "The way you've been working so hard, trying to turn things around . . . Your parents would be proud."

Correction: My parents would never buy a bit of this BS. They also would've believed me six months ago, when I came home covered in dirt and needing stronger meds.

I force a bite of oatmeal: steel-cut oats, soaked overnight in almond milk, and freshly ground flaxseed. My aunt is a health nut. *Clean body, clean mind.* There's no place for my dirty, pill-popping self.

I pour a layer of maple syrup over the oatmeal, much to Aunt

Dessa's distaste. I can see the irritation twitching on her lip. To her, maple syrup is the devil's food, right up there with sugar, flour, and hydrogenated oil. To me, it's holy water because it reminds me of my mother.

"Aren't you going to have some?" I ask her.

My aunt pushes in her chair, even though she never sat; the legs make a scratching sound against the floor. "I'm going to head out for my run, but I'll be back in an hour, okay?"

She pokes her earbuds in before I can respond, then forces a smile—the same off-centered grin as my mother's. My aunt Dessa looks a lot like my mother too—same honey-colored hair, same wide brown eyes and pointed chin. Even her voice sounds similar: delicate, like tinkling wind chimes. Sometimes, when I hear her talking on her cell, I'll linger a few seconds, imagining it's my mother's voice, that Mom's still here with me.

Other times, I'll pretend it's my dad's coffee cup on the table, that he just stepped away for a second, to answer an email, to change his shirt. *He'll be right back,* I tell myself.

After my aunt leaves, I retreat to my room, wishing my parents were here for real. Five years ago, I lost them in a blaze. And for the eight days that followed, I refused to speak a word. I slept at the foot of my aunt's bed, two towns away, cuddled up with a bottle of maple syrup, while the smoke rose up within me. I could taste it in my mouth; it burned my tongue and scalded my will to live.

Sometimes I remember random details from the night they died, like the pink pajama bottoms I wore. And the root beer floats Mom and I had made earlier that evening. Plus, the word problems Dad had helped me with, including the one about train stops and gallons of fuel that neither of us could figure out.

I remember sounds too: the loud, hard crack that finally woke me up; the shattering of glass; and the pleading wails. So much screaming. But I'd been deep in sleep; my brain had registered the wails as part of a dream.

A burning-rubber scent filled the room. Clouds of smoke filtered through the space at the bottom of the door. I jumped out of bed and flicked the light switch.

But nothing happened.

The switch wasn't working.

And meanwhile, the wailing continued. It took me a beat to realize it was my mother's voice: my mother's screams.

I heard my father shout, *Terra, can you open your bedroom door?*

Where was he?

At the end of the hall?

I tried my bedroom doorknob as he continued to yell. The metal seared my skin, radiated to my heart. Smoke filtered through the shiny grain, turning the panel black. I stepped back, just as another cracking sounded.

The house was coming apart.

My head was caving in.

"Dad?" I called.

He didn't answer.

I grabbed a sweatshirt and used it as a makeshift glove to try the knob again. But it was still too hot. And the air was way too thick. I brought the sweatshirt to my face to keep from hacking up. But I couldn't stop wheezing. The burning-tire smell seeped into my lungs, caused my eyes to sting.

I bolted for the window, threw the pane and screen open, and climbed on top of my desk to access the sill. Sirens blared from streets away. As crazy as it sounds, it hadn't even dawned on me to call 9-1-1.

But maybe my parents had.

I could no longer hear their voices. *Maybe Dad had gone back downstairs. Probably, they'd already gotten out.* Their bedroom was on the first floor, behind the kitchen pantry, not far from the patio doors.

Beneath my window was the driveway pavement. Neighbors had come outside, into the middle of the street. Mr. Jensen, who used to sit on his front lawn whittling stakes for his garden, came running in my direction with a tall metal ladder. Neighbors say he helped coach me down.

That Mr. Chung got out his garden hose.

That Mrs. Wheeler knelt down in the middle of the street to pray with her rosaries.

My memory has holes, so there's a lot I don't remember. But one major thing I do: the bright ball of fire coming out the side of the house like something you'd see in movies, and the black clouds of smoke as they drifted up toward the sky—too big to be real, too much to take in.

"What's happening?" I shouted to whomever would hear me.

Where were my parents?

Why couldn't I find them?

Fire trucks showed up. Bright flashing lights turned the pavement red and blue. Someone draped a jacket over my shoulders.

Someone else whispered into my ear, "The firefighters will do the best they can."

What did that mean? What was "the best"?

I ran toward the front entrance, where the firefighters had gone in, heat pressing against my face, smoke wafting up my nostrils. But people held me back—hands and fingers and shoulders and grips— despite my kicking and screaming and pushing and pleading.

I woke up sometime later in a strange room, on a strange couch, unsure how I'd gotten there.

"Terra, are you awake?" Mrs. Wilder's voice. She stood in the doorway with clumps of tissues balled up in her hands.

I was in my neighbor's house, in my neighbor's living room. I recognized it now: the picture window that faced my driveway with the stained-glass sun that hung in the center.

"You blacked out, honey," she said.

Blacked out? Was that even a thing? Why were her eyes so red?

I got up and peeked through one of the sun's rays, at first thinking the tempered glass must create a distorted effect, because the image across the street—my childhood home—was no longer the way it should've been.

"Where are my parents?" My whole body shook. I looked back at Mrs. Wilder, waiting for her to tell me that my parents were in another room or being checked out at the hospital.

"Sit down," she said instead, her hand clasped over her mouth. Tears dripped down her face. She pressed her dead husband's slipper against her chest (a security blanket of sorts, she'd told my mother once).

"*Where are they?*" I repeated, covering my ears, bracing myself for the words.

Mrs. Wilder shook her head, unable to explain it. And I couldn't understand it—why my parents were gone, why there was nothing else left except rubble and dust: a heap of lifeless ashes, including inside my heart.

4

I follow Dave-the-tour-guide over a footbridge and to a tree-lined clearing. I chose Dave specifically, because people say he's an expert on Hayberry Park, that he knows these woods like the back of his hand: every tree, shrub, rock, and burr.

A woman on a review site wrote that Dave was so "well acquainted with these woods, he'd know it if a single log had been kicked from its beaver dam from one visit to the next."

I doubt that's really true, but he definitely sounds like an expert, and that's exactly what I need.

Dave stands at the front of our group and asks us more of his nature-inspired questions, this time about the age and type of the oldest fruit tree. I don't really care. I'm not here for nature trivia. I just want to find the place where I was being kept.

There are fifteen of us on tour today, a larger number than most of the tours I've taken, likely due to the fall foliage. Nobody in the group seems to recognize me, maybe because of my sunglasses and baseball cap. Or maybe my story has already been forgotten.

The air is cool, so I've dressed accordingly in a fleece jacket and hiking boots. Bright orange leaves quiver from the branches of cherry and maple trees. As the sun strikes down, the leaves appear to glow, lighting up like shimmering ornaments. One time, back in elementary school, my dad took me here for a hike around the frog pond. The woods had seemed so enchanting then with their towering oaks and winding trails. I couldn't hate them more now.

This is my sixth guided tour since my release from the hospital three months ago. When I made the mistake of talking in group about wanting to come back here, the group leader—Winnie was her name—said it wasn't a good idea.

"I'll be fine," I told her.

"You don't understand," she insisted. "When something traumatic happens, the brain has a way of storing details from the event—details you may not even consciously remember, like certain sounds, smells, textures, tastes . . . When exposed to those same details, sometime later, the individual can become overwhelmed and stressed. It can trigger a fight-or-flight response."

Post-traumatic stress. I knew all about it. I'd already had my fair share of practice with it. "Didn't you read my chart?" I asked her. "It says that I'm delusional, that I make things up, that you're not supposed to believe a single word I say."

Her mouth parted open, perhaps at a loss of words. I almost felt bad for her. She couldn't have been more than twenty-two years old (just a few years older than I was) and completely unprepared for an attitude like mine.

"Please, just be safe," she said quickly, quietly. "None of you should go anywhere that might prove upsetting—or worse, *triggering*—unless it's under the guidance and supervision of a licensed therapist."

I've been coming to this park under the guidance and supervision of no one other than the park ranger assigned to give the tour.

Is it upsetting?

Yes.

Does it trigger me?

Most definitely.

But I *want* to be triggered. I *need* to be upset. How else will I know I'm not delusional like everyone says?

"Hello?" calls a voice.

I look up. Dave's waving at me. He and the group have moved away; there's at least thirty yards' distance between us now.

A woman with a fuzzy brown coat whispers something to her partner. It's only then I realize . . . The stick in my hand; I'm rubbing it against my cheek. The cool, coarse sensation flashes me back to the cocoon I made in the woods—of brush and burrs—and trying my hardest to curl up tighter and get myself smaller; *just a little bit more and he won't see me.*

Rub, rub, rub.

Tuck, tuck.

Sniff, sniff. The musty scent of dirt.

Is someone whistling? The tune to "Mary Had a Little Lamb"?

"Is she going to be okay?" A voice asks. "Shall we take a water break?"

Dave asks, "Can you confirm that you're still with us?"

I drop the stick, forcing myself back, plugging myself in. The cocoon cracks open. Who was just whistling?

"Hello . . ." Dave says. Is he talking to me?

I search the faces of the group. But no one's whistling. Only one girl is smirking. Dave starts talking again, holding a pine cone, staring in my direction. Finally, after a few moments, he turns away, leading the group over a footbridge.

I follow along, curious to know where the bridge came from. The maps don't show it anywhere, plus it seems misplaced; it doesn't stand over a stream of water.

I grab my phone to check the online map, but I have no cell reception. We're in too deep. I search my pockets for the paper map. I have my knife and my mini can of wasp spray, but my map is missing. Did I leave it at home? Or inside my car?

Did I even take my car?

No, I took the bus.

Right.

The thought of driving here makes my insides race. My nerves twitch. I swivel from the bridge, trying to get a new perspective.

Have I been here before—to this part of the park, that is? Is there anything distinguishable?

Dave continues chattering away, something about tree bark now . . . about which bark one could eat if ever caught out in the wild, apparently pine, red spruce, and balsam fir. "Does anyone have any questions before we move on?" he asks.

I raise my hand. "Why doesn't the online map show this footbridge?"

"A good question." He grins. "I see someone's done her homework. Does anyone want to take a stab at the answer?"

Most of the faces in the group remain blank. But then a woman at the front raises her hand to offer a guess: "Because the map was made before the bridge was placed here?"

"Excellent theory," Dave says, "but not quite right. Anyone else? No? Okay, so the bridge was built by a local homeschool group as part of a hands-on math project. The group often likes to take hikes in this park, and so when they were finished building the bridge, they donated it, requesting that it be placed by this clearing—what they refer to as their outdoor classroom. If you look closer, you can see the bridge's dedication plaque just under the first step. When our cartographer was making our most current map guides—about two years ago now—he knew about the bridge, but wasn't sure its placement would be a permanent fixture."

I move closer to get a good look. The bridge appears to be about twenty feet long by six feet wide. I take a snapshot, including of the dedication plaque, mentally noting the homeschool group as a possible resource.

"Are there any other questions before we wrap up our tour?" Dave asks.

Wrap up?

Already?

I check my phone for the time. How is it that nearly two hours have passed?

"Anyone?" Dave scans the group.

I raise my hand again. "How well do you know this park?"

His eyebrows shoot upward, as though taken aback by the question. "Well, I'm the tour guide, aren't I? It's my job to know this place. But to answer your question, I practically grew up in these woods. I camped here, hiked here, volunteered to do cleanups here . . ."

"Do you know every square inch?"

He folds his arms and widens his stance: defense mode. I know it well.

"I'm not even sure I know every square inch of my own apartment," he says. "Why do you ask? Is there a question I haven't answered for you today?"

Yes. There is. "Where is the water well located?"

His face furrows. He doesn't know. *"Water well?"*

My heart sinks.

I look around at the others to see if any of them might be familiar with the well. "People say it's hidden under brush and brambles, and that it's tucked behind a grove of elm trees . . ."

"Really . . ." He smirks. "Well, as you can see, these woods are *full* of brush, brambles, and elms." He motions all around us. "But I can assure you there are no water wells."

"That you know of," I say, correcting him.

"No." He draws the word out for emphasis. "There are no water wells *period*. You can check your map."

"I don't need to check. I know the map. Every square inch of it. The well isn't on there. The footbridge isn't either."

"I know Hayberry Park," Dave argues. "It has eight water fountains and two fishing holes, miles of hiking and biking trails, the most species of deer and birds in the New England area—"

"And a water well," I insist.

"Could it be that you have this park confused with another?"

"I'm not confused." Part of me wonders if the well had been built just for me. But that doesn't make sense either—doesn't explain the overgrowth of brush or the aging of the well bricks.

"Hey, wait," Dave says. His face brightens, the look of recognition, of puzzle pieces fitting together. "I think I may've heard about you. You've been on a lot of these walking tours, haven't you?"

"No. I don't think so." My face flashes hot.

"Yes. You have." He's smiling now, his suspicions confirmed. "You're *that girl*."

The people in the group are gawking at me now.

"Is she okay?" a female voice asks. Which one of them said it? The lady in the brown coat?

"I'm not," I say. "That girl," I mean.

"Your name is Terra, right?" Dave takes a step closer. "You're Terra, the girl who was on the news?"

"I'm not." I'm no one. I turn away and keep on walking.

NOW

5

Later, in my room, behind an art desk that's loaded with the sharpest of tools; beneath a blanket that reminds me of the pink one my mother knitted me; and with all the windows closed, locked, booby-trapped, and duct-taped, I log on to the Jane Anonymous chat site. My chat name, NightTerra, pops up on the screen to announce my attendance.

JA Admin: Welcome, NightTerra. Remember the rules: no judgments, no swearing, no inappropriate remarks. This is a safe space for honesty and support.

Paylee22: Hey, NightTerra! So glad to see you!!!

NightTerra: Is anyone else on here?

Paylee22: Logged on maybe but not chatting. It's been pretty quiet, so I'm binging my way through Season 3 of Summer's Story. Have you watched it yet?

NightTerra: No, but I tried those Swiss Rolls you recommended.

Paylee22: And?

NightTerra: So good.

Paylee22: Told you! Sometime, we should go into a private chat room, watch Summer's Story, and eat Swiss Rolls, so it'll be like we're together.

NightTerra: Definitely. :)

NightTerra: Can I ask you something?

Paylee22: Of course. Anything.

NightTerra: Do you think I'm crazy? Like, for real, beyond mentally unstable.

Paylee22: Seriously? Again??? What's with you and the c-word?

Paylee22: If you were really, truly crazy, you wouldn't be asking if you're crazy.

NightTerra: Do you really think that's true?

Paylee22: I really, really do.

NightTerra: Sometimes I just feel so completely alone, even when others are around, which I know sounds crazy coming from someone who was trapped in a well.

Paylee22: The crazy part is that it doesn't sound crazy at all, not to someone like me who's been through something similar. For me, other people make the lonely feeling worse—the fact that I can't really relate to them, and they don't relate to me.

Paylee22: Just the other day, with my mom . . . I was trying to describe what it was like for me, trapped in that shed, not knowing what was going to happen or if I'd ever get out . . .

Paylee22: I was telling her how thoughts of my little brother Max came up, how I felt like his spirit was with me somehow, in the shed, how I imagined doing card tricks with him . . . His favorite trick with the Aces and the Queens . . .

Paylee22: But I couldn't really share much because my mom started crying as soon as I said Max's name. So, then I felt bad, like I had to soothe her, and lonely because I had no one to tell those Max memories to.

NightTerra: You'll always have me.

Paylee22: xoxoxo

Paylee22: I really miss him. His giggly little laugh, his obsession with Polymer clay, all those snails he used to sculpt . . . He made a DIY video tutorial. Sometimes I watch it just to keep him close.

Paylee22: His heart just wasn't strong enough for his larger-than-life spirit.

NightTerra: I'm really sorry, Peyton.

NightTerra: Sending you a virtual hug.

Paylee22: Thanks, Terra. What would I do without you? I don't ever want to know.

Paylee22: Now, back to you. Are you feeling a little less alone and unstable? I hate the c-word, btw. Delete crazy from your vocabulary.

Paylee22: And while I'm prescribing, don't go surfing online for symptoms. Need I remind you that I'm way better than Dr. Google.

Paylee22: I'm Dr. P. :)

NightTerra: What's my diagnosis, Dr. P?

Paylee22: Paranoid, with a side of mistrust, a hefty helping of isolation, and a scoop of low self-esteem.

Paylee22: In other words, you're just like me.

NightTerra: Thank you for being there.

Paylee22: Let's not leave each other yet. Let's be alone, together.

NightTerra: What do you mean?

Paylee22: When we go to bed . . . How about we stay logged on, in case either of us needs to chat?

NightTerra: I actually love that idea.

Paylee22: Great! Let's exit this chat. I'll send you a link for a private room, where we can "sleep." Lol.

NightTerra: Ok. Sounds good.

NightTerra: xo

Paylee22: xoxo

Paylee22 has left the chat room.

NightTerra has left the chat room.

There are currently 3 people in the chat room.

6

Unable to sleep after the sorority party, I rolled over in bed and stared at the wall, remembering a time when I was seven or eight and my father used me as a makeshift barbell. With one hand wrapped around my ankle and the other holding my shoulder tightly, he lifted me high above his head—again and again, up and down—as I squealed, and laughed, and begged for more.

Sometimes, I imagine he's in my room, watching over me as I sleep. I imagined it that night as I cuddled one of my mother's old sweaters (one she'd left in her car on the night of the fire). Once I'd nodded off, I pictured my father—in my dream—standing by the window wearing his favorite sweatpants, the blue ones with the torn back pocket.

Eventually, as I slept there soundly, I felt him grow closer, his fingers gliding over the wounds on my forearms, the ones from sliding onto the pavement in front of the convenience store.

Terra, he whispered into my ear, inside my brain. *It's time to get up.*

It's weird: sleep. Sometimes you can get caught in that murky place between wakefulness and slumber. Sleep paralysis: a state of restful unrest (if that makes any sense). You feel as though you're on the verge of waking up, but the claws of slumber hold you in place, keeping you from gaining full consciousness. I asked a therapist about it once—about why it was always happening. She said it's typically caused by anxiety and fatigue, not to mention the meds I'd been taking for said anxiety and fatigue.

In that moment, lying in bed, after the party, my brain told me to get up, to do as my father had said. But sleep wouldn't let me, and so I remained snuggled up, somewhat comforted by his voice.

Terra . . .

I felt his weight then—on the mattress—as though he'd sat down beside me. I felt more of his patting too—over my shoulder and down my arm as he tried to rouse me to full consciousness.

Now, his voice insisted. *You need to wake up.*

I remember the sensation of smiling, still caught in that cloudy place. Who would ever want to wake from it? There, in dreamland, I had my father back—could hear him, feel him, and smell him too: the scent of the black licorice he used to snack; Sunday afternoons, on the sunporch, we'd sit side by side, reading books and nibbling licorice sticks and pretzel rods.

In my dream, I wanted to talk to him so unbelievably much. I think I moaned from the effort. In my mind, I told him I was sorry for not opening my bedroom door on the night of the fire.

Get up, he persisted. *It isn't time for you.*

Time? For what?

I tried to wake up. At one point, I could've sworn I'd sat up in bed, that I'd been able to see the room around me—my blue checked covers, my maple dresser, my bulletin board full of pictures, and my fuzzy green chair . . . But, in reality, I was still curled up in bed, with my mother's sweater nestled beneath my cheek.

"Don't you wake up now, pretty girl," a male voice said. But it wasn't my father's; this voice sounded gruffer, deeper, and had a singsong quality.

Where had my father gone?

Why wasn't I waking up?

I heard a zipper then—*zip, unzip*—followed by a clattering noise and the jangling of keys. In my dreamy state, I pictured my dad's gym bag—the lime-green one. He used to keep a stainless-steel water bottle tucked inside. Was he removing the lid and handling his locker keys?

Something thin and light draped over my face, tickling my skin. I pictured the bedsheet game Mom and I used to play, when I'd lie on the mattress while she made it up. She'd toss the top sheet high in the air and let it float down over me, again and again.

Was Mom here too? Were she and Dad like two sleep angels?

I rolled over, still trying to force myself awake, feeling something gritty against my cheek, like a dishcloth or rag. It wasn't a bedsheet, wasn't my mother's sweater either.

A moment later, I heard it. A loud popping noise jolted me awake. My eyes snapped open. I turned over.

And saw him—his broad chest, his thick arms.

A black ski mask covered his face.

A hot, sweltering heat flashed over my skin.

He hovered by my bed, partially concealed by the dimness of the room. The light in the hallway was still on, as I'd left it.

"Well, hello there, pretty girl." His breath slithered like silverfish over my skin. "Feel like making a fairy tale?"

I went to sit up, but he kept me pinned in place, one hand over my mouth, the other clamping down on my thigh. He pushed the cloth in deeper, using his finger. I could feel his knuckle against my teeth. I started to bite down, but more fabric filled my mouth, and I gagged.

"Don't panic," his voice continued to slither. "If you just relax, everything will feel smooth like butter."

His eyes were pale blue, like the jogger's at the park. Was it the same person? Were his fingers just as long? They were covered by thin black gloves. Were there light reflector stripes?

"Do you like fairy tales, Terra?"

Fairy tales? How did he know my name? Why would he ask me that?

"What's the matter? Has a cat got your tongue?" He stuck out his tongue—straight through the hole in his mask—and waggled it back and forth like a bright red dart.

I reached outward, toward his face, not knowing how this happened when I'd followed all the rules and done everything right: called a friend, locked the door, brushed my teeth, didn't go with strangers.

Looked both ways.

Used my instincts.

Armed myself.

Didn't leave my drink unattended.

But none of that mattered now, as he ground my head against the mattress; as his fingernails dug into the front of my neck.

My arms dropped. A choking sound burst from my mouth. A mix of bile and purple punch shot into the back of my throat.

"Do you know where that expression comes from?" he asked. "The cat having your tongue?" He started to explain—something about Egypt and tongue-eating cats.

My mind grew foggy. The room was getting blurry. Still, I tried to fight back, drawing upward with my leg, wanting to knee him in the groin, flailing outward with my arms.

He removed the rag—one quick pluck. My teeth clanged down, and I let out a wheeze. Something tasted sweet. Why did my tongue feel so lumpy?

"Now, tell me the truth," he said. "What do you think about fairy tales? Which one is your favorite? *Tell me yours, and I'll tell you mine . . .*"

My heart pounded.

"Want to give me a little hint?"

Just then, I remembered. On my bedside table, I had a glass of water. I turned my head slightly and started to look over.

But he grabbed my jaw and forced it open, stuffing something else into my mouth—something softer than before; bulkier, like sweatshirt material.

Still, I reached a little farther.

My fingers grazed the night table. *Just a little bit more.* I felt the surface of the glass. I searched for the rim. Why was he letting me?

I just needed another inch as he continued to stuff—*in, in, in, filling my cheeks, deep into my mouth* . . .

Was he poking my eyes?

Was that water on my forehead?

Drip, drip, drip. Like a baptism.

My fingers curled over the rim of the glass. I got a good grip and swung outward, toward his head. The sound of glass shattering echoed inside my brain.

Had I hit him? Did I stab him?

The minty scent of mouthwash filled my senses, brought tears to my eyes. Was I still fighting? I could no longer tell.

A patch of gray flashed in front of my vision. A picture of Hemingway, my calico cat that'd died ten years before, pressed inside my mind's eye.

Had a glass really broken?

It was all too much to process: what my body parts were doing, what was really, truly happening.

A blazing burst of light shot out inside my brain like the lights of a fire truck—bright red and blue flames, burning up my thoughts, painting splotches on the pavement.

"Sleep now, sweet girl," the voice said right at my ear as though he were nestled beside me. "There will be time for fairy tales later."

He continued to talk, telling me a story about a water well and a forest girl until eventually his voice melted like wax in a fire, just a puddle of muffled sounds.

My consciousness melted too: a hot, dripping mess. I pictured the door in my bedroom, in my childhood house, four years before. Beyond it, I saw a pile of yellow ashes and clouds of maroon smoke, as though through the ray of my neighbor's stained-glass sun.

7

The following day, after my aunt leaves for work, I go outside to my mom's old Subaru. It'd been parked on the street on the night of the fire. My aunt kept the car, assuming I might one day want to have it. I'm glad she did, because aside from fading memories, it's one of the few things I have of hers.

I unlock the door and crawl into the back. Mom's yoga blanket is here—a thick wool one that smells like the lavender oil she used to carry home from her vinyasa classes. I drape it over me and pull my old bedroom doorknob from the pocket of my sweatshirt. The knob is from the house that burned. It's discolored from the fire, but a star is still in the center of it, drawn with little-girl hands and a red Sharpie marker. Back when I was five, I believed that drawing the star there, in the center of the chrome, and coloring it in, would somehow magically create a keyhole. Needless to say, it didn't work, and my parents were not amused. But I'm grateful for drawing it now, because weeks after the fire, when I went back to the scene, the star helped me recognize the knob from the heap of what remained of my childhood home.

I open up the podcast app on my phone and play *Star Up,* the series my parents and I used to listen to on long car rides. It's currently on its eighth season. With the blanket snuggled close, I curl up on the seat, with the doorknob pressed against my palm, where the burn mark used to be. And as I listen, I ask myself questions about the characters, like what Mom would say about Maisie's choice to go off to boarding school, or what Dad would think about Thomas's father's drinking problem. Would it remind him of his own father?

When I close my eyes, I can almost trick myself into believing that we're just stopped at a gas station en route to New York City or the lake house in Maine, that Dad's using the restroom, that Mom's buying snacks—licorice sticks and pretzel rods. *They'll both be back in a few moments,* I tell myself.

I inhale a deep breath and try my best to hold on to these thoughts—to keep back the fire inside my head. But when the *Star Up* episode ends, reality creeps back and I remember who I am: someone who's not at all ready to go back to being me. And so, I advance to the next episode, eager to get back to make-believe.

8

JA Admin: Welcome, NightTerra. Remember the rules: no judgments, no swearing, no inappropriate remarks. This is a safe space for honesty and support.

Paylee22: I tell my parents I'm fine because they don't want to hear anything different. Yes, everything's great, tra la la.

Cobra-head43: Same here. My parents look at me like I might spontaneously combust, like at any second I'm going to come apart. When anything bad happens, they don't share it with me because they don't think I can handle it.

TulipPrincess: At least your parents care about you. All my mother cares about is payback. She's on a mission to take down the guy who screwed with me, a.k.a. her ex-boyfriend.

Paylee22: Go, TulipPrincess's mom!

TulipPrincess: Not really. I wish she'd care as much about me as she does about payback. I almost feel more alone

now than I did when all that stuff was happening. How
screwed up is that?!

Cobra-head43: I'm really sorry. :(

NightTerra: Yeah, me too.

TulipPrincess: I think this is her way of getting over the
guilt she feels about bringing that scumbag into our lives
and ignoring the signs that something messed up was
going on. In other words, it's all about her—still, after
everything. Her, her, her . . .

Darwin12 has entered the chat room.

LuluLeopard has left the chat room. There are currently 7
people in the chat room.

JA Admin: Welcome, Darwin12. Remember the rules: no
judgments, no swearing, no inappropriate remarks. This is a
safe space for honesty and support.

A message from Peyton pops up on my screen. Private chat?
She and I have been using the private chat feature quite a bit.
For one, they're a lot less monitored. For another, not everyone
wants to spill their guts in an open forum. We've hinted once or
twice about going "off-site" to chat or FaceTime, but the Jane
Anonymous administrators have a strict policy that forbids the
swapping of personal information (aside from first names), stress-
ing the layer of protection provided when chatting exclusively
through a website.

Are you still there??? Peyton asks.

I type back Yes and click the private link she's sent.

NightTerra: Hey, I'm here.

Paylee22: I'm seriously about to lose it.

NightTerra: Why? What's going on?

Paylee22: I've already taken a dose of my just-in-case meds and eaten an entire box of Swiss Rolls.

NightTerra: ???

Paylee22: I went out earlier.

NightTerra: But that's a good thing, right? Getting out of the house . . . Isn't that what you want?

Paylee22: What I want is to be able to go to a store and not end up with a full-on panic attack because of it.

NightTerra: Tell me what happened.

Paylee22: I needed more contact solution and my mom refused to get it for me. She gave me the whole tough-love routine: "Baby steps, Peyton. A trip to the store. It's only two blocks over. I'll even walk a block behind you if it makes you feel more confident blah, blah . . ."

Paylee22: Anyway, I went to the store myself. And I felt like someone was following me the whole time. I kept seeing a patch of dark blue fabric out of the corner of my eye, like part of someone's jacket.

Paylee22: I ended up leaving, without buying anything, then had a panic attack outside, on the sidewalk.

Paylee22: I seriously feel like he's going to come back for me, like he's waiting for just the right moment, when I least expect it.

NightTerra: Wait. Slow down. Perspective, remember?

NightTerra: Were you at a pharmacy? Because those places usually have way too many mirrors, which means way too many reflected images.

Paylee22: Yes, a pharmacy.

Paylee22: For real? Do you think that could be it?

Paylee22: Omg, maybe you're right.

NightTerra: Deep breath.

Paylee22: I'm being completely paranoid, aren't I?

NightTerra: I can relate to that. How do you think I know about reflected images in a pharmacy? #BeenThereDoneThat

Paylee22: Damned triggers, right?

NightTerra: An understatement.

Paylee22: Thank you, once again, for talking me off the ledge.

Paylee22: I can't share this stuff with my parents. It hurts them too much. They just want me to be better. I can't really blame them tho. I'd want me to be better too.

NightTerra: You'll get there.

Paylee22: I try to look at things from their perspective. Parents who lost their son earlier than anyone ever should and then whose daughter went missing just eight months ago . . .

Paylee22: A couple that stays together, probably because of me, because I'm still living in their house and they don't want me to have to endure any more change . . .

Paylee22: And then I think . . . Who am I to complain about drugstore visits or having to come out of my room?

NightTerra: You can complain all you want to me.

Paylee22: And that, my friend, means more to me than you'll probably ever know. xo

NightTerra: xoxo

NightTerra: Has anyone ever doubted what happened to you?

Paylee22: That I was taken, you mean?

NightTerra: Yeah.

Paylee22: Who would ever make that kind of thing up?!

Paylee22: Plus, everyone knew I was telling the truth. For one, because I'm not a liar.

Paylee22: For another, because they found the shed where I was being kept. It'd been dismantled by the time the investigators uncovered it, but still . . .

NightTerra: Did they find any clues?

Paylee22: Nothing that went anywhere and all leads fizzled out.

NightTerra: After how much time?

Paylee22: Just a couple of months, which almost felt as bad as getting taken. Now that I'm back home, with no physical scars, it's as if the crime no longer matters.

Paylee22: Why do you ask? Do people doubt your story?

NightTerra: Pretty much everyone does. For all the reasons you said. I returned home, physically unscathed—for the most part, anyway. There wasn't much proof.

Paylee22: Except your word!!

NightTerra: My word doesn't hold much weight. The people close to me think I'm pretty messed up.

Paylee22: Which is obviously why you're always asking about your mental stability . . . All is beginning to make sense now. #TerraMysterySolved

Paylee22: Does your aunt believe you, at least?

NightTerra: She did at first but not anymore.

NightTerra: Things would be so different if my parents were still here.

Paylee22: I know. I'm sorry. :(

Paylee22: Sometimes I wonder how you even deal.

NightTerra: Obviously, not well.

NightTerra: Remember how you said before that when you were held captive it felt like your brother was there with you somehow—his spirit, that is?

Paylee22: Yeah . . .

NightTerra: I feel like that with my father too, that he visits me in my dreams.

Paylee22: I totally believe it, that stuff like that can happen.

NightTerra: I wish it happened with my mother too, that she'd talk to me in my sleep.

Paylee22: Can you talk to your aunt about her?

NightTerra: Not really. She says it's too hard reliving the past.

NightTerra: For me, it's too hard not reliving it—at least parts of it.

Paylee22: I haven't wanted to ask . . .

NightTerra: But . . .

Paylee22: Did you ever find out how the fire started?

NightTerra: Faulty wiring, plus smoke detectors with dead batteries.

Paylee22: It's pretty amazing you got out.

NightTerra: Most days I wish I hadn't.

Paylee22: You can't blame yourself for surviving.

NightTerra: I can and I do.

Paylee22: I guess I do the same, punishing myself, I mean. Like, why Max? Why not me?

Paylee22: I'm really grateful you survived, btw.

NightTerra: Thanks for being there, Dr. P.

Paylee22: I'm glad we found each other. Seriously, you have no idea.

NightTerra: Yeah. Me too.

NightTerra: It'd be great to meet one day.

Paylee22: I'd like that too.

Paylee22: Come to the Midwest!! You can stay with me and my depressed parents. How fun does that sound?!

NightTerra: Where in the Midwest?

Paylee22: A tiny, sleepy village-town outside Chicago, where barely anything happens . . . except abduction in broad daylight.

NightTerra: I'm East Coast, just outside Boston.

Paylee22: Chat later?

NightTerra: Sounds good.

Paylee22: xo

NightTerra: xoxo

I log out and reach beneath my pillow. The kitchen scissors are still there—the serrated kind, with the jagged teeth. I chose them specifically, figuring if my aunt were to ever find them, I could say they're for my one of my mixed media creations, that after cutting and pasting in bed one night, *I must've accidentally forgotten to put them away.*

And the carving knife on my windowsill, tucked behind the curtain . . . ? *It's just for my wood-whittling,* I'd tell her.

The duct tape around my windows? *It's because of the draft.*

The wasp repellent on my night table? *It's for the wood-boring bees I've seen flying outside my windows. There must be a nest somewhere, and I can't take any chances. I'm highly allergic. Don't you remember? Back in elementary school, when I got rushed to the hospital . . . ?*

Fortunately—and unfortunately—my parents aren't around to confirm the story.

My aunt isn't concerned enough to put two and two together.

The authorities aren't reliable; otherwise, I wouldn't have to resort to such tactics, which also include a booby trap above the door; a collection of fire extinguishers, strategically placed around the room; and an artillery of art supplies for the primary purpose of trying to stay safe.

Sometimes I remind myself of Crazy Sally—pretty shameful to think about it now, but that's what we called her—a girl at the hospital during my first stint there, who wore pink party dresses claiming it was her birthday all but three days of the year. Sally used to set traps around her bed, complaining that each night, after she'd gone to sleep, someone would sneak into her room and snip off a lock of her hair. She'd usually blame one of the nurses for doing it, but sometimes she'd say it was a therapist or one of the custodians.

So many mornings, she'd come tearing out of her room, desperate for a tape measure so that one of us could check the length of her hair, proving that some minuscule amount had been trimmed while she slept.

"They take a little bit each night," she'd say. "Just enough that I won't notice. But I *do* notice. Don't you see it too? Can't you tell?" She'd grab the ends of the hair and shove them into our faces.

But no one believed her. Sally's hair always looked the same: a brown stringy mess that hit just above her shoulders. Still, she'd set cups of water over her door as a trap; sleep with balled-up tissue paper littered around her pillow, hoping the rustle might alert her to a "burglar"; and sprinkle peanut M&Ms all over the floor (because she didn't have marbles), as if peanut M&Ms could ever make anyone slip.

Everyone said she was certifiably nuts, including me. I'd giggle right along with the others as someone would measure Sally's hair and agree that, *yes,* it *did* seem shorter (even though it didn't). And, most definitely, she *should* wear a hat, because she'd probably be bald soon.

I feel badly about it now—badly that I laughed, guilty for playing into Sally's paranoia, and scared shitless that if Sally was supposedly the poster girl for "crazy," then I must be "crazy" too.

9

When I woke up again, I noticed right away: I was no longer in my room. I was surrounded by dirt walls, lying on a dirt floor.

In a circular space.

About six feet in diameter.

I sat up, trying my best to process the whole scene, still dressed in the clothes I'd worn to bed: my dark blue sweatpants, my long-sleeved tee, and a pair of knitted socks. A smattering of dried-up leaves littered the ground, along with a handful of broken twigs.

Where was I? What had happened?

But just as fast as the questions hit, the memories hit too: the stranger in my room, his ski-masked face, the smell of mint . . .

Somehow, I could still feel the cloth inside my mouth, though it was no longer there, and the ache in my jaw.

Hadn't I broken a glass too?

Weren't his fingers extra-long?

His eyes were a pale shade of blue; those I remember, along with his tongue—the way it'd waggled back and forth out the hole of his mask.

Where was he now?

Why was I here?

My body trembled. Still, I told myself, *Just get a grip. Don't lose it yet. You can figure this out.*

A spotlight dangled down, from a chain, enabling me to see; the dirt walls were at least twenty feet high. There were no doors or windows. No ladder to climb out.

There appeared to be a ceiling at the top of the hole; it looked partially open like a lid of sorts. Out the other half, I spotted a patch of blue. Was that the sky? Were those tree branches?

What was this place? A giant pit, dug into the earth? A root cellar? An old bunker?

I stood up. In the stream of light, a couple of feet above my head, I saw that the wall had a brick-like pattern.

Was this a water well?

That's when I remembered: all the questions about fairy tales . . . The ski-masked stranger had said something about a water well and a forest girl.

Was I in the forest? Did I know where a well was?

My head felt dizzy. I stumbled on my feet, literally spun around in circles, eventually noticing: the spotlight chain. It snaked through the opening in the ceiling, meaning anyone could easily pull it out, and close the lid, and let me die here.

My body twitched like I'd been given a shock—over and over—as a warming sensation spread between my legs, spilling over my thighs. It took me a moment to realize I'd lost control, peed my pants. Tears filled my eyes.

Don't panic. Rule number four.

Still, how much time had passed since the scene in my bedroom? Were the two things connected: being in the well and the guy hovered above my bed? As obvious as the answer was, I hadn't wanted to believe it, because of what it would've meant—that he'd taken me, that he'd put me there.

Chills ripped through my core as the pieces came together. I screamed at the pieces. The sound vibrated inside my ears. I pictured a hunter hearing my cries. I prayed a hiker might be somewhere nearby. I imagined a pack of search dogs sniffing their way to me.

Where could there be a well? Was it anywhere near home? Had anyone seen what happened? A neighbor, maybe . . .

Had my aunt gotten home from work yet? Did she check my room? And spot the signs of a struggle? Were the police already looking? But then I remembered: the text I'd sent to my aunt about staying the night with Jessie . . . and a shot of terror flooded through my veins.

Would my aunt even know I was gone? Would anyone come looking?

I ran my fingers over the ground and clawed at the walls, not even sure what I expected to find—a clue, a tool, an answer, a way out . . .

That's when I saw it.

Angled against the wall, only partially concealed by a layer of dirt . . .

An illustration of a little girl.

I brushed the dirt away, revealing a children's book cover. It looked old, circa nineteen-freaking-ancient, with cursive loopy letters that spelled out *The Forest Girl and the Wishy Water Well*. The girl in the picture wore a long blue dress and her hair in two braids. She carried a pail; water splashed out of it as she ran from a well in the middle of the woods. A worried expression hung on her face: bulging eyes, gaping mouth.

With trembling fingers, I opened the cover.

At the same moment, the light went out, stopping my heart. The sound of something solid and heavy, like the lid of a tomb sliding closed, came from above, sending panic through my bones.

I screamed for help over and over again, until my throat turned to blades and each inhalation felt like a cut. How long did that take? Five hours? Five minutes? Until I could swear that blood was seeping out my mouth, dripping over my lip. I pictured the droplets drizzling onto the ground. Eventually, I folded forward and hugged the book like a friend.

Was I really, truly here?

Was this absolutely happening?

A thirsting noise gasped from my mouth. I tried to breathe, but I couldn't get enough air. I cried like I'd never cried before—like a wounded animal left behind by its pack: a sound so shrill and pleading, I didn't recognize it as mine, kept thinking that someone or something was in the well with me. Was that true? Was he here somehow?

I sat up straight and kept my eyes wide, as if that would help me see in the dark.

Don't panic, Logic said. *You need to hold it together—need to be so much smarter, so much stronger.* But all I could manage to be in that moment was a pathetic forest girl in a dark water well.

10

Having spent most of the night on the Jane site, I get up the following day, sometime after four p.m., and slip into the same pair of dark-washed jeans I wore on the night of the sorority party. I also pull on the same top (with the ruffled hem). My hair is the same too: down and wavy. My lips are colored mauve (Rosy Vixen), just like that night, to match the eye makeup I'd been wearing. And my vintage Gucci cross-body bag (circa 1980-something) is around my shoulder and hip, to complete the precise look.

Into the purse, I stuff a pocketknife, my mini-can of wasp spray, and my own personal set of house keys—all things I should've had with me on the night of the party. The spray can shoot up to eight feet. The knife has a jagged edge. And the keys are because there's no longer a spare set kept hidden outside the house. Rule number five on my parents' list of survival tips: Go with your gut. Keeping house keys in a planter on the front stoop, as had been my aunt's practice, always conflicted my gut, but before that night, I hadn't done anything to change it.

My aunt knocks on my open bedroom door, dressed in her pale green hospital scrubs. I hate seeing her wearing them, hate flashing back to my first stint in the hospital, after the fire—to how ripped open I felt, like a walking bundle of severed nerves. The nurse wore scrubs the exact same color. I remember pressing my face against them, feeling the sensation of thin starched cotton against my cheek as I cried so hard it felt that blood, rather than tears, was running from my eyes.

"Going somewhere?" she asks.

"A work thing," I lie.

"At the library? Dressed like that?"

"It's a social event. A book reading."

"Are you going to take the Subaru? Or do you want a ride?"

"I'm going to walk. It's nice out." Luckily, it is: mild for October, with clear skies and a setting sun.

"You're not planning on walking home in the dark, are you?"

"Katherine said she'd drive me." Another lie, but I know Aunt Dessa won't check.

Sometimes I wish I had a magical ring that could time-travel me back to that brief period, after the well, when Aunt Dessa believed my story, when she'd make mochaccinos with cocoa powder and ask me crossword puzzle riddles—the only time we've ever been close. We hadn't even been close before the fire, when my mom was still alive. Though they'd once been inseparable, back when they were kids (according to my dad), my mom and Aunt Dessa never saw each other much.

Then, after the fire, when my aunt began to piece together how the night had played out, things just got more distant: *So, you heard your mom screaming, but you didn't wake up? How is that even possible? And what does it even mean? You thought you were* dreaming *about your mother's screaming? That makes no sense.* I couldn't exactly argue.

I leave the house and head toward town. This isn't the first time I've taken one of these jaunts. Maybe it's my fourth . . . Or could it be my ninth? I've gone over the details of the night of the sorority party at least a million times in my head, wondering who he was and how he found me. Had he been at the Theta Epsilon house? Or did he pick me off the street? My hope is that retracing my steps, taking the same streets, and wearing the same clothes will somehow bring me closer to finding out.

I assume he must've seen me snag the house key on the outside stoop, as I'd been talking to Felix; that he must've watched as I unlocked the door and went inside. The bigger questions: Had he been watching me even before that night? Had he been waiting for just the right moment? He knew my name, after all; though he could've seen it in my room, spelled in bubble letters over my desk.

According to investigators, the person who took me left no traces of DNA, and yet I don't recall any kind of protective suit.

Just that ski mask.

And those sleek, black gloves.

I turn the corner, cross a main road, and proceed over the bridge, watching cars pass by. *Swish, swish.* My anxiety revs. I've never been in a car accident, but ever since I got back from the well, I haven't wanted to drive any more than I absolutely have to, particularly long distances, and especially after dark.

A man jogs in my direction—slim, medium height, and in his midtwenties. I meet his eyes, noticing how dark they look, nowhere close to blue. At the same moment, a car horn honks. I'm standing still, in the middle of the crosswalk.

I scurry forward and proceed into town, crossing the grassy field where the runner and I collided on the night of the party. The police tried to locate that guy, checking surveillance cameras at local shops and restaurants, unable to find any trace of him, aside from my word, which quickly lost all credibility.

The field is a smallish space, about the size of a basketball court, connecting two roads. I've been back here at least ten times, as if seeing it again—the grass, the trees, the rocky path that leads to the Lightning Bolt gas station—will reveal something new. But so far, it hasn't.

I move toward the path, just as I had that night, hearing a car door slam. I reach into my purse and wrap my hand around the wasp spray—just in case—as I approach the back of the gas station.

A woman is filling her tires, having just exited her car. I let out a breath and cross the street, picturing the van that nearly hit me—its bright white lights. As I stand in front of Sandie's Mini-Mart, the motor inside my chest begins to race. I run my palms over my forearms, still able to feel the scars—tangible proof. *I really fell here.*

"Excuse me?" a male voice says.

I turn to look. Someone's standing there: a tall guy, with dark hair and tanned skin. He props his sunglasses atop his head, enabling me to see his pale blue eyes and thick, hooded lids.

A gasping-sucking sound escapes out my mouth.

The guy says something, but I don't hear the words. My eyes are locked on his thin red lips and slight overbite. A darkish mole sits on his chin.

Is it him? *Could it be him?*

My mind flashes back, picturing the guy with the ski mask cramming a cloth into my mouth. *Did he have an overbite? Or hooded eyelids?* Would I have noticed?

"Excuse me," he says again, studying my face. "I'd like to get in."

I'm standing in the way, in front of the door handles. My heart hammers so hard inside my chest, I can feel it against my bones. It makes my lungs compress.

The guy scoots around me and starts to go in, grabbing the handle, before letting it go.

The door falls closed.

He turns to me as I wheeze.

"Terra?"

I take out the spray.

"Are you okay?" he asks.

I can't respond, can't seem to get enough breath.

"You're not okay." He reaches for my forearm and starts to pull me away.

"No!" I shout; the word bubbles up from somewhere inside me. I take a step back, losing his grip. I hold the wasp spray outward to keep him back.

The guy raises his hands. People in the parking lot turn to look.

A woman with a baby comes out of the store. She backs away when she sees me.

"Terra?" the guy says, his hands still high. "Don't you know me? Do you recognize me?"

I picture the ski-masked face, the bright red tongue waggling out the hole . . . My arm shakes, holding the spray. I use my other hand to steady it, clutching the can like a gun, like the way you see on crime shows, with a wide-legged stance.

"It's me," he says. "Connor Loggins . . . You used to live on my street. Bailey Road . . . Our parents were friends."

Bailey Road?

The house that burned.

"I've been away for a bit," he says. "I was in college, then med school . . . I'm just finishing up my residency. Do you remember me at all? Connor Loggins," he says again, louder this time as if that will make a difference.

And maybe it does, because I *do* remember Connor. His bright green Jeep. His millions of gaming cards. The way he topped his pizza with ketchup and string beans. My parents once had dinner with his, in the Logginses' backyard. But Connor was older than I was by at least ten years. We didn't really have too much in common.

"Do you remember my parents?" I ask him.

"I do." His face brightens. "Your dad let me borrow his drum pad and sticks when I wanted to learn."

Did my dad play the drums? Why don't I know? What else can he tell me?

"I heard you were having a rough time," he continues, before I can ask. He takes a step closer. His hands extend to the spray can, the way you see in movies: the good guy tactfully maneuvering the gun from the villain's hands.

My face crumples as I let him. Why am I always the villain? Why do I never get to be the hero of my own story?

ere, parked in the drive. I crawl into the back and curl up on the
r, beneath the yoga blanket. It feels somewhat safe here with my
s closed and the doors locked. There's just me and my breath, me
whatever story I want to tell myself about where I am and how
t to this point.

Except the stories aren't coming.

My mind won't stop reeling.

It isn't as easy as it was, freshman year, when Charley, a boy
mo who loved fantasy as much as I did, would engage me in
-playing and storytelling in an effort to escape reality. As soon
break time hit, we'd flee into the quiet room—where we were
er actually quiet—and sit on beanbags, spinning tales inspired by
ryday items, like the mood ring I'd won as part of Dr. Beckett's
ia challenge.

"Let's use it as part of a story," Charley said. "Imagine the
g gives the wearer a superpower. Which power would you
k?"

"Time travel. No question."

"Except practically all our stories are about time travel. Pick
in."

"Invisibility?"

"Now you're talking. So, think. What's our story?"

The question is just as relevant now. What's *my* story? About
rret? About whether or not he saw me tonight? Does he think I'm
roubled as everyone says?

I reach for my phone and log on to Jane, hoping to find
ton.

JA Admin: Welcome, NightTerra. Remember the rules: no
judgments, no swearing, no inappropriate remarks. This is a
safe space for honesty and support.

Paylee22: Hey, Terra! I'm so happy you logged on!!!

"I'm sorry," I tell him. "I thought you were someone else." Does
he still have the drum pad? Would it be weird to ask for it back?

"Don't worry about it," Connor says. He waves to the onlook-
ers—a horde of people—telling everyone that everything's fine.
"Why don't we sit down for a second?" He motions to a bench in
front of the store.

I move toward it. The fumes from a car heat my face. The smell
of diesel fuel and something else—hairspray, maybe—fills my
senses, makes my throat close up.

"Is there anyone you want me to call?" He sits down beside me.

I shake my head, just wanting him to go. "I have my own
phone." I pull it out and hold it up as proof.

"I really think you should call your aunt. That's who you're
living with, right?"

"I'm fine, really." I manage a full breath.

"How about I call you a cab? My treat."

I clench my teeth, unsure how things went so horribly wrong:
Connor Loggins, from Bailey Road, with the ketchup-and-string-
bean-smothered pizza . . . After the fire, his parents sent a $500
check to the local bank, where a relief fund had been set up. Did I
ever send the Loggins family a thank-you note?

"Well?" he asks.

"Thank you," I say, maybe a little too late. I stand up. My head
feels woozy. I peer all around, checking my surroundings. Isn't there
a bus stop on the corner? Didn't Detective Marshall mention that
once, when she asked if I'd considered taking it home that night?

I go to text my aunt.

But I spot someone else first: Garret, the guy from the sorority
party, the one who'd wanted to drive me home.

He's going into the store.

"Terra?" Connor asks, still waiting for my reply.

"My ride's here," I tell him.

"Are you sure?"

"Yes." I nod, not sure of anything. Still, I head inside the store.

Garret stands at the coffee station with his back toward me. Ever since that night, I've wanted to talk to him—to ask what he saw or who he knew. According to investigators, his alibi checked out. After the party, he and his roommates went to an all-night diner, ate platefuls of pancakes (the waitress can attest), then returned to their apartment.

But what if investigators got the details wrong? What if the waitress had confused them with another group? Or might she have remembered them from a different night?

I've spent so many shifts, working at the library, at the same college where I went to the sorority mixer, searching the faces of students, waiting to spot his. And now, here he is: same dark rumpled hair, same square black glasses.

A loud crash sounds.

My chest constricts.

I turn to look, only to discover the crash was from me. A display of juice cans, taller than I am. At least twenty of the cans have toppled to the floor. One has busted open. Dark liquid comes shooting out, like a hose, spraying my legs, coloring the floor red. Contents under pressure, just like me.

The guy working behind the counter comes darting out, grabbing a bin.

"I'm so sorry," I tell him, at least that's what I mean to say.

I look up. Garret is staring straight at me. His mouth parts. Did he just say something—to the worker? To me?

I open my mouth to speak, even though I have no words and know no answers, so nothing comes out. I turn back around and hurry out the door.

11

I walk back to my aunt's house, taking the mai[n] back to the night of the sorority party and talkin[g] long walk home. A year ago, at this time, we [made an] agreement: to be one another's emergency cris[is] ever either of us needed it. So many nights, h[e] issues about his mom's new husband or his fathe[r] to spend time with him. I did the same, waki[ng from] sound sleep to talk about the fire, how I wish i[t had] gone up in smoke.

"Then who would I cheat off of in health clas[s?]"

"It's *health* class; you shouldn't even need to ch[eat.]"

"Still, I wouldn't survive without you, Terra-[] I love you deeply."

"Yes, and I love you too."

Before he left for college, we made a pact. [We ate] onion rings in a café not far from the Emo moth[er] to text, call, or FaceTime at least once a day or [when either] of us needed. But that pact petered out after h[e settled] at school. For me: It hurt to hear how much fu[n he had in] college. For him: I'm not really sure, but he s[topped returning] my texts.

Finally, I reach the house. My aunt isn't hom[e]

NightTerra: Who else is on here?

Paylee22: I think it's just you and me for now. No one else is chatting.

Paylee22: So, what's up?

Paylee22: Have you watched Summer's Story yet?

NightTerra: Not yet.

Paylee22: What are you waiting for? It's sooooo good!!!

Paylee22: Do you have recs for me? I'll need something else to binge once I've blasted through all the seasons.

Paylee22: ???

Paylee22: Hello?

Paylee22: You there?

NightTerra: Yes, here.

Paylee22: Is everything ok?

NightTerra: Define ok.

Paylee22: What happened?

Paylee22: ???

NightTerra: I retraced my steps again.

Paylee22: In a word: Why?

Paylee22: Why?

Paylee22: WHY is that a good idea?

NightTerra: I never said it was.

Paylee22: So, then why do you do it?

NightTerra: Sometimes I'm not even sure myself.

NightTerra: Other times, I feel there are too many reasons.

Paylee22: Give me one reason.

NightTerra: Maybe if I found some clue or made some connection, people would have to believe my story.

Paylee22: FYI, the people who love you are supposed to believe you regardless of proof. #Fact

NightTerra: It's just pretty isolating when everyone thinks you're a liar. #Truth

Paylee22: I'm in your life and I don't think you're a liar.

NightTerra: Maybe doing enough of these searches will help to reassure me that everything happened the way I remember.

Paylee22: Why do you need reassurance?

Paylee22: Are negative voices causing you self-doubt?

Paylee22: I'll never doubt you, ok?

NightTerra: I really wish you were here.

Paylee22: I'm always here, whenever you need.

Paylee22: And I'll always believe you.

NightTerra: xo

Paylee22: xoxo

NightTerra: I should probably get something to eat. My stomach keeps growling.

NightTerra: Except I don't want to log off yet.

NightTerra: You help keep me sane.

Paylee22: So, take me with you!

NightTerra: While I make my food?

Paylee22: Why not? I can open a private room. It'll be like I'm right there in the kitchen with you in case you want to chat.

NightTerra: Are you sure?

Paylee22: Of course. I know you'd do the same for me.

NightTerra: I would!

Paylee22: Exactly. I'll send you a link now. Ok?

NightTerra: Thank you again!! xo

Paylee22: xoxo

NightTerra has left the chat room. There are currently 3 people in the chat room.

12

When I woke up again, I couldn't see. I blinked a bunch of times, but the darkness remained. Was the lid still closed? How long had I been there? More than a day? Was anyone searching for me?

I crawled to a seated position, with my back pressed against the dirt wall, and closed my eyes, trying to trick myself into believing that it wasn't so dark, that my lack of sight was of my own choosing.

In that tarry stillness, I asked myself questions, like who he was, and why he picked me, and how long he would keep me there.

Was I his prisoner? Like that movie I saw where the woman locked her daughter's killer in a cage, behind her house . . . She brought him food and water, keeping him alive. Would the guy who took me do the same? Or was he planning to do other things?

What other things?

What could I do?

I drew my knees upward and gnawed at my kneecaps, straight through my sweats, breaking the skin, as my mind continued to reel. Was he going to come back? What would be worse: seeing him again or being left there to die?

To stop myself from thinking, I hummed out loud. Sound in place of thoughts.

The taste of blood instead of food.

The sensation of touch because I needed to feel something

besides the ache of my bones against the dirt floor and walls. And so, I touched the parts of myself I'd never consciously touched before— the lines on the arch of my foot, the bump on the back of my ear, the bones of my bloody knees, and the smooth tissue inside my cheek.

When, finally, sometime later, the light came on again and the tomb-like lid tremored at least partially open, I made like a cockroach—the way roaches scatter when you turn on a light switch, the clattering of their legs across the tile countertop, like the ones at the summer house my parents had once rented; the shock of light was too much to bear, and l curled up in the corner, shielding my eyes, yet wanting to see.

Who was there?

What was happening?

I tried to scream out, but a weird sputtering-hacking sound spewed from my mouth. My throat stung from the sharp edges of my voice. I needed water—more than anything else. I looked up, just as bursts of light shot out in front of my eyes, distorting the images.

Was he leaning into the well, over the opening? Looking down at me? Was that his arm? Was he dangling something?

I closed my stinging-stabbing eyes. When I opened them again, I noticed almost instantly: A blanket sat at my feet—a gray fleece square, about four feet long and wide. Where had it come from? When had it gotten there? While I'd been sleeping? *Or just now?*

"Let me out!" I tried to shout.

When nothing happened and no one answered, I slid the story-book toward me, across the ground, suspecting a message might be hidden among the pages. I searched the cover for the author's name, but it didn't list one. No name was included on the spine or in the interior pages either.

I flipped the book open, my fingers fumbling, the pages sticking. The illustration showed the girl from the front cover, with the braided hair and the long blue dress, leaning over a chicken coop. The book tells the story of Clara, a girl who lives on a farm and goes to a one-room school. Clara wishes to be invited to a classmate's twelfth birthday party, as all the other girls were. She soon meets William, a troll-like character and the minder of the magical Wishy Water Well, who says he can help her wish come true.

I turned another page just as a banging noise startled my heart.

A gun?

A firework?

I stood up. Was it possible the police had finally come?

"I'm down here!" I screamed as best I could, over and over again, jumping up and down, slapping against the walls, pounding with my fists . . .

Finally, I tossed the book upward, picturing it popping up from the top of the well. But I couldn't tell if the book was hitting part of the roof or soaring into the air.

Was no one seeing it?

Nothing was happening, even when I yelled some more, screaming myself sick. Before I knew it, I was hacking up. Bile burned the back of my throat. I sank to the ground and curled into a ball with my cheek resting against the blanket. The stench of my puke—like week-old garbage that'd been baked in the sun—made my stomach churn. Meanwhile, hot, bubbling tears ran from my eyes. I directed them into my mouth, hoping to coat my throat, desperate to escape back to sleep.

NOW

13

Days later, in my room, unable to sleep, I grab my art book and start to draw yet another sketch of the guy who took me. I still picture him hovered over my bed. That's how I described him too—at the police station, to the sketch artist. But the final product looked far too generic, especially with his masked face and dark clothing; there was nothing distinguishable.

Except those eyes.

I've spent countless hours working on them, experimenting with various mediums, trying to get the right shade of blue—not like the sky, or the sea, or any of my pastels. His is a custom color. The closest I've come to achieving it is by mixing acrylics—teal, royal blue, and white—and even then . . . It's not quite right, not nearly brilliant enough.

Using colored pencils this time, I shade in the chest. It's too wide in my sketch, but that's how it felt—wide like a wall. His forehead was wide too, or maybe that was just the mask, and his chin appeared pointed. In my mind, I imagine a heart-shaped face with high cheekbones and smallish ears. But that's part of the problem: what my mind envisions, the place where creativity intersects reality. What did he truly look like beneath that mask?

How tall was he really?

How big were his hands?

"Did you see his eyebrows?" the sketch artist asked. "Did any of his hair peek out? Could you tell if the outline of his ear hit above or below the line of his nose?"

I really didn't know. "I wish I could remember."

"I'm almost surprised you don't picture him as more of a monster," Winnie-the-group-leader told me once. Because obviously monsters don't come in disguise. Obviously, they're as clear and cliché as those in storybooks and movies. And so, I played along, telling her about his serpent tongue, his clawlike hands, and his icy stare, further affirming what she already believed—it was all in my head, all concocted by me.

The ironic part: I kind of wanted to believe that too. When people tell you long enough that your story can't possibly be true, that it's the result of post-traumatic stress because your parents died and you don't know how to survive, it feels less isolating to agree, especially when those people are the "sane" ones: the police, the investigators, the doctors, the therapists . . .

There was no physical evidence.

They checked me out.

I opened myself up.

"No fingerprints."

"No signs of forced entry."

"No DNA."

"No water well within a twenty-mile radius of Hayberry Park."

There was no broken glass in my bedroom either; the tumbler of water I'd set by my bed that night—that I'd reached for in self-defense—was still fully intact; still sitting, half-empty, on my night table.

"Are you sure you picked it up and threw it at the guy?" my aunt asked me. "You heard the glass shatter?"

Did I? Could I really be sure?

Believing everyone else's stories—their versions of what happened—would make my life so much easier. So what if I'd had a brief bout of temporary insanity?

Of delusional delirium?

Of post-traumatic dissociation?

Of whatever else they were calling it today?

Big deal.

The only problem: There was no bout. I *did* get taken. "Why else would I get panic attacks just going to bed at night?"

"Why *wouldn't* you get them?" Dr. Mary asked, sitting across from me on her "safe and sound" sofa. "Don't forget: Five years ago, you went to bed and woke up to a fire that took both of your parents. You lived, while both of them died . . . I'd almost be surprised if you *didn't* experience the occasional panic attack."

"Okay, but how about the fairy-tale book? My mind wouldn't have just conjured that up."

"Or wouldn't it have? Think about it. The fairy-tale book centered on a sinister wishing well tucked away in a menacing forest. Is it so hard to believe that the well represents the death of hope (literally, wishes, in this case) and a prison your mind's created to trap yourself in, because you feel the need for punishment?"

"Punishment?"

"Have you ever heard of something called survivor guilt?"

I shook my head, but it didn't take a psychology degree to guess what it meant.

"Might you be punishing yourself for surviving the fire, something your parents weren't able to do? Might the vast, thick forest symbolize an overwhelming situation—one you can't find a way out of?"

Except I did get out. "That's not it."

"The burning house is gone now, Terra. But perhaps your mind's creating its own version of a fire."

"I *am* my mind. It's governed by me." I squeezed the belly of my troll key chain over and over, making the eyes pop.

"The mind processes information to the best of its ability," she continued. "It isn't perfect. It protects itself—and protects *you* . . . It perceives events and situations as both real and unreal."

"I know what's real."

She mustered a patronizing smile. "Think of it this way: getting abducted, surviving the well . . . It brought you closer to your aunt, didn't it? Isn't that what you said?"

"Because that was the truth."

"Maybe you manifested that truth because you longed for that closeness. Maybe prior attempts didn't get you what you needed."

"Prior attempts?"

"It's my understanding you had a history of ditching school, disappearing for days, not telling anyone where you were. Isn't that correct? Didn't you also get in trouble for shoplifting?"

"It was just a notebook. I needed it for school, and I'd forgotten my wallet. I would've paid the store back somehow. Plus, I didn't *disappear*. It was just two days at a friend's house."

"The point is those attention-seeking strategies didn't seem to work. So maybe you found another way—a more effective strategy. That's survival by pure definition. Embrace it. Be proud of that will."

I continue to sketch, burned out on everyone's theories, but knowing they aren't all completely untrue. At some point, during the fire, after the firefighters had arrived, all reality faded away. I know I was there, but I don't remember watching the scene unfold: the mounting flames, the irreparable damage . . .

Supposedly, I was checked out by a medic. But I don't remember that either, or the phone call I had with my aunt in the back of the ambulance.

My patchy memory—like an abyss of its own—is just one of the many reasons I ended up in the hospital after the fire, and probably a major reason why no one believed me, years later, after I got back from the well.

"You woke up in a neighbor's house with no recollection of how you got there," Dr. Mary persisted.

"What does this have to do with the fairy-tale book?"

"It has to do with the mind, with how the brain regulates trauma. Does that make sense?"

I shook my head. "The book is real. I'll prove it."

But I've yet to prove anything. Because I can't find the book (or evidence that it exists), which is why I've started writing the story myself. I've asked librarians far and wide, both online and in person, to help me find a copy.

"Reality Bites Press?" most of them ask. "I've never heard of it."

A reference librarian in the town next door asked if it was a self-published title. "But even still," she continued, "it would've been copyrighted, unless the author published it with his own 'Reality Bites' printing press, without registering the title first. Do you think that could be a possibility?"

But even she knew.

I could see it in her smirk.

I was that crazy girl from the Emo school, who'd made the false allegations and wasted everyone's time.

One week prior, the news had reported about the dropped case with no leads or substantial evidence. I'd spoken to a journalist about the fairy-tale book. In that same interview, a university professor, a supposed expert in legends, folklore, and fairy tales, was quoted as saying he'd never (in his thirty years of research and having written two dissertations on the subject) heard of *The Forest Girl and the Wishy Water Well*.

So, where does that leave me? With zero proof and a bunch of generic sketches of a darkly clothed man with eyes the wrong color.

I check the Jane site, but Peyton isn't on and I really don't feel like chatting with anyone else. I log on to Hulu to watch an episode of *Summer's Story*, hoping that wherever Peyton is, she's doing the same, that we're watching the show together. The mere idea helps make me feel a little less alone.

14

On the night I got home from the well, I fished the hidden key from the ivy planter by the door and used it to enter the house, just like any other day, like nothing bad had ever happened.

There were no police cars parked out front.

No news trucks.

No missing-person signs.

No one was investigating inside the house.

I went inside, locked the door behind me, and saw the reflection that stared back in the entryway mirror. Layers of dirt painted my face, outlined my eyes, and encrusted my lips. My hair hung down in clay-like clumps.

Somehow, I managed to drag myself up the stairs, straight to the bathroom, where I turned the shower valve to the highest setting and stepped inside, without a second thought, still fully clothed.

The sweet, hot water pounded against my chest, soaked through my shirt. I opened my mouth and drank the water up, nearly choking on the liquid. Dirt and pebbles slid down my throat. My teeth ached. My jaw throbbed.

Once my thirst had finally been quenched, I spat some of the water out as I washed my teeth. I also gargled to clean my throat. Blood and dirt ran from my bare feet.

I scrunched down to the floor of the tub, closed my eyes, and pictured a ball of flames burning up inside me. My hands screamed, the skin raw, blistered, and broken. Where had my socks gone? When had I peeled them off: my protective gloves?

Despite the soap and water, I couldn't seem to get the nubs of my fingers clean. They were just so dirty. My ears were still so itchy. Was that a rock embedded beneath the skin of my palm?

I watched as the water filled the tub basin. Dirt from my body had clogged up the drain. But I didn't want to move, didn't care that my skin was wrinkled like a prune.

Sometime later, a floorboard creaked. My heart instantly clenched. I grabbed a razor and watched the bathroom door through the crack in the shower curtain, listening for the sound of footsteps up the stairs, like a wild animal awaiting its predator.

"Terra, is that you?" My aunt was home. Her voice didn't sound urgent.

I heard the clamor of her keys against the hallway table, followed by the clapping of her heels up the stairs.

I closed the gap in the shower curtain.

"Hey, stranger." She rapped on the open bathroom door. "What have you been up to? I called Jessie's grandmother. She said that you and Jessie were still at Jessie's sister's sorority house, but you didn't answer my calls. I was starting to get worried."

Just starting? "What day is it?" How much time had passed?

"Seriously? It's Wednesday."

How was that possible? "Are you sure?"

"What do you mean? I think I know what day it is."

I'd only been gone for four days?

"Wait, do you have a cold?" she asked. "Your voice sounds funny. Are you not feeling well?"

When was the last time I'd felt even fine?

"Terra?"

Rule number six: Take your time to think things through. Except I couldn't really think. My body froze, and yet my mind raced.

Logic wanted me to tell her what'd happened. But it felt too big to convey. What words would I use?

When had I taken off my clothes? Was it me who'd wound the leg of my sweatpants around the tub faucet? Had I also rolled up my tee and set it on the soap dish?

"What's that?" she asked.

It was only then I noticed: the stains of dirt on the rim of the bathtub, the glob of mud on the edge of the shower curtain. Had I also made a puddle on the tile floor?

"Terra? What happened here? Why won't you answer me?"

I bit my knee, making a circle of tooth marks, still unsure what to say.

"Terra?" she repeated, peeking inside the curtain. Her eyes widened at the sight of me. My dirty self. In the dirty tub.

The water looked like the dirt soup I used to make back in my sandbox when I was four and five.

I watched her mouth move, but I couldn't process the words. Her face contorted into shapes—wide, gaping, scrunched, shriveled. So much expression; I'd never seen it from her before, not even after my parents died.

She grabbed a towel and got my robe, then sat with me on the ceramic tile floor; its hardness reminded me of the ground in the well.

Aunt Dessa held me tight and patted my back, asking over and over again, "What happened?"

I remember the sensation of her pendant charms against my forehead: the letters *O* and *M*, for O'Dessa and Maeve (my aunt and my mother), two sisters who'd once been so inseparable they wore each other's initials around their necks.

"*What happened?*" she repeated. "You can tell me anything, sweetie."

Sweetie. The word didn't make sense, because she'd never used it on me before, had never held me so close either—not even after the fire.

"Tell me," she repeated. *Did she always smell like cinnamon? Was this softer version of her voice the one she reserved for her patients at the hospital?*

Over the next several hours, I told her everything—every last bit. She acted like she believed me, grabbing her phone, calling the police . . .

"Is that why you called me that night?" she asked. "You didn't leave a message." Because her mailbox was full. "I assumed it was because you were going to stay with Jessie, just like your text said . . ."

We spent the blur of days at a hotel in the city—one with a king-size bed and soft white sheets—while investigators collected evidence from the house. When we got back, Aunt Dessa continued to shower me with love, brushing my hair, reading me books, and apologizing over and over: *I'm so sorry. I should've known better. Should've made sure to talk to you. Shouldn't have listened to Jessie's grandmother . . .*

She drew me salt baths (I still hadn't felt clean) and set up the living room sofa with fresh sheets and a pillow and blanket.

And made me food.

And urged me to talk.

But my answers weren't good enough. Investigators told her I wasn't reliable enough. Doctors shook their heads and said I wasn't strong enough:

"Don't you hear it? She's still humming."

"You know she needs serious help, don't you? You need to consider the repercussions five, ten, even fifteen years from now when she still hasn't received the support she needs."

Enough. Enough. Enough.

Need. Need. Need.

"Terra . . ." Detective Marshall's voice.

I'd come to know it well. It sounded extra loud, as if being abducted meant I could no longer hear well.

"I need you to answer a few more questions now, okay?"

Not okay.

She asked anyway. "When you exited the park, did you pass through the city square?"

"I did." I nodded.

"The police station is on the corner of Main Street and Langley Terrace. The fire station, as well. These are places that are open twenty-four hours. Are you aware of that?"

"Yes. I'm aware." I only stopped for water at the fountain, by one of the park's entrances. I'd already told them this; why did we have to go over it again? "I wanted to get home." My eyes slammed shut. My hands wouldn't stop shaking. "I really just wanted to clean myself up."

"Do you think the police would've cared that you weren't looking your best, that you needed a shower?"

I shook my head. "I wasn't thinking about them."

"We've talked to some people and gone through your records," Detective Marshall said. "We know about the shoplifting, as well as your habit of disappearing. According to your principal, you have a record of ditching school, taking off, not to be found again until several hours later. Might this habit of making yourself scarce be the situation in this case too?"

"Tell us the truth now, Terra," another voice said. "If you're honest, you won't get in trouble."

I could no longer argue. What could I possibly say? It seemed that everyone had already gotten my story figured out.

Everyone.

Except me.

15

JA Admin: Welcome, NightTerra. Remember the rules: no judgments, no swearing, no inappropriate remarks. This is a safe space for honesty and support.

TulipPrincess: The warped part? I blame myself.

RainyDayFever: For your mother's BS?

TulipPrincess: For letting everything happen to begin with.

CityGirlSal: Do you realize how screwed up that sounds?

TulipPrincess: Screwed up or not, I shouldn't have been hanging with my mother's bf. I should've said no when he insisted we watch movies together every Tuesday night, then twice a week.

Paylee22: It wasn't your fault.

TulipPrincess: It was my fault I didn't trust my instincts. I should've suspected he was garbage when he started giving me money to spend on the weekend.

RainyDayFever: Paylee's right. It wasn't your fault.

CityGirlSal: My therapist says the victim almost always blames herself.

TulipPrincess: The victims are also the ones who have to relive the trauma over and over again with everyone's questions and with the consequences of whatever happened.

CityGirlSal: You can pretty much tell what people are thinking just by the questions they ask. "Why didn't you tell someone?" "Wasn't there a parent or teacher you could talk to?" #Gross

CityGirlSal: What's the right answer anyway? "Yes, there was someone, but I was too stupid to think of that"? Or, "Yes, there was someone, but I didn't go that route so I probably deserved what I got"?

TulipPrincess: On top of everything else, my bf broke up with me because he couldn't understand why I took that guy's money, why it didn't set off warning bells.

TulipPrincess: The thing is, it did, but I took the money anyway. I'm not even sure why.

TulipPrincess: Maybe because I felt like not taking it would've hurt his feelings. How messed up is that?

RainyDayFever: It isn't your fault, Tulip!!

Paylee22: Def not!

NightTerra: I'm really sorry.

NightTerra: But I'm also really thankful for everything you're sharing. It's helpful to know I'm not the only one feeling stupid for her choices.

TulipPrincess: You're def not the only one.

TulipPrincess: But you shouldn't feel stupid. None of us should. We've all been through enough crap.

TulipPrincess: Notice I can say that clearly, but feeling it is something else entirely. #SelfBlameIsABitch

JA Admin: Remember the rules. Please, no swearing.

TulipPrincess: Sorry! #pottymouth

TulipPrincess: I need to get some sleep.

TulipPrincess: Thanks for listening, everyone.

NightTerra: Thank you!

CityGirlSal: We're here for you, Tulip!

RainyDayFever: Always here!

Paylee22: Always willing to listen!

TulipPrincess: Thank you, thank you, thank you.

TulipPrincess: G'night.

NightTerra: Good night, TulipPrincess.

Paylee22: Sweet dreams.

TulipPrincess has left the chat room.

Instead of logging out, I send Peyton a direct message: Exit to private chat?

She replies: YES! I'll send you a link.

When the link pops up for the private room, I click it, excited to tell her I watched an episode of *Summer's Story*.

Paylee22 has left the chat room.

NightTerra has left the chat room.

There are currently 4 people in the chat room.

16

A couple of weeks after I got home from the well, Aunt Dessa took me to the grocery store. Despite her obsession with all things healthy, she told me to pick out whatever snacks I wanted, and led me down aisle after aisle, pointing out chips, chocolate, and cartons of ice cream.

As we headed for the checkout, I spotted Jessie's car pulling into the lot and parking by the entrance. A gaggle of Emo girls burst out the back, laughing at something funny. Jessie lagged behind, pulling on her jacket, trying her best to keep up. I hadn't seen her since I'd gotten back from the well, but we'd exchanged a few texts just days before:

Omg, Terra!?! I can't believe what happened!

Is it true? Everything I'm hearing???

Everyone's talking about it, asking me questions, like if I've talked to you and what I saw.

Do you think it was that guy you
were talking to at the party?

Omg, you totally should've crashed
with me at the Theta house.

> I'm pretty sure it wasn't him. He
> was already questioned.

So was I!!! Which made me feel
guilty, even though I wasn't.

Totally freaky!!!

How are you, btw? People are
asking.

Is there anything I can do?

> Maybe you could come visit.

Definitely. Just tell me when.

> Friday?

Sounds good.

It did sound good. But Jessie never came. And I never called to
ask her why. And so, days later, at the grocery store with my aunt,
when I spotted Jessie's car pull into the parking lot, I was looking
forward to seeing her.

But the group of Emo girls spotted me first through the window
glass.

"Are those friends of yours?" Aunt Dessa asked.

I shook my head because, aside from Jessie, they honestly weren't. I'd had classes with a couple of them, had gone to group therapy with a few more . . . But none had been girls I'd spent any real time with.

"Are you sure?" Aunt Dessa persisted. "That dark-haired girl looks a little familiar."

Hannah Cahill. She blew me kisses.

Juanita, class dancer, came right up to the glass, smooshing her nose against it.

As soon as we stepped outside, the gaggle of girls swarmed me like flies to roadkill. Jessie fought her way to the forefront, wrapping her arms around me. "Hey, friend! I've missed you," she said. "I'm so glad to see you."

They stood all around me, trembling, teary-eyed, and clutching one another. It took me a beat to realize their tears were for me.

"I'm so relieved you're okay," one of them said.

I turned toward the voice, not knowing where to look.

Asia from English class reached out to touch my shoulder.

Juanita couldn't stop crying.

Betsy from bio held out her potato chips: therapy in a bag.

Their voices competed, talking over one another, mixing together, and stirring like chicken soup inside my hungry soul:

"I was so scared when I heard the news. Thank god you got away."

"My older sister was at that party too. Do they know who did it yet?"

"I can't even believe how amazing you look."

"Rock star amazing."

"I think I'd be hiding under my bed right about now."

"Oh my god, me too."

"Me three."

"Please, don't even think twice; if you need anything, call me. I'll be there in a second."

"I'll be there in a millisecond. We're practically neighbors."

"I'm here for you, Terra."

"We're all here for you."

"Terra . . . You're so, so brave."

"So strong."

"So unbelievably heroic."

I found myself spinning in circles, in the center of their love, feeling more accepted than I ever thought possible.

But where was Jessie? No longer part of the gaggle. Instead, she sat on the pavement, several yards back, sucking her pinkie finger (a nervous habit she'd given up years before).

In the days that followed, I tried texting her, but she didn't respond. And then, a short week later, on a dark and desperate night, when Aunt Dessa had been working and Felix couldn't be reached, I called blowing-kisses Hannah, hoping for that shoulder she'd offered, imagining all of us (her, Juanita, Betsy, Asia, and Jessie) meeting at one of their houses—one big, happy gaggle.

Hannah picked up right away. "Who's this?" she asked, not having recognized my number.

"It's me. Terra. I was hoping that maybe we could get together to talk."

"Are you kidding me?" she snapped. "How could you lie like that? Some people have *real* problems."

My chest tightened. What was she talking about? "What are you talking about?"

"On second thought, I'm not even that surprised. I knew you were a liar as soon as you opened your mouth at Emo—all that talk about your parents, in the present tense, as if they were still alive and you weren't the fire girl . . ."

"Wait, *what*?"

"I saw Jessie's post. Actually, I've seen a lot of posts. Famous yet?" The phone clicked off.

I went online to see what she was talking about. Jessie had blasted me on social media, saying I'd once told her I'd do almost anything to be famous: *I never thought she'd stoop this low and waste everybody's time and money,* she wrote. *But obviously I was wrong. #FireGirl*

My heart caved in.

My tears poured out.

Had I said that? Or anything remotely close to it? Maybe once, after a talent show, when a group of us, Jessie included, sang an a cappella version of "Lean on Me." We'd gotten a standing ovation. Everybody loved it. Maybe I'd said something about being famous then?

I tried calling Felix again. Still no answer. "Please call me back," I said at the beep, my voice all gravelly.

I crawled beneath my bed with my bottle of maple syrup and the doorknob from my old bedroom, wishing I could go back in time to the night of the fire and have another chance. I wouldn't have fled out the window, climbing down a neighbor's ladder. I would've tried to save my parents instead of thinking solely of myself. But there are no do-overs in a crisis situation: rule number seven.

It's dark under my bed, but not nearly dark enough to erase all time and space—not dark like the bottom of a dark, dark well, with the light turned off and the lid closed tight.

17

It wasn't long after Jessie's post that word began to spread about who I was: the daughter of parents who'd died in a house fire; a girl who'd spent months on the mental health floor of a hospital; a student at the school for emotionally disturbed kids . . . To those I knew—and others I didn't—I was a liar, a loner, and an absolute loon.

An anonymous former teacher told the local news I was "the kind of girl who sets little fires as a distraction, so you'll never see the blazing inferno inside" me. Another no-name source said I moped the school halls like "a walking dead girl: there but not; present but absent. It was really kind of creepy."

A Facebook page for the town where I live had a whole thread devoted to me and my case. I made the mistake of reading the comments: people complaining what a waste of taxpayer money it was to investigate the fantastical claims of someone as confused and disoriented as I am.

My aunt's home became the one place I could escape from all the voices—until one night, sitting across from Aunt Dessa on the living room sofa, thinking we were going to discuss takeout options for our girls' night in, I felt her staring at the side of my face.

I looked up from a menu, focused on the gold pendants around her neck—the initials *O* and *M*—wishing more than anything that my mom were there. "Is everything okay?"

She scooted in closer, took both of my hands, and asked the burning question: "Is there something you want to tell me?"

"What do you mean?" I asked.

"I mean, did you really get taken?"

A match struck inside my heart, burning a thick, black hole. I gazed down at our clasped hands, noticing the trembling of my fingers. Did she feel it too?

"Tell me the truth," she continued. "Is it possible you might've spent those nights at a friend's house, someone I don't know? It wouldn't have been the first time. Remember last summer, not to mention this past Christmas . . ."

How could I have forgotten? The time I fell asleep in the back of my parents' car, because Aunt Dessa wasn't home and the house had felt too vacant. And then this past Christmas, not wanting to be alone, I escaped to Felix's grandparents' place. I hadn't told my aunt, mostly because Aunt Dessa had to work on and off that weekend anyway, Christmas Day included, so what was the point in being "home"? It took two days for her to notice I wasn't around. And eight additional hours for the police to find me.

And so, flash forward to after I got home from the well, and there was no actual evidence I'd been abducted to begin with, my aunt began to doubt my story. I knew it too—could tell from the twitching of her lip and the narrowing of her eyes each time she asked me a question.

In a last-ditch effort, I told her the story of my tooth—how, while I was in the well, a piece had broken off and I'd nearly choked swallowing it down. "Could you take me to the dentist?" I asked. Because x-rays didn't lie. The dentist would be able to see.

We drove into the city the following day. The hygienist sat me in the chair and took a bunch of x-rays.

The dentist came in and inspected the photos.

An assistant inserted a metal instrument into my mouth to keep

my tongue from flailing, which was harder than I'd expected, because it flashed me back to the night I was taken, the cloth over my
mouth, the poking and prodding . . .

"Open up a little wider," the dentist ordered, using her long,
gloved fingers to pull my cheek back.

I did as she said, pressing my eyes shut, noticing the trembling
of my limbs.

"How are you doing?" a nurse asked, giving my forearm a
squeeze.

I pictured a balloon inside my chest, filling up with air. Eventually, the balloon popped, and I let out a loud, retching gasp from
the back of my throat.

The dentist withdrew her fingers.

The metal instrument was snatched away.

The overhead light clicked off.

"Are you okay?" someone asked.

I reluctantly opened my eyes as the dentist stepped away. Could
she read my mind? Was she giving me space?

She checked and rechecked the x-ray pictures, enlarging them on
the screen before coming to her conclusion: "There are no cracks or
fractures that I can detect."

How was that even possible?

"That's a good thing," the hygienist said, unclipping my bib.
"Everything looks great."

"How come you don't look happy?" The assistant frowned.

"Maybe she wants to rinse," another voice said.

What I wanted was to curl up into a ball with my bottle of
maple syrup and shut them all out. Being told I didn't have a broken
tooth—after the story I'd shared about getting it lodged in my
throat—just made me look crazier.

"That's great news," Aunt Dessa said, but her lip quivered when
she said it. Had she been hoping for a fracture too . . . some outward
sign, a shred of evidence to prove her only sister's daughter wasn't
absolutely nuts?

Investigators thought I was nuts too.

"How is it you were able to get away without barely a scratch? And the scratches you did get—they were from a fall at the mini-mart, not from anything your perpetrator did. Not from the place where you were allegedly being kept."

"How about the dirt?" I argued. "I came back from the well covered in it. Plus, my palms were cut up . . . from the chain."

"Right. Yes. The medical report says there was evidence of a manual struggle."

Nothing more? "What does that even mean?"

"There were no signs of breaking and entering. So, how do you propose the perpetrator was able to get in?"

"Your aunt states she came home early from her shift that morning, just before four a.m.," someone else said. "That would've put you alone in the house for less than two hours. Is it a coincidence the perpetrator knew when that short window of alone time was?"

"Life can be a real bitch," Dr. Mary said weeks later in her hospital office. A fleece blanket lay across her lap. It reminded me of the blanket I'd had in the well, distracting me. Why did she have it?

Aunt Dessa was there too. We sat in a circle of seats for what was supposed to have been a "family meeting." But that obviously wasn't true, because Detective Marshall was there as well. Her face had a perma-scowl.

Dr. Mary angled toward me, running her fingers over the pale gray fabric. Her voice was the physical equivalent of powdered sugar, nauseatingly sweet. "Maybe I shouldn't be so crass as to use the b-word, but I don't believe in sugarcoating. Say it like it is, right? Sometimes when we really need something, and the conscious mind isn't making it happen, the subconscious one takes over. It finds a way; it may not always be an admirable way. But this isn't about admiration, is it, Terra? It's about survival, and you know what? We're wired for it. You're wired for it."

I peered at my aunt, hoping to snag her attention, but she wouldn't look up from her lap; she just kept fiddling with the drawstrings on her pants: tie, untie, tie, untie. Why wasn't she coming to my defense?

"I'm not lying," I told them. "I showed you the place where I was being kept."

"What you showed us was Hayberry Park," the detective said. "Do you know how big it is?"

Over a thousand acres. Hayberry is roughly four miles long and two miles wide. Some locals refer to it as the Land of the Lost, the perfect place to hide a body.

"Do you know how many people get lost in all that space per year?" Detective Marshall asked.

Eleven people last year—at least, according to the park rangers I've spoken to.

"But not you," she continued. "Despite a lack of food and water, which, by the way, we were unable to confirm because your medical exams looked good."

"I'm not lying," I repeated.

"No one's accusing you of anything," Dr. Mary said. "This is a safe space." Perhaps the biggest lie of all.

"There's never been a single dwelling in Hayberry," Detective Marshall persisted. "No cabins or shelters, not even a forest ranger station. Do you know what that means?"

I did. I nodded. We'd been through this before. It meant there was no need for water wells.

Detective Marshall scooched her chair closer, puncturing a hole in the circle. "The person who took you . . . You say he may have been a jogger you bumped into, but you're just not sure . . . If you felt like you were being followed, why didn't you call the police? You called your friend Felix that night, correct?"

"Yes."

"But according to him, you never mentioned being followed, colliding with anyone, or nearly getting hit by a car. Is there a reason you never told him those things? Or that you'd texted your aunt earlier that night saying you'd be staying over at the sorority house?

Did you have some other plan that you don't want to tell us about now?"

"I don't . . . I just . . ."

Dr. Mary continued to paw the blanket. "Do you need a moment?"

"I took photos of the license plate," I said to whomever would listen. "Of the van that almost hit me."

"Too bad your phone is now untraceable."

Too bad I had to sit there.

Too bad no one believed me.

Too bad I got taken at all.

"I'm not lying," I said yet again, still staring at the top of my aunt's head. Why wouldn't she look up?

"Right now, I think you should focus on resting and recharging." Dr. Mary leaned in closer. "What do you think?"

Did it matter what I thought? "That sounds good," I lied, sucking back tears.

"I'm glad you think so." She smiled.

I stood up, more than ready to go. "So, are we done?"

But my aunt wasn't moving. And she still hadn't spoken. She sat slouched in the seat, unable to look me in the eye, to tell me what everybody already knew: They wanted me to stay there. They wanted to lock me up again.

"It'll only be for a little while," Dr. Mary said. "You'll be able to rest and recoup."

I reluctantly agreed, hoping that doing so would fix things somehow. Penance for surviving the fire? Time away while proof of my crime surfaced? I'm not really sure. But saying yes seemed like the right thing to do. And so, I did.

18

At work the following night, Katherine, the head librarian, places a steaming cup of coffee on the desk in front of me. "Still getting acclimated to working the zombie shift? This will help: straight black with a shot of espresso and a few droplets of garlic oil."

"Seriously?" I ask, curious about the garlic.

She winks at me in lieu of an answer. The mug is winking too: a big bloodshot eye sits above the words *Wake Up*.

"Thank you." I sit up straighter.

Katherine hired me despite my "bad-girl" reputation (her words, not mine), saying that my "three-dimensional backstory" was actually a bonus. To hell with the cookie-cutter caricature of the ho-hum librarian with glasses and a bun. She swiveled out from her desk, revealing Ruth Bader Ginsburg tattooed on one leg and a black version of Wonder Woman on the other. But the factor that really sealed the deal and earned me the job was my willingness to work the graveyard shift. And why not? Aunt Dessa is never home. And I don't like being alone at night.

Katherine rolls a cart full of book returns in my direction. "Feel like reshelving for a bit? Movement equals momentum."

"Sure." I take a few sips, then grab the cart and spend the next full hour reshelving books. Most everything is on the main floor, but a handful of nonfiction titles belong upstairs. I check their call numbers, then take the elevator up a flight.

The majority of tables are populated by groups of students, but there are also a handful of "singles" (as Katherine calls them), basically people working alone. I start to return the remaining books to their spots: a jumble of science titles. I grab one of the last books from the bottom rack, spotting the front cover right away. It features a picture of a water well with cobblestone walls.

I blink hard, sure I must be seeing things.

But I'm not.

The title of the book is *Water Wells and Septic Systems*.

I look up and peer around the room to see if anyone is watching. No one is. So, is it just a sick twist of fate, the universe playing games with me?

I flip through the pages, searching for the cover shot. At last, I find it: a water well located on a farm in Roca, Nebraska, nowhere near the spot where I was being kept. The rest of the book is filled with diagrams of water channels and underground pipes, as well as photos of wind turbines and generators.

I take a deep breath and return the book to its place on the shelf. I start to reach for the next title, but stop short.

My eyes slam shut.

My insides shake.

I recheck the title. *The Hiker's Guide to Hayberry Park.*

I look up again. The room has gone hazy. A veil of gray casts down over my eyes, in front of my vision. At the same moment, my body lurches forward.

What happened?

Someone bumped me from behind: a girl texting on her phone. "Sorry," she says, moving on her way.

I count to five. Slowly, the images begin to fade back in. I scan the room: the shelves, the carrels, the singles and study groups. But nothing appears off. And no one's looking this way, checking for my reaction.

Only one more book remains on the cart. I take it, my fingers trembling. The cover of the book features an illustration of a girl wearing a long red dress and carrying a sparkling wand. She stands beside a dagger-wielding cat. The title reads *The Beechwood Encyclopedia of Folklore and Fairy Tales*.

I try to open the cover, but the book slips from my grip and lands with a thud against the floor.

Girls working at a nearby table snicker to themselves, peeking in my direction. One of them is the texting girl.

I pick the book up and flip to the index, searching for *The Forest Girl and the Wishy Water Well*. I run my finger over the list of titles, unable to find it. Meanwhile, one of the girls in the group lets out a laugh. Did she do this? Do they know about me?

I retrieve the water-well book from the shelf where I returned it, set it atop the others, and make my way to the group's table.

A dark-haired girl with bright green glasses looks up from her laptop screen. "Can I help you with something?"

"I heard you laughing over here," I tell them.

"Yeah, because something was funny," the texting girl says. "That's usually what happens when one hears a joke. Are you the library police, here to slap us with a no-laughing fine?"

I spread the books faceup on the table. "Are any of you familiar with these books?"

"*Excuse me?*" Texting Girl says.

"Can any of you explain them?" I ask.

Another girl—with her hair in braids, just like Clara, the forest girl from the Wishy Water Well—glances up from her textbook. "They look like books to me."

The texting girl uses her phone to shield her lips, so I can't see what she's mouthing. Moments later, another girl comes and takes her seat at the head of the table. Her baseball cap—with the college's wolverine logo—partially obstructs her face, so I don't notice right away . . .

"OMG!" she shouts, noticing me too.

It's Jessie, from Emo, from the sorority mixer. From her social media post about my desire to be famous. I can still picture the accompanying photo: a snapshot of me doing a silly pageant wave, hamming it up for the camera at Emo's annual spelling bee.

"Do you guys know Terra?" she asks the others. "Remember that story last year, at the Theta Epsilon house? Terra is *the one. So* famous."

I can't quite tell: Is she being sarcastic? Is she happy to see me? Her enthusiastic tone doesn't match her words.

"You go here now?" I ask her.

"Well, yeah." Her eyes bulge. "It seemed like a no-brainer. I mean, my sister still lives in the sorority house, so I can basically stay with her whenever I want to crash. The real surprise: I'm studying psychology. I know, *right*?" She laughs. "Coming from Emo and all . . . I figure I already have a lot of experience—*literally*. But how about *you*? Are you a student here too?"

"I work here. Part-time. Shelving, returns, and stuff."

"Okay, that makes more sense. Because I heard you went *back in*."

Back in, as in locked up. I bite my lip.

"I'm really sorry," she keeps on going. "Totally rough. But onward and upward, right?"

I bite harder as if that will make this all go away, transport me someplace else.

"Terra?" Someone touches my shoulder from behind.

My insides jump. I turn to look.

Katherine's there. "Is everything okay?"

"Yes. I was just . . ." I go to take a breath; the words are caught in my throat. The air feels trapped in my lungs. I collect the books into a single stack: *one, two, three.*

"Is something wrong?" She gazes at the cover of the Hayberry Park book: a dirt trail that cuts through the woods.

"Do you know why these books were on the reshelving cart?" I ask her.

Her eyebrows dart upward. "Besides the obvious reason?"

"Did you see anyone with them?"

"I see *you* with them."

"Right, but do you know who took them out last?"

"Come," she says, leading me away, back into the stacks. "What's going on?"

"These books," I begin. "All together . . . they tell a story—*my* story, what happened to me."

Katherine takes another look, putting her glasses on. "I don't understand."

"All *together*," I repeat. "The well, the park, the collection of fairy tales . . ."

"I thought all of that well business *didn't* happen." She removes her glasses, meeting my eyes again. "You think someone's playing a joke?"

"Maybe." I swallow hard, desperate to get away.

"Have you considered the possibility that an environmental science student is doing a project on water and waste systems? Or that someone studying English is writing a paper on the evolution of fairy tales? And perhaps a student in Professor Jameson's local history class is researching the park."

"Maybe," I repeat.

"Look, I just shelved a biography of Justin Bieber, a baby name book, and a copy of *At Your Cervix*. But you know what? It doesn't put a Belieber in my belly."

"Excuse me?"

"If you're going to work in a library, you're going to see all sorts of research going on, including topics that hit close to home. Believe me, when my aunt was diagnosed with Alzheimer's, it seemed every title I touched had to do with memory and neuroscience."

"Okay, but that's not this."

"It is, in fact. The books are talking to you. It's an old librarian's expression. Now, why don't you do us both a favor and microwave some popcorn. I'll be down in a few, and we can check out the new movie releases."

While she heads off to the copy room, I make a beeline for the bathroom and lock myself in a stall. I breathe here—in and out—sitting on the toilet, with the books stacked in my lap. My phone vibrates. A reminder to take my meds. I log on to Jane instead.

JA Admin: Welcome, NightTerra. Remember the rules: no judgments, no swearing, no inappropriate remarks. This is a safe space for honesty and support.

Paylee22: Too funny!! I mean, seriously?! A ladle?

TulipPrincess: Lol!!

Paylee22: Hey, NightTerra!

NightTerra: I'm so glad to find you on here.

Paylee22: Is everything ok?

Paylee22: ???

RainyDayFever: What's going on?

NightTerra: I'm at work . . .

NightTerra: And it's filled with triggers.

TulipPrincess: A.k.a. demons.

Paylee22: What kind of triggers?

NightTerra: Books that reminded me of what happened six months ago. The titles, I mean . . .

RainyDayFever: ???

NightTerra: They were on the return cart. Three titles that reminded me of everything I went through—about the park and the well . . . There was also a collection of fairy tales.

NightTerra: I'm trying really hard to hold it all together . . .

NightTerra: But I feel like I'm coming apart.

NightTerra: I just never know what to think.

NightTerra: Or who to trust, including myself.

NightTerra: Am I just reading into everything, making connections that aren't really there?

Paylee22: I agree. It's def hard.

NightTerra: Sometimes I feel like I'm my own worst enemy.

Paylee22: I feel like that too. Believe me. Just remember you're not alone.

TulipPrincess: You have us!

RainyDayFever: You also have ice cream and doughnuts. Lol.

NightTerra: I should probably go. My boss is going to be looking for me.

Paylee22: You sure you're ok to go back???

RainyDayFever: Can you go home early? Just say you don't feel good.

NightTerra: I think I'll be ok.

Paylee22: Terra, I'm worried about you.

Paylee22: Come back on later, ok?

NightTerra: Ok.

Paylee22: Promise? I'll be waiting for you.

NightTerra: Yes. Promise.

NightTerra: xo

Paylee22: xoxoxo

I log off, exit the bathroom, and go downstairs. Back behind the circulation desk, I scan each title's bar code into the computer. It seems the fairy-tale book was taken out two months ago. But both the water-well book and the park guide haven't been checked out at all, meaning someone in the library pulled them off the shelves but then decided not to borrow them.

I look around again—at people working, students studying, everyone just going about their business. So maybe it *is* a coincidence that all three titles ended up together on the same cart, on the same shelf, on the same night I was asked to put them away.

Or maybe not.

JA Admin: Welcome, NightTerra. Remember the rules: no judgments, no swearing, no inappropriate remarks. This is a safe space for honesty and support.

TulipPrincess: Exactly my point! My mom started going to a support group for victims of domestic violence. The thought of that makes me want to puke because, once again, she's the victim.

Paylee22: I'm really sorry.

TulipPrincess: And I'm really done. Two months until I'm legal. Then I'm moving out.

TulipPrincess: NightTerra, I'm so glad to see you back on here. I've been thinking about you!

RainyDayFever: How did the rest of your work shift go?

NightTerra: I got through it, at least.

Paylee22: NightTerra, I've been thinking about those library books.

Paylee22: Are you worried they might be more than just triggers?

NightTerra: I'm not really sure.

Paylee22: I'm sort of in a similar situation.

Paylee22: When I came back into my room after breakfast this morning, I found the window behind my bed cracked open. It hadn't been like that before, so it triggered me.

Paylee22: Should I have a) recognized the open window as a trigger and moved past it? Or b) considered the open window a possible clue that something threatening might take place?

NightTerra: How about c) asked your parents if either one of them had opened your window?

Paylee22: I actually did that, and both said no. But they offered to take me to my therapist, saying I'm driving myself crazy.

TulipPrincess: Are you??? (Insert suspicious grin here.)

Paylee22: I just have this feeling that the guy who took me is going to come back. I don't think he's finished with me yet.

NightTerra: Deep breath, remember?

TulipPrincess: Paylee, your crime was totally random, right? He grabbed you off the street?

Paylee22: Yes, random, at least that's what everyone believes, which is one of the many reasons I don't like to go out now.

Paylee22: I'd been on a hike and taken a detour onto a back road, having heard about an old, abandoned elementary school, which seemed like a cool idea at the time—to check out, I mean—but in hindsight it was really stupid.

Paylee22: A car pulled up beside me at the school. Some guy got out and said he was a cop. He was wearing a uniform and flashed me what looked like a badge. But I couldn't really tell.

Paylee22: He said I was trespassing, and that I needed to go with him. I went to get a closer look at the badge, and he grabbed me, snapped my head back, and put something over my mouth. He shoved me into the car.

Paylee22: I blacked out, then woke up later, in a shed, in the middle of a cornfield.

TulipPrincess: Wait, so you saw his face?

Paylee22: Not really. He was wearing these big mirrored sunglasses and a hat, so I couldn't really see much. Plus, he was a lot taller than me and I was so focused on that bogus badge.

TulipPrincess: Was anyone else in the shed?

Paylee22: No. Just me.

TulipPrincess: For how long?

Paylee22: It took me three days to escape. I found a loose floorboard. I was able to pull it up. Beneath the floor was dirt. I made a tunnel, like a groundhog, and dug my way out.

TulipPrincess: With your bare hands???

SugarRush911: Is that even possible?

Paylee22: I found a pointed rock that helped. I still have it. I keep it on my night table.

Paylee22: Now, looking back, I kind of wonder if he wanted me to escape—if that's how he gets his kicks . . . Like the way hunters sometimes catch their prey then let it go just to keep on hunting.

Paylee22: I saw a movie like that once—about some guy on an island who kept catching and releasing a girl who'd gotten stranded, just so he could continue to hunt her.

NightTerra: Wait, is that seriously a thing???

SugarRush911: Can we talk about something else now, please?

TulipPrincess: I feel like I read a short story like that once. About a guy who hunted humans . . .

Darwin12: "The Most Dangerous Game" by Richard Connell.

SugarRush911: And I'll say it again: Can we talk about something else now, please? Paylee22 isn't the only one going through stuff.

Paylee22: You're right. I've monopolized the chat.

Paylee22: I should probably go anyway.

NightTerra: Wait, I want to talk to you more.

Paylee22 has left the chat room. There are currently 5 people in the chat room.

I send her a direct message to move to a private chat room and follow it with a link, hoping she hasn't logged off. But she doesn't respond, even several moments later.

SugarRush911: Sorry (not sorry). It gets a little (a lot) tiring with her constantly playing the victim. She's not the only one with issues.

TulipPrincess: No, but she's the only one with her issues.

SugarRush911: Let's be real. She's a total attention whore. No one's after her.

NightTerra: You don't even know what you're talking about.

SugarRush911: Says the girl who's always asking if she's crazy.

JA Admin: Intervening here. We have rules on this chat site. Let's review them now.

My face burns hot because I didn't see that coming: SugarRush knowing my weak spot when I never directly shared it with her.

It's called a chat site for a reason, Logic says. *Lots of people lurk and "listen" without making themselves known.*

I go into my JaneBox and type Peyton a message:

Hey there,
I tried to catch you before you logged off. I'm sorry about
SugarRush. After you left the convo, the Jane police
stepped in, as did many of us. We all love you immensely,
especially me. I hope to chat with you soon. I'm also happy
to sleep in a chat room again if you want the company.
Xoxo,
Terra

I hit send. But still I don't feel better. I stay logged on, in case Peyton comes back, then click the Hulu app to watch another episode of *Summer's Story*—not exactly my favorite (a series about a girl named Summer whose mother abandons her at a camp commune). But I know watching the episode will make Peyton happy, and so I do.

20

I wake up later, feeling a hollowness inside my heart, an absence so heavy that it presses against my ribs and makes it hard to breathe.

The door is closed.

The windows are locked.

I reach for my laptop, at the foot of my bed, to check if Peyton is logged on to chat. She didn't come back on last night—not through four full episodes of *Summer's Story*. It doesn't appear she's on now either, and I have no new messages in my JaneBox.

Now what?

I grab my bottle of maple syrup and hold on tight, trying to think of a safer time, like Dr. Mary used to advise, like the visit to Story Land with my parents when I was six or seven, when Mom pulled a packet of maple syrup from her bag and drizzled it over her fries. The woman at the table beside us was so inspired, she asked Mom for an extra packet so that she could try it too. The memory helps, but it isn't enough. My chest still feels tight. My insides won't stop racing. And I've already taken my meds.

Sometimes, when I'm feeling this way, I'm not even sure what causes it. A thought? An image? A nightmare I don't remember? I gaze up at my bulletin board over my desk—at the photo of Felix and me, posing at the Emo relay race in potato sacks, sophomore year. I miss his superpower ability to inject me with me a much-needed dose of reality when the thoughts inside my brain would spiral me out of control.

"What am I going to do without you?" I asked him shortly before he left for college.

Felix was the one person who hadn't called me a liar, who'd never seemed to care what everybody else was saying.

"Don't worry," he said. "It's all going to work out for you too. You'll finish school, check that box, and get on with your life. What do you want to do? Where do you want to be?"

The questions were too big. "Do you know those answers for yourself?"

"I know that I don't want to be *here,* in this microscopic town, with only one flavor. I want to *do* stuff, make a difference, not get held back by old ghosts. That's your problem too. Everybody in this town knows you. You need to get the hell out of Dodge and start fresh." His eyes were fired with excitement, as if there wasn't a single doubt he was going to do something great.

I open up my phone and search for his name. Is it crazy to think he might want to talk to me too? I press his number anyway, desperate to hear him call me Terra-saurus, to slip back into the way things were before, when we'd debate about stuff like longest-lasting gum flavor and fizziest seltzer brand.

Felix picks up on the fourth ring. The screen looks dark; there's just a sliver of his face. *"Terra Train?"* His other nickname for me.

"Hey." I fake a smile.

"Did somebody die?"

"What do you mean?"

"It's five thirty in the morning. Has someone been hurt? Stabbed? Killed? Has there been a national catastrophe?" He sits up farther, enabling me to see that he's still in bed, that the light's turned off.

"I'm so sorry," I tell him. "I forgot you had a roommate."

"What does a roommate have to do with calling me at the ass crack of dawn?"

The question is a direct hit, straight to my heart. "I'm sorry," I say again. "Nothing's wrong. I just haven't talked to you in a bit. We can catch up another time."

"No, wait." He rubs his eyes. "I'm up *now*."

"Are you sure?"

"Sure." He yawns.

"It's nothing, really. I just woke up in a panic. I was going to go online, but then I remembered our pact, and how *you* used to be the person that I called in a panic."

"Remember that?" He smiles. "Night chats, little sleep, red eyes in the morning, and caffeine shots just to get through the day . . . And even then . . . Recall the time I started ugly-snoring in group, complete with bobblehead and a vibrating tongue."

"Just as Morgan was confessing to having suicide fantasies."

"Good times." He laughs. "It feels like a lifetime ago now."

"It's only been months."

"And speaking of Emo," he segues, "how's it going there? Does Ms. Strazinski still bleach her leg hair behind the desk?"

"I'm finishing up online, remember?"

"Right." Another yawn. "Online is better. You can sleep in as late as you like."

"And some days I don't even need to get out of bed at all. It's not necessarily a plus."

"Speak for yourself. I had no choice but to register for two eight a.m. classes. Talk about bobbleheads and bloodshot eyes."

"I should let you go."

"Not yet. It's good to hear from you. How's everything else going?"

"Everything else?"

"Yeah, are you feeling better about stuff?"

"Are you talking about the fire?"

"No. I'm talking about all that drama from last year."

"When I was taken, you mean?"

"Okay."

Not okay. My heart forms a crack.

"Are things becoming clearer?" he continues, making the crack worse—longer, deeper; it spider veins to my gut.

"Hey, you know who goes here?" he asks, steering the conversation again. "Remember Hannah Cahill? From Emo?"

"Of course, I remember." Hannah Blowing-Kisses Cahill, from the grocery store parking lot. Hannah, who wrapped her arms around me and told me to call her for anything, but then who hung up on me just days after that.

"Yeah, she's actually pretty cool. We hung out at a party last weekend and your name came up. Who knew, *right*?"

Who knew? *He* knew. Because I'd told him. Because I'd cried on his shoulder—for two hours straight—after Hannah had called me a liar and brought up that stuff about my parents.

"I should let you go," I say once again.

Felix sits up straighter, wearing the T-shirt he bought last fall in Onion Square: the one with the camouflaged unicorn. It's the only thing I recognize.

"Don't go yet," he says. "It's been too long."

I've been too damaged.

Too much time has passed.

"I really have to go," I tell him. "I've got a bunch of stuff I need to do."

"At five thirty in the morning?"

I peer over my shoulder at absolutely nothing. "I just wanted to say hello."

"Well, hello back, and I'm really glad you did. It was good to talk to you, Terra Train."

"Yeah, you too."

I shut the phone off and fold into the bed with my old bedroom doorknob pressed against my chest. Seeing how evolved Felix seems just makes everything worse: much more stifling, totally and completely isolating. Why do he, Jessie, and Hannah get to move on and be normal, while I'm stuck here?

Alone.

And crazy.

21

In the well, using the point of a rock as my crayon, I drew pictures on the walls: murals to feed my brain and keep me distracted. It didn't matter if the light wasn't on, I still drew: flowers, faces, abstract designs with diamonds and stripes . . .

The walls felt smooth beneath my fingertips, the dirt compacted like studio clay, turning my skin orange and brown. Sometimes I made up stories to go with the pictures, flashing me back to the quiet room with Charley, freshman year, and the storyboarding we used to do with markers on whiteboards. I pretended my drawings were like ancient hieroglyphics, weaving tales of princesses being punished for lying or stealing and stuck in a root cellar for days on end. I role-played that *I* was the princess and that the servants would let me out just as soon as they got the okay from the queen.

One time, so proud of my work, I didn't want to erase it. And so I lay down on the ground in the center of my creations and closed my eyes, imagining I had long princess hair and an apron-covered dress, hoping the story would continue in my dreams. And continue it did, because later, when I felt something pelt the side of my face, I thought it was one of the servant boys tossing stones into the well to taunt me. It wasn't until a larger, heavier stone struck my eyelid that I startled awake.

I sat up, shielding my face, peeking out between my fingers, able to see: There were no stones.

The lid was open.

Rain hurled down against the walls of the well, over my mural and over me.

I tilted my head back and opened my mouth wide as the droplets dripped over my dried-apple lips, my sandpaper tongue, and down my desert throat.

More.

More.

More.

I wanted so much more, and so I drew up my sleeves, peeled off my socks, and rolled up the bottoms of my sweats, exposing my bare skin, and suddenly remembering.

The water-well book.

Where was it?

I snatched it from the ground, wiped it with the blanket as dry as I could, and set it on a ledge two feet above the earth to protect it from the rain.

The rain. How long would it last? How high would the well fill? The ground didn't seem to be absorbing the droplets completely. Instead, they were beading up in places. Was the dirt too dry, too compact? Would I be able to preserve any of the water?

Using the pointed rock as the blade of a shovel, I dug into the ground. My shoulder ached with every drag of the rock, but still I kept going, sculpting a bowl of sorts, about six inches deep and eight inches wide: my makeshift sink, my own personal well. I lined it as best I could with a few of the fallen leaves, the ones that weren't too brittle. I also made a channel to feed the well, one that sloped down from the wall.

After several moments, rainwater started collecting inside the hole—not a lot, but at least it was something—and I moved to higher ground, a patch that angled upward, and sat back on my heels. My skin had thoroughly pruned. My teeth wouldn't stop chattering. I rotated my shoulders back in an effort to stretch.

That was when I spotted something about eight feet up, positioned on a ledge. What was it? I stood up to get a better look.

A colorful figure, like a tiny doll. I grabbed a rock and threw it at the figure over and over again, like a carnival game.

Finally, I hit it. Bull's-eye. The figure toppled from its spot and fell to the ground.

I picked it up. It was the size of my thumb. A squishy, rubber troll-like doll, with a flash of white hair, a long bushy beard, and a scrunched-up face . . .

Chills ripped up my skin as I made the connection. It was William, the character from the water-well storybook, the minder of the Wishy Water Well. The figure's eyes were wide and gaping just like in the book. It appeared that someone had painted on the clothes: the green-and-white-striped suit, the same one William wears.

Why was it here?

Had it been there all along, from the start? Wouldn't I have noticed? Or had someone placed it on the ledge somehow, while the light was out, when the blanket came down?

I squeezed the rubber belly. The eyes bulged even more, bugging out of its face. I rolled it over in my hand; it looked practically new. I gazed upward, desperate to see something, to find some answer. "Hello?" I called.

No one answered.

Nothing happened.

Meanwhile, the rain pelted against a spot on the wall, where the water had washed away a layer of dirt, revealing a smooth rock. I outlined the rock with my finger, pressing into the earth, trying to deepen the perimeter around the rock's surface. The water helped. But it wasn't until I was knuckle-deep that the rock started to loosen and I was able to pry it free, leaving a crevice.

How many more crevices could I make?

The spotlight blinked a bunch of times. Was it shorting out? Or was the battery dying? I snatched the rubber troll and huddled against the wall with my wet baby blanket, waiting for something to happen.

But nothing did.

Until the light went out again.

After I got back from the well, I told Dr. Mary about the William doll.

"Did it scare you?" she asked.

I shook my head. "It turned out to be a comfort, like the water-well book."

"And yet you didn't bring either item home with you." Dr. Mary tapped her chin as though in thought. "And the troll was a doll or action figure, you said?"

"Maybe, but it could also have been a squishy. You know . . . For stress relief . . . Like the Panic Pete doll Sally used to carry around. Remember her?"

"Sally had a toy troll too?"

"It was a Panic Pete doll," I said as if the distinction even mattered.

"A doll that provides both comfort and relief . . ." She grinned. "How lucky that one practically dropped into your lap during a very dark time. You had a blanket in the well too. A baby blanket . . . It doesn't get more comforting than that now, does it?"

"I didn't make it up. The doll was there. William," I said to be clear. "He was the minder of the Wishy Water Well, the character from the storybook . . . The troll who collected all the well coins and made people's wishes come true."

"You know what's amazing, Terra? The mind. It has a remarkable way of manifesting exactly what we need at very dark times."

In other words, to her, the troll wasn't real; my mind had created it as a way to self-soothe. She continued to explain, but
everything else she said went unheard; it was just words in the air,
passing over the invisible grave I'd made where hope and trust had
died.

22

The following morning, in my room, with a hand mirror clipped to the side of my easel, I dip my paintbrush into a glob of glue and paint the hair of my self-portrait: long, wavy strokes over the golden-brown color. My laptop is open. People are chatting away on Jane. But not Peyton. Where is she?

Into a mixing bowl, I've added equal parts dirt and soot. I sprinkle a handful of the mixture onto the glue. I need to get the face as well—to make dirty cheeks and soot-encrusted eyes. But first I want to finish the mouth. I take my lit candle from its dish and let the hot liquid wax drip onto the lips, imagining words that hurt—burning truth, brutal honesty, all the things I no longer feel safe enough to say.

"*Hello, hello . . .*" My aunt knocks on my open bedroom door. "Didn't you hear me calling you?"

Calling me?

"I'm home for the day." She flashes me her swollen knuckles. "This is what nine hours of drawing blood and administering IVs will do."

She looks toward my pillow. Mom's sweater covers it. For a second, I think she might ask me about it, that we might talk about my mother.

"What's going on *here*?" she asks instead, nodding to my laptop, to the feed of conversation climbing up the screen.

"It inspires me." I could probably say anything.

She doesn't question it, just continues to look around. Her focus lands on my basket of rubber trolls; it's filled with squishies, key chains, cat toys, ornaments—all the items I've collected in my quest to find the same troll as the one in the well (with or without the painted-on suit). The things in my basket come close, but there's something off about each of them (the color, the size, the shape, the feel . . .).

"Did you eat?" she asks.

"Yes." Though I didn't have much of an appetite. I forced down some yogurt earlier; it's burning like lava in my stomach now.

"Okay, good. So, I'm going to go for a run, then I'm going to sleep. Do you need anything?"

She's already dressed in her running clothes. Her hair is pulled back. If I don't answer, will she even "hear" me?

Her eyes zero in on the doorknob on my night table. She knows what it is. She was there when I salvaged it from the debris. She's also seen me toting it around the house, stuffing it into my bag, and turning it in the air as though in an invisible door. But she's never asked why—why I keep it, what it symbolizes.

"Is everything okay?" I hold my breath, half hoping she'll ask me now.

Instead, she asks if I really need to have *six* fire extinguishers in my room. "I thought I moved these out of here," she says.

"You did, but I got them back." Lugged them up from the corner of the basement.

"*Really?* Even though we have perfectly good smoke detectors that I test every six months? And even though I don't smoke and barely cook? There's no fireplace or wood-burning stove, no funky lights or heat-generating blankets . . ."

"Still. I need them," I tell her.

Aunt Dessa comes a little closer, nodding to my canvas. "What are you working on?"

"Not what, *who*."

She makes a face like she's looking at a monster. "Not anyone I want to bump into late at night, *that's* who."

I gaze back in the mirror, almost surprised she doesn't see the resemblance: my light brown eyes, my dimpled chin and hollow cheeks.

"Before I forget," she continues, "I met someone, a woman at the hospital who does hypnotherapy. She helps people who have false memories."

"False memories?"

"She works specifically with trauma victims. She said that sometimes the brain creates stories as a coping device. It's all so fascinating . . . the brain's ability to preserve and protect. Anyway, when I heard the word *stories,* I perked right up and thought of you. Would you like to meet her?"

I drip more wax over the mouth—a dark red glob that seals the lips shut. The last time I met one of her doctor friends, I ended up back in the hospital.

"*Terra?* The therapist's name is Cecelia Bridges. You can look her up, check her out. She has a website. I really think it'd be a good idea. Terra?"

"Do we still have cocoa powder?"

"*Excuse me?*"

"Remember?" I ask. "The mochaccinos you used to make after I got back from the well? And the crossword puzzles we used to do?"

Her face fuzzes with confusion. "That was a really difficult time."

And this isn't?

"We were talking about your therapy," she continues. "It's not a bad word, you know. I've been seeing my therapist for more than twenty years. Your mom saw a therapist too."

I knew my mom had. She had too many dark days not to warrant the need for outside help. I'd watch her from the hallway, outside her and Dad's room, as she lay in bed staring at the wall. For years, whenever she was having one of "those days," Dad would say Mom just needed a little extra space. But eventually he told me the truth, that Mom had been dealing with depression.

"It started back in high school, after she was attacked at a party," he'd explained. "She got trapped in a room by a boy who was drinking. It's why we're always so vigilant with you, why we taught you our rules—so we can help keep you safe."

The night he told me, I wrote the rules of survival all over my arms, picturing each rule like a scratch Mom might've gotten at that party, from her struggle. I wanted to feel the scratches too, to help share her pain.

"Life is hard work," my aunt continues. "But having a therapist you can trust, whose style works for you, can make all the difference. Mine's been like pure gold for me. What if it could be that way for you as well?"

"Could we please go back to talking about my mom?"

"What about her?" Aunt Dessa takes a step back. "You know your mother is a difficult topic for me."

"Because she's gone?" Or is there something more? Why don't I remember my mother ever wearing her and Aunt Dessa's pendant initials too?

"I'm going to make that appointment for you," she says.

"Okay." I nod, hoping the agreement will make a difference, make things better.

But she leaves the room without another word, making me feel that it doesn't.

NOW

23

Later, when I join the chat room, I find that it looks mostly vacant. No one's typed a message in the last couple of hours.

NightTerra: Hello??? Is anyone else on here?

Paylee22: Terra!!! I'm so glad to see you.

NightTerra: Omg, me too!

NightTerra: Did you get my message?

Paylee22: Yes. Thank you.

Paylee22: I've been seriously freaking out.

NightTerra: Why? What's up?

Paylee22: It's gotten worse.

NightTerra: What has?

Paylee22: I found a torn page in my mailbox. It'd been ripped out of a book.

NightTerra: Ok . . .

Paylee22: Not ok. It means he's getting closer.

Paylee22: He's warning me.

NightTerra: Ok, slow down. Perspective, remember?

Paylee22: The page is from a book about junkyards. I searched online for one of the paragraphs . . .

Paylee22: The book is nonfiction, about a guy who gets most of what he needs—furniture, TVs, computer equipment, appliances—from junkyards.

NightTerra: Like a dumpster diver?

Paylee22: I guess.

NightTerra: So, pretty random?

Paylee22: I think it's a message.

NightTerra: A message about what?

Paylee22: There's too much to explain.

NightTerra: Not too much for me. I have plenty of time.

NightTerra: ???

NightTerra: Peyton???

NightTerra: Is it possible the page got into your mailbox by mistake? Maybe it tore from a book your neighbor ordered and your postal guy didn't notice, and so now it's a trigger.

Paylee22: It wasn't a mistake. We'd already gotten the mail for the day, meaning someone made a special trip to put it in there.

NightTerra: Maybe a kid playing a joke . . . I once found someone's math homework in our mailbox.

Paylee22: It's not a joke.

Paylee22: Like I said, there's a lot to explain . . .

NightTerra: Ok, well, I'm here for you, and I want to know.

NightTerra: Pretend I'm sitting right beside you.

Paylee22: Ok, deep breath . . .

Paylee22: Where I was being kept, in that shed . . . The only things in there, aside from myself, were a sleeping bag, a jug of water, some trail mix, and a book.

NightTerra: Wait, how come you never mentioned that before?

Paylee22: Which part?

NightTerra: The book.

Paylee22: I don't know. It just never came up.

NightTerra: What kind of book was it?

Paylee22: From what I could tell, it was about a bunch of people who came together as a family.

Paylee22: They lived in the middle of the woods, in tiny one-room shacks, with their own set of rules, so off the grid, basically.

Paylee22: I didn't read the book all the way through. And I'm not sure why it was there. Like, did he want me to read it? Was there a message inside it? I was too focused on escaping to give it much attention.

Paylee22: But think about it . . .

Paylee22: A book left in the shed, a page left in my mailbox . . .

NightTerra: What was the title?

Paylee22: If only I could remember. I've been searching for it online, under topic and special interest. To be honest, I don't even know if it was true or fictional.

Paylee22: But I think the page is his way of letting me know he's close.

NightTerra: If that's the case, then why not leave you a page from that same book—about the family living off the grid—or one about abduction . . . ?

Paylee22: I don't know. Too obvious? Maybe the page about junkyards is a clue for something that's going to happen . . .

Paylee22: I have no idea.

Paylee22: What do you think???

Paylee22: ???

Paylee22: Are u still there??? Why aren't you talking?

NightTerra: I'm not really sure what to think.

NightTerra: But I have to go.

Paylee22: Wait, why? I thought you had plenty of time.

NightTerra: I'll come on later, ok?

I close the lid on my laptop, trying my best to breathe. A motor clicks on inside my heart, flaring my nerves, jumbling my thoughts.

Is the book page just a trigger—for her? For me?

Is it simply a weird coincidence? Both of our captivity quarters having books? And both of our books at least somewhat related to our captive situations? Mine, with the well; hers, with the shed . . .

Plus, the two of us managing to escape after a handful of days . . .

I log back on, but she's no longer there. Meanwhile, my phone alarm chimes. A reminder to take my meds—the fastest way to quiet my mind. Obviously, I ignore it.

24

In her memoir, Jane Anonymous, the creator of the chat site, describes her experience of being abducted. Among the items she had while in captivity, there was a book. A romance novel. Jane says she read it over and over as a way to pass the time, just as I did the water-well book. So, the fact that Peyton was given a book in captivity too . . .

Is leaving reading material for victims a thing that predators do? The idea of that seems completely crazy. But so is the shrine that's become my bed, with the sweater, the syrup, and my parents' list of rules; I've written the rules on card stock and set them beside the doorknob from Bailey Road.

I type Peyton's name into the search box on my computer, along with the words *missing woman* and *Chicago.* Lots of missing-persons links pop up, but none with the name Peyton, and only a few seem to be from the greater Chicago area. Some of the links are for cases I've heard of—"famous" ones. Several of them involve younger kids, not even necessarily from the Midwest. But most of the stories seem to be over a year old, at least—nothing from the last eight months or even a year involving a twenty-four-year-old woman.

I try another search, using the words *shack, suburb of Chicago, cornfield,* and *missing woman found.*

A case in Northbrook, Illinois, keeps popping up, but it involves two girls—both thirty now—who'd been gone for ten years.

Another well-known case in the Chicago area concerns an eight-year-old boy believed to have been taken by his father, who's also missing.

I click on a story involving a nineteen-year-old college student who disappeared while on a road trip with some friends. I start to scan for details, only to discover that the girl is still missing; it's been eight years now.

None of the cases I find mention a cornfield or a shed. So, what am I doing wrong? Was there not much written about Peyton's case? Did it somehow get even less attention than mine? Is this what happens when you're over eighteen and taken? No one really cares. Especially if you resurface with no visible wounds?

I go to take a breath, but the tightening sensation has returned to my chest like shrink-wrap around my ribs. I reach for my bottle of pills and shake one onto my palm, over the phantom burn mark. I swallow the pill down, just as an alert jumps up on my screen: I have to be at work in an hour.

Downstairs, Aunt Dessa is in the kitchen, standing over the stove. She takes a sip from her wineglass. Something must be bothering her; she almost never drinks. "I made a fresh pot of carrot-and-ginger soup." She stirs the pot with her back toward me. "Would you like a cup?"

"Maybe tomorrow. I have to work."

She takes another sip. "How's that going?"

"The library?"

"Yes. Are you getting anything out of it?"

"Well, I'm getting paid. It's an actual job, not volunteering."

"I'm surprised you want anything to do with that place."

"What do you mean?"

"I mean, I can't imagine many victims going back to the scene of their alleged crimes to get a job, volunteer or otherwise."

"It's a paid job," I tell her again as if it even matters. "And *this* was the scene of my crime. He took me from this house."

Doesn't she remember? Redecorating my room? Back when she believed me, when my crime wasn't just alleged, she desperately tried to clean things up, to make everything look new. And so, while I stayed on the living room sofa, not even wanting to get up to pee, Aunt Dessa repainted the walls of my room—slate blue from the former yellow—and rearranged the furniture with the help of neighbors. In the end, the room was barely recognizable. Even the windows looked different: Velvet curtains replaced stark-white blinds. My bed was draped in purple satin instead of blue-and-white checks. Gone were the pale wood floors; they'd been refinished, stained a dark cocoa color.

"Well?" she asked once the room had been finished. She stood beside me in the doorway. "What do you think?"

I couldn't really think. I could only feel—palpitations inside my heart, wooziness in my head, and unsteadiness on my feet. I liked what she'd done, but it didn't change the fact that I didn't want to move. I only wanted to curl up into a ball—if not on the living room sofa, then in the corner of the redecorated space.

And so that's what I did.

For weeks on end.

Not so much unlike when my parents died.

"Do you have the night off?" I ask, assuming she does, given the wine.

"I *always* take this night off."

This night? I peek at the wall calendar, only just remembering. Today would've been my mother's birthday.

"Did you forget?" she asks.

"No. It's just . . ." I'm more attuned to her death. On the anniversary of the night of the fire, I walk around like a ghost, half wishing I were one, thinking the powers that be—whichever god is true—made some horrible mistake by leaving me behind. "I remembered the date last week," I tell her, "but somehow it fell off my radar today."

She continues to stir the pot, to take another sip, and then to refill her glass with sparkling pink, the same wine my mother drank on occasion; I recognize the rosy label. The soup is the same too, one of my mother's favorites, *made with only three ingredients,* my mother used to boast.

"I really, really miss her," I say, my voice thickening with the words.

Aunt Dessa swivels from the stove, finally making eye contact. The initials *O* and *M* dangle around her neck. After the fire, when we went back to the scene to try to salvage what remained, I remember her searching for my mother's necklace, wanting to find the shiny gold pieces amid the piles of soot and ash.

What I wouldn't give to talk about my mother. But I look away instead, avoiding the blow of her stare, the potential bang of her blame.

"Sometimes you remind me of her," I venture, gazing toward her feet—sheepskin slippers. "Especially your voice." I peek up into her face, waiting for her to say something similar, like that I have my mom's smile, her bony fingers, or her pale ivory skin. But maybe she doesn't see any traces of her sister in this person I've become.

"Too bad you're working tonight," she says.

"I could call out sick. Katherine would understand. We could go shopping for snacks and have a girls' night in, just like old times."

"Maybe some other night." She turns her back again to stir the soup.

"Are you sure?" I persist. "It'll probably be a slow night anyway."

"Some other time." She grabs a thermos and fills it with the soup, then slides the container toward me, across the counter. "For your snack break."

I open my mouth to thank her, but she's already turned away

again, already taken her wineglass and headed into another room, further widening the gap between us.

Once outside, I lock myself in the car and start the engine. My face feels hot, like I've just been slapped. I grab the yoga blanket and scream into the fabric—over and over again—hating myself, hating this life.

When my lungs give way, I struggle to take a breath and look out the windows, almost expecting to have shaken the Earth, woken up the town. But the neighborhood appears just like any other day.

No one's looking this way.

Not a single soul's disturbed.

I log on to Jane, hoping to find Peyton, but she isn't in the chat room. I open up my JaneBox and type her a message:

Hey, Peyton,
I'm on my way to work. I hope you'll be on later because I'd really like to talk to you. I'm sort of having a rough time.
Plus, I want to hear more about the page and the book. I'm sorry I ended our last chat early. Xo.
Love,
Terra

I click Send, feeling a smidge better. Because, though she may not be here for me in this moment, I know she will be soon.

25

I'm not sure when it was, but at some point, when the light was off, and I lay faceup with the blanket bunched beneath my head, I saw a bright ball of light hovering at the top of the well: a fiery globe that rotated around and around, illuminating the brick. I blinked a bunch of times to check that I was awake. Because this couldn't be real.

Still, the globe remained: mesmerizing, especially as it began to grow in size, taking up the entire space of the lid. A fusion of colors swirled inside it—red, blue, green, and yellow—eventually morphing it into what appeared to be a rainbow-colored bird, the kind of mystical shape-shifting creature I'd have imagined with Charley, freshman year.

The bird lingered at the opening of the well, flapping its wings, casting bright strips of color over the dirt walls (the pictures I'd drawn of Clara and William). I raised my arms to see if the rainbow might reach my hands, but I was too far down.

Could the bird see me?

How was this even happening? It simply had to be a dream.

Slowly, the bird began to float higher. The strips of color rose too, traveling up the walls, getting farther away. I wanted to go with them and tried to sit up, but I was frozen in place, unable to move.

"Don't go," I tried to call, but no sound came out.

I noticed then: The bird was holding something—a sticklike object—in its claws. A fallen branch? A magical wand?

The bird hovered for several more seconds before flying away, taking all the light with it, leaving me in the dark, still paralyzed in place.

Moments later, something landed against my chest, startling me awake. I sat up, feeling something topple into my lap. I picked it up, recognizing what it was: a sparerib. Bits of charcoal encrusted the top layer of skin. I pressed the sparerib to my nose, able to smell the meat: a sweet and spicy scent. My mouth watering, I brought it to my lips, half expecting it to disappear just as magically as it'd come. But instead I tasted the rib with my tongue—so unbelievably good. I tore into it with my teeth, barely stopping to chew. Thick hunks of charred meat pushed down my throat, plodded into my esophagus.

I told myself to go slow, but I wanted more, and spent the next several minutes huddled on the ground, searching for any remaining shreds, even gnawing on the bone. I let out a mournful whine when there was nothing else left.

Would more be coming? I looked up again, suckling the bone like a popsicle stick. Did the person who took me throw it down? Was it a way to tease me? Or keep me alive? Or what if it hadn't been a person at all? What if it *were* a bird that dropped it? Could the deprivation of light cause some neurological response that produces a spectrum of color? Maybe something happens to the pupil upon the elevation of blood pressure . . .

I had no idea.

But I had the bone: my proof.

If only I had that proof with me now.

Later, curled up against the wall with the troll doll and the fleece blanket, I told myself I wouldn't fall asleep. I needed to keep on working, searching for more boulders. But I let my head rest down on the fairy-tale book anyway, imagining it as a pillow.

Just five minutes, I promised myself.

The spotlight was on. The rock I'd managed to pry from the wall sat within view. It'd left a six-inch gouge. I needed to dig more.

But I felt so tired. My lids were so heavy. My bones and muscles ached.

I stuck my fingers into my mouth and suckled the bloody tips; they tasted like salted chips. I pictured a plate of waffle fries from Gaga's Grill, with the creamy dill sauce. My mouth ached for the sweet-and-sour taste coupled with the oily crunch of deep-fried potato. Meanwhile, I chewed at my waterlogged skin, remembering lunchtime with Felix at Iggy's Market—the turkey-, stuffing-, and cranberry-layered sandwiches smothered with gravy, and the time the owner had us sample from a tray of recipes he'd been trying. And so we ate: hunks of garlic knotted butter rolls, gooey mac-'n'-cheese balls with bread crumb crust, filo dough–wrapped asparagus bundles, and four-cheese manicotti with plum tomato and basil sauce.

My body quivered for food. I scooped up a handful of muck, like wet clay, imagining the brownie batter Mom and I used to make with the chocolate chunks. I tried to re-create the look, sprinkling bits of the drier dirt on the top of the heap like caramel drizzle. "Just one spoonful of batter," Mom used to say. "Then they're going in the oven."

I reached out to touch the walls, noticing how much they looked like chocolate too, dampened from the rain. I closed my eyes, willing them to morph into thick hunks of fudge. They felt slick, like glass, like the slabs of cheese at the gourmet shop in the center of town—the provolone, the Parmesan, the Jarlsberg, and the creamy pecorino . . . But when I opened my eyes again, there was only dirt.

And only me.

With no food and little energy.

There's no time for sleep now. My father's voice played inside my ear. *There's so much you could do.*

He was right. I could toss the book upward again, so that someone might see it. I could also try yelling some more, stretching my vocal cords. My throat was feeling better, coated with rainwater. What I thirsted for now: sound that wasn't mine—gunfire, whistles blowing, birds cawing, animals barking . . .

Any kind of sound.

Some type of noise.

If only the troll doll made a squeak.

I snatched a couple of rocks from the ground and knocked them together—*knock, knock, knock*—just to remind myself I could still hear, that my ears were continuing to work. I also tapped a rock against my teeth, radiating sound through my body, which felt enlivening at first, but I was still so tired.

I snuggled the blanket. Just five minutes. My eyes burned with dirt. I let the lids fall closed.

Don't fall asleep, my father's voice continued.

I tried not to, and I told myself I wouldn't. But before I knew it, I was back in my childhood bedroom on Bailey Road.

Open up! Dad shouted.

I dreamed that I was glued to the rug as the flames ate away the roof of the house.

Terra? Mom's voice.

In my dream, I tried to call back, stretching my mouth wide. But no sound came out. My vocal cords seared, despite the rainwater. And the smell of burning leaves hung heavy in the air. I reached outward, toward my bedroom door, zeroing in on the Sharpie-drawn star.

At the same moment, something slid between my fingertips.

A piece of paper?

A page from the fairy-tale book?

I brought it to my nose. It smelled like campfire, like toasting marshmallows.

A loud, cracking noise startled me awake. I sat up with a jolt. Were the rafters splitting? Was the ceiling caving in?

No. Because I was still in the well, surrounded by dirt. There were no rafters, no wooden structure either.

So, what was that sound? A tree falling over? Was someone chopping firewood nearby?

Clenched in my hand was a piece of paper, but it wasn't a page from *The Forest Girl and the Wishy Water Well*. This page was whiter; the corners seemed sharper. The texture was different too, matte rather than glossy.

I turned it over, anticipating text or an image, but it was a blank sheet. Where had it come from? How did I get it? It hadn't been here in the rain; it was as dry as the sparerib bone I could no longer find.

A corner of the sheet was as black as the night sky, as though from a fire. I brought it up to my nose, able to smell smoke.

I stood up. My pulse raced. Did the sheet of paper float down here by accident? I gazed toward the opening of the well. Were campers nearby? I inhaled the night air, desperate to see if I could smell fire. "Hello," I called, but the word came out a gasp, barely audible enough to hear.

Aside from the burn mark, the paper looked completely pristine—so bright, barely wrinkled. How was that even possible?

Maybe it wasn't. Maybe the guy who'd taken me had burned the paper himself, then dropped it into the well just to let me know that I wasn't a random pick—that I was the girl from the burning house who'd let my parents die.

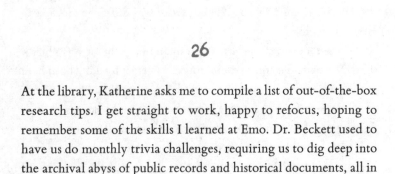

NOW

26

At the library, Katherine asks me to compile a list of out-of-the-box research tips. I get straight to work, happy to refocus, hoping to remember some of the skills I learned at Emo. Dr. Beckett used to have us do monthly trivia challenges, requiring us to dig deep into the archival abyss of public records and historical documents, all in a long and laborious effort to find the answer to some seemingly impossible question.

I start to take some notes, just as a bell dings. My insides jump. I look up.

To my complete and utter shock, Garret's standing there, behind the checkout desk.

"Well, hello, stranger." He grins. "So, it's true."

"True?"

"I heard you were working here."

I stand from the computer, reminded once again how blue his eyes are, like the color of the sea. What would they look like behind a ski mask? "I was wondering if you were still a student here."

"This is my last year. How about you? How have you been?"

"I'm still trying to finish up high school."

"Oh, right." He smirks. "Little did I know you weren't in college when we met."

My face flashes hot. "Sorry about that."

"Are you kidding? *I'm* the one who should be apologizing. I never should've let you go off alone that night."

"As if I gave you much of a choice."

"Well, I'm just glad you're okay."

Is there a reason he's not saying anything about my juice can disaster at the convenience store? Should I mention it first? Before I can, he pushes a book toward me across the desk.

"I'd like to check this out," he says.

The cover shows a shrouded figure standing on the fringe of a forest. I blink hard, sure I must be seeing things. But I'm not. The title, *Girl Missing,* stares up at me in big, bold lettering. Meanwhile, Garret is still smiling. The joke's on me.

"Why?" My voice shakes. "Did you leave those other books too?"

"Other books?" His eyes go wide.

"On the return rack the other day . . ."

He takes a step back, holding up his hands as if I'm putting him under arrest. "I'm really sorry, but I have no idea . . ." His words stop there.

Some guy comes over and stands by Garret's side. "Hey, man. Is everything okay over here?"

Both he and Garret stare at me, as though I'm the one with the problem. And maybe they're right, because Katherine comes over too.

"Terra?" she asks. "Do you need some help?"

One of the singles at a nearby table—some guy in a puffy jacket—keeps stapling papers together: *staple, staple, staple.*

Clobber.

Clank.

Swish.

The noise is grating. My head is pounding. Did I take my medication? I remember spilling a pill onto my palm, over the spot that's lost its lines. But did I swallow it down? Yes, I think I did.

"Did *what*?" Katherine asks.

"Terra?"

I open my mouth to speak, spotting a textbook tucked under Garret's arm, *The Art and Science of Forensic Psychology,* prompting me to remember. He's a criminal justice major. We talked all about it. He wants to be a cop.

I look once more at the title he wants to check out. It's changed now, not *Girl Missing* but *Gil Messing: The Autobiography of a Former ATF agent.*

"Can I help you?" Katherine asks him.

"Terra's been plenty of help already," Garret says. "Thanks again." He gives me a wave and turns away, heading upstairs, leaving the book behind.

"What was that?" Katherine asks, her brows raised high.

I go to take a breath, trying to get a grip, but the air is caught in my lungs. "Just an old friend," I manage to say.

"A friend I wouldn't go kicking out of my sandbox, if you get what I'm saying." She keeps on talking—something about a sand pail and shovel.

I'm not really listening.

Katherine nods to my coffee mug, asking if I need another cup. What I really need: a moment to breathe. And so that's what I do, turning away, closing my eyes, picturing Story Land and the maple syrup packets.

When I open my eyes again, Katherine's gone. The door to her office is shut.

I sit down and grab the key ring from my bag. Was I wrong about those other titles too? The ones on the return rack?

No, I wasn't.

Because Katherine saw them too.

Plus, I scanned their barcodes into the computer.

I squeeze the troll charm again and again, making the eyes bulge, hoping the motion will soothe me. Still, my insides race.

In the bathroom, I splash water onto my face. My eyes are swollen from a lack of sleep. I pat them with my dampened fingers. The sensation flashes me back—to my time in the well, the night it rained, my waterlogged skin, the quenching of my thirst . . .

"It really happened," I tell my reflection in the mirror, popping one of my meds just to be sure.

My skin has chills, and yet every inch of me feels like it's sweating. Still, I go back to my desk. My article on research is still up on the computer screen. I start to type, only just noticing.

What is this?

A folded piece of paper sits on my keyboard. It's not exactly small, about the size of a cocktail napkin. How did I not see it?

How tired must I be?

I peer over my shoulder, toward Katherine's office. The door is still closed but maybe she came out to leave me a to-do list. I unfold the creases and flip the paper over, feeling a knot form in my gut.

How can this be?

Be logical, Logic says. *Remember: The mind plays tricks. Obviously, the eyes do too. Recall the magical rainbow bird that hovered at the top of the well, that brought you a sparerib and lit up the walls like a night-club . . . You had the common sense not to tell anyone about that bird. And you know why? Because it sounded like one of those fantastical stories that you and Charley used to make up, freshman year, in the quiet room, to pass the time.*

Charley.

Was it a coincidence he disappeared not long after I gave him the mood ring with its power of invisibility? Weeks after his departure, when I brought up his name—to see if anyone knew where he'd gone—none of the other students were able to place him, as if he were just an imaginary friend, like TumTum, the monkey I had in preschool.

"There's a big difference between reality and fantasy," Dr. Mary used to tell me time and time again. "But sometimes perspective gets skewed, and the difference can feel quite small."

Sitting at the computer, I blink hard—once, twice, three full times. But nothing changes.

The reality remains: A paper map of Hayberry Park lies stretched across my keyboard.

I stand from the desk. Blood rushes from my face. *Who did this?* I look out over the room. People's heads snap up.

A girl turns from the printer.

Some guy spins around in his chair.

"Terra?" Katherine comes storming out of her office once again. "What's wrong? What happened?" Her mouth's parted; her eyes are gaping.

I look toward the fire alarm light. It isn't flashing.

Katherine asks, "Why were you shouting?"

Was I? *Shouting?*

I look out at the students. Did one of *them* shout? They all appear to be awaiting an explanation. From me?

From me.

"Sorry, I just . . ." I have no words. I turn away, avoiding the pressure of their glares, the questions in Katherine's gaze, the judgment in everyone's mind. I fold up the map, quickly, quietly, and keep it clenched in my fist.

"Look, I get it," she says, softening her voice.

I want to block my ears.

"The transition to working the overnight shift isn't an easy one," she continues. "It can make everyone a little off-kilter."

Is that what this is? If so, what does it mean? That when I look at the folded-up piece of paper again, after some rest, it won't be a map?

Katherine continues to talk, but I'm no longer listening. I'm focused instead on the table of girls by the photocopy machine. Jessie's there. They're all laughing at something, sneaking peeks in my direction. Did one of *them* do this?

Katherine's still talking: "It isn't right for everybody. Why don't you take the rest of the shift off and try to get some sleep? I don't mind. Miguel's here early anyway."

I manage a nod, sucking back tears. I don't even clock out. I just head for the door, eager to get inside my car.

But I'm intercepted along the way. A dark-haired girl with big purple glasses, one of the girls from the laughing table. I look over from where she came. The others are watching. Jessie pulls down the visor of her cap to shield her face as though I haven't already spotted her.

"Do you know this book?" the girl asks me.

It's only then I notice. The front cover. The blazing title. *Burning Down the House.* It doesn't go away, no matter how many times I blink.

My head starts to spin. I take a step back, able to feel the cover's penetrating heat.

"I'm really sorry," the girl mutters. "My friend put me up to this. Can you just give it a good look and then I'll get out of your way? Sorry," she says again. "This wasn't my idea. I'm not even sure what it means."

I cover my ears and back away some more, able to hear a blaring siren inside my head.

Fire, fire, fire.

Fire: inside my heart, searing my lungs, collapsing my ribs.

I struggle to take a breath as the girl goes back to the table.

Someone asks, "Terra, are you okay?" A male or a female.

I can't quite tell. I don't stop to check. Somehow, I end up back in my car, where I turn on the engine and lock all the doors.

Why, why, why?

Why would Jessie do this?

Why do I let it burn me? It's not as if I don't know Jessie's secrets too, as if I didn't sit with her on the floor of the locker room as she cried about being abandoned by her mother at ten months old. This obviously wasn't the first time she betrayed our friendship. Back at Emo, when Ms. Melita, one of the group counselors, pulled me aside and suggested I seek out more compatible peers, I still glommed on to

Jessie's sparkling ways—one day getting me out of cleanup duty, the next sneaking us into the teachers' room, where we scarfed down pound cake and cheese puffs.

"You have to choose who you allow to hear your story," Ms. Melita said, after Jessie had made a comment in group about "some of us" being pyromaniacs.

"It was a *joke*." Jessie laughed when I called her on it later. "Lighten up. Why do you always have to be so serious?"

I miss Ms. Melita a lot. But, even sadder, I miss Jessie too.

The folded-up piece of paper is still wadded in my grip. I open it up, hoping that here, in the safety of my mom's Subaru, things will look so much different, become so much clearer. But unfortunately, they don't.

The map is still a map.

And I am still me.

27

As soon as I get back to my aunt's house, I grab the yoga blanket and go upstairs to my room, where I log on to Jane. Peyton isn't in the chat room, but she's left me a message.

Hey, Terra,
I got your msg. You aren't on right now, so I'm thinking you might be working (???). I'm about to take a nap, but as soon as I get up I'll go in the chat room and stay until I see you. I hope things have gotten better. I'm still freaking, btw. At least we're freaking out together.
Xoxoxo!
Love,
Peyton

As I wait, I start season two of *Summer's Story.* But I'm not sure how far I actually get, because the next thing I know, the episode's stopped.

It's light outside my window. Somehow, I managed to drift off to sleep. I check the chat screen:

RainyDayFever: I ended up feeling so overwhelmed that I ate two pints of ice cream.

LuluLeopard: Which flavors?

RainyDayFever: To be honest, I'm not even sure. I wasn't paying attention. I just kept shoveling cold and sugary goodness into my mouth.

LuluLeopard: Lol!

NightTerra: Hey, everyone.

Paylee22: Terra, so glad to see you!!!

A message bubble from Peyton pops up on my screen: an invitation to go into a private chat room. I click the link.

Paylee22: Hey, are you there?

NightTerra: Yes, here.

Paylee22: Sorry I missed you before.

Paylee22: How are you? What's going on?

NightTerra: You first.

Paylee22: You sure?

Paylee22: Ok, so, I found something. That page in my mailbox . . . About the junkyards. It had a message.

Paylee22: It said, "To be continued."

NightTerra: Wait, what?

Paylee22: When you look at the page up close, you can see that some of the letters have been shaded in with pencil. When you put all those shaded letters together, in order, they spell out "to be continued"!!!

Paylee22: But don't take my word for it . . .

Peyton posts a photo in the chat box. I click to enlarge it; it's a picture of the page from the nonfiction book about junkyards. I give the page a quick scan. The author explains his ranking system for junk.

I enlarge the photo more, able to see that some of the letters have been shaded in, ever so lightly, with what appears to be pencil. I grab my sketch pad and copy the letters, deciphering the message right away.

Paylee22: Believe me now?

NightTerra: It can't be what you're thinking.

Paylee22: It's exactly what I'm thinking. He isn't done with me yet.

Paylee22: The question is when will things be continued? In a day? A month?

NightTerra: Have you told anyone about this?

Paylee22: Not yet.

NightTerra: Are you going to tell anyone? Because I really think you should.

Paylee22: Well, I just told you.

NightTerra: Yes, but you don't even know me, really—at least not in real life.

Paylee22: Are you kidding?!

Paylee22: !!!

Paylee22: I feel closer to you than most of the people in my real life.

NightTerra: I feel the same.

Paylee22: So, then . . . ???

NightTerra: I need to ask you something.

Paylee22: You can ask me anything.

NightTerra: Are you really from Chicago?

Paylee22: ??? What?!

NightTerra: You told me you were from Chicago, but when I went searching for your case I couldn't find details that matched what you've said.

Paylee22: Where did you search? Online? As if investigators put all those details out there for anyone to find.

Paylee22: Why were you searching for my case anyway?

NightTerra: I was just curious.

NightTerra: Does that bother you?

NightTerra: I searched under your first name, plus the fact that you were locked up in a shed, in the middle of a cornfield, in a suburb of Chicago . . .

Paylee22: I was put in a shed, but it wasn't in a cornfield.

Paylee22: It was in a remote area, though, in the woods. That's all I want to say about that.

NightTerra: What happened to burrowing through a hole?

Paylee22: I did burrow through a hole.

NightTerra: In the Chicago area?

NightTerra: Are you really 24?

Paylee22: Ok, to be completely honest . . . I haven't wanted to reveal everything, esp. online.

Paylee22: And, yes, you're right. It wasn't in the Midwest. But does where really matter?

Paylee22: I've been through a lot, so you can't really blame me for being guarded about what I put out there, esp. when it comes to specific details.

NightTerra: I've been through a lot too, but I've told you the truth from the very beginning.

Paylee22: You may want to reconsider how open you're being, esp. online. The internet isn't exactly a trustworthy place. I've had to learn that the hard way.

Paylee22: And, btw, I'm 22, not 24. The stuff about the shed is true. I just changed the location because I don't want people knowing where I am.

Paylee22: Can you understand that at all? I have to be careful about who to trust and what I make public.

NightTerra: Even in our private chats?

Paylee22: The private chats are a little bit safer, but still . . . You never know.

Paylee22: I hope you understand.

Paylee22: I'm just trying to protect myself.

Paylee22: Hellllloooooo???

Paylee22: ???

Paylee22: Are you still there?

Paylee22: I can tell you're upset.

Paylee22: Hello again???

NightTerra: Let's chat about this later.

Paylee22: Promise???

Paylee22: I'm really sorry, Terra. I should've told you sooner. I'd never do anything to intentionally hurt you. You're like a sister to me.

NightTerra: I'll talk to you soon.

I exit the chat and close the lid of my laptop, feeling like I've just been punched in the gut. Am I hurt that Peyton lied to me? *Jealous* she follows my parents' rules of survival★ so much better than I do? Or angry for defying my *own* rule—the one about not sharing my truth, not letting people in?

Cut.

Cut.

Cut: the list of survival rules. How did these scissors even get in my hand? I continue to use them, cutting out a paper heart, as if serrated scissors (or any of my defenses) could ever possibly save me from the blazing inferno that's swallowed me whole.

★ Rule number eight: Be careful who to trust.

28

I still couldn't find the sparerib bone, as hard as I looked . . .

Where was it?

The spotlight was on, but it was still dark—so dim. And there were so many rocks now—those I'd managed to prod out.

I raked my fingers over the ground to search. The book and blanket were there; the troll doll and sheet of burned paper were too. So, what did it matter? I knew the bone existed. I'd eaten the sparerib meat.

Hadn't I?

How many days had I been off my meds? What were the side effects of missing so many dosages? Delusions? Hallucinations? What was the difference between the two again?

Eventually, when I could no longer see straight, I pulled my socks over my fingers like gloves and dug a four-inch crevice into the wall—enough to fit the width of my foot. I tested it to be sure, wedged my foot right in.

I kept working, making more crevices, creating a ladder of sorts. How high could I go? If I used the rungs as leverage . . .

The spotlight blinked, snagging my attention. I looked up. It was daylight now; there was a patch of gray.

The light blinked again—three more times—before shutting off altogether.

I froze in response.

Was he up there? Would he pull up on the chain? And close the lid? Did he know what I was doing?

A whistling sounded: the tune to "Mary Had a Little Lamb."

I clenched my teeth—so hard one chipped. A jolting pain shot through my gums. I went to spit the piece out, accidentally swallowing it down. It got caught in my throat, choking me. My chest convulsed.

I shoved my fingers into my mouth, reaching toward my throat, trying to force myself to throw up. But it wasn't working. And meanwhile, my body was shaking. I couldn't breathe. My face felt chilled.

I scrambled for the book, tore half a page out and crammed it into my mouth. The muscles at the back of my throat strained as I worked to swallow the paper down—to get the piece to move, taking handful after handful of water from the makeshift basin I'd made. I splashed the water into my mouth until there was no more left and I was just clawing at dampened dirt.

My tooth ached where it'd broken—a throbbing pain that radiated to the crown of my head. The chewed-up paper moved downward into my throat, making me gag. I threw up. A stream of acid spouted out my mouth and nose. Somehow, I could feel it inside my ears. But at last, I could breathe.

Exhausted, I lay with my cheek pressed against the ground. The whistling was gone. Was it ever there to begin with? Eventually, I fell asleep and dreamed of drowning—of dirty beach water filling my sandpaper lungs as I floated out to sea.

When I woke up again, the light was still off. I slid my cheek over the ground, making sure that I was still in the well, that he hadn't brought me someplace else. I ran my palms over the wall, feeling for the crevices I'd dug. I found the first one and moved my hand upward, able to feel the second.

Using the spine of the book as my pickax, I began digging again. My shoulder ached. My fingertips tingled.

I stepped into one of the crevices, able to reach upward and feel the bumpy brick surface. The spotlight hung down from the chain about two feet above that. But what was the chain attached to, outside the well? Was it something sturdy enough to hold my weight?

I continued working, keeping stability in mind. I'd need to anchor myself to the wall so I wouldn't fall off. I dug extra deep into the highest crevice—the top rung of my makeshift ladder. With stinging-stabbing fingertips, I maneuvered a rock toward me and let it fall to the ground.

The crevice was elbow-deep now. I reached my arms inside it, steadying myself on the wall. But I was so slouched over. How was this going to work? What would I have to do?

Keeping one arm secure, I swung outward with my hand extended, trying to feel for the chain. No luck. I jumped back down, then climbed up again. I did this over and over, trying to grab the chain.

Where was it?

Just a little bit higher.

I could swing out farther.

Finally, my hand hit the rim of the light, producing a gong sound. My heart soared. The chain rustled. I performed the same motions over and over: climbing up the wall, securing myself with the top crevice, then swinging outward, until eventually I was able to grip the chain.

Keeping steady, I grabbed hold with my other hand too, and continued walking up the wall—left, right, left—moving up the chain.

I told myself, *If I can get to the very top, I can crawl back inside my bedroom window (the one on Bailey Road). I can reverse time, and turn the knob, and open the door, and save my parents.*

So many stories as I continued to climb—one step at a time, up the brick, hand over hand.

I was almost there.

Just a little bit more.

I could smell how close I was—the scent of forest trees and fresh blooms . . . I took another step, just as my foot slipped off the brick.

My legs dangled like monkeys on a tree.

The weight of my body slipped me downward at least a few inches.

Hold on, I screamed inside my head, swinging back and forth, as my palms seared and my biceps quivered. *Don't fall.*

I clenched my teeth and slipped a little farther. Droplets of sweat rolled down my face. Rule number ten: Don't panic. *You can do this. It's all a head game:* If I could get to the top, I could win my prize, I could save my parents, I could live happily ever after.

But I felt myself sliding farther. My sweaty palms . . . if only I could've wiped them. *Maybe one hand at a time . . .* Did I have enough strength?

No. I didn't.

I slid a few more inches down.

My feet clonked against the light. What did that mean? How much height had I lost? I held my breath and clung on to hope. But hope wasn't enough because moments later I dropped to the ground with a hard, heavy thud.

29

Unable to sleep, I lie awake in bed watching the rain droplets pelt against the windows and throw dart-shaped shadows on my bedroom floor. I'm missing my mother tonight—so hard it hurts. I clench her sweater, wishing the fabric still carried her scent, the rose oil she used to dab behind her ears and the lilac-scented hand cream we used to stuff into her stocking at Christmas.

I picture her dark gray eyes and the scar through her eyebrow (from a scooter accident as a kid) and imagine that she can hear my voice: "Is there a rule that could help me now?" I ask aloud. What are the chances she'll answer in a dream?

Eventually, after what feels like hours of tossing and turning, failing to fall asleep, I fish a pocketknife from my night table and go downstairs, seeking a little fresh air. Aunt Dessa's backyard is fenced in on all sides. Sliders lead to an open deck. I step outside. The cool fall air bites the back of my neck. It's probably no more than forty degrees.

I sit down on the floor of the deck and roll up my sweats as far as they can go to expose more skin. My feet are bare. My arms are too. I stretch out, facing up toward the sky, remembering how exhilarating the rain felt, when I was in the well. What I wouldn't give to feel that same way now, as crazy as that sounds, as messed up as it is.

The rain soaks through my clothes and sprinkles inside my

mouth, but it doesn't taste nearly as good as it did in the well, like liquid sugar. Instead, it's bitter like acid, like the water from old and rusted pipes. I roll over and rest my head against the crook of my arm.

What am I doing? Why am I out here?

And what is that?

On one of the side tables. A figure of some sort.

I sit up to get a better look. It appears to be a ceramic statue, about a foot tall, painted green, white, and red. I move closer, scooching across the deck, able to see what it is: a garden gnome, dressed in a green and white suit, exactly like William, the troll-like character from the water-well book.

Wait, Logic says. *Don't jump to conclusions. Rule number nine: Never guess. Always be sure.*

Am I sure? Is this a dream? *Pinch, pinch, pinch.*

The gnome is wearing bright red boots that curl up at the toes, different from William's shiny black shoes. This gnome also has a pale pink face, rather than an orange one. Its hat is different too: tall and red rather than black and rounded.

But still . . .

It has a long white beard just like William's, and similar enlarged eyes that take up most of its scrunched-up face. Its perma-smile chills me even more than the rainwater. If Aunt Dessa were home, I'd ask her where it came from, but for now I leave it here on the deck table and go back inside the house, locking the door behind me.

NOW

30

The following day, when I log on to Jane, I search the chat feed for Peyton's name. Her message pops up just a few seconds later: Do you want to talk? I click the private room link.

Paylee22: Hey.

Paylee22: I hope you're not still upset with me.

NightTerra: Honestly, I think I'm more upset with myself.

Paylee22: You're more upset with yourself because I lied???

NightTerra: I'm more upset with myself because I trusted you were being honest with me. And, like you said, why would you be? This is an online chat site. How naive can I be?

Paylee22: Please don't be like that. I'm glad you trusted me.

NightTerra: Trust is for people who haven't been burned.

NightTerra: I trusted my parents would always be with me. I trusted my aunt would believe my story. I trusted the people in my life would stick by my side.

NightTerra: I trusted you, because we'd both been through something similar and because maybe you knew how I felt . . .

Paylee22: I do know. You can trust me. I was just trying to protect myself.

NightTerra: I know and I can't blame you for that, not at all.

NightTerra: But now I need to protect myself.

Paylee22: So, what does that mean for us?

Paylee22: Please, Terra, you have to believe me when I say that your friendship has been the one thing that's kept me going these past couple of months.

Paylee22: Will you still confide in me?

Paylee22: ???

NightTerra: I'm still going to chat with you.

Paylee22: I'm really sorry I hurt you.

Paylee22: You have no idea how much.

NightTerra: Don't be sorry. You were just being smart, following all the rules. I should've done the same.

Paylee22: Please, Terra. I really need you.

NightTerra: I'm right here. I'm chatting with you, aren't I?

Paylee22: But it's not going to be the same. I can already tell.

Paylee22: Please, don't give up on me. You're like the sister I never had.

NightTerra: Let's talk about something else, ok? Like the book that was in your captivity quarters . . .

NightTerra: The one about the family that lived in the woods, in tiny shacks, off the grid . . . You said the setting was the woods, right? And that you were in the woods too, rather than a cornfield . . . ?

Paylee22: I'm really sorry, Terra. I really need you.

Paylee22: There are things I want to tell you . . .

Paylee22: Like that my family is from Maine, from a small coastal town that's known for having one of the oldest lighthouses.

Paylee22: And that the hike I went on the day I was abducted to look for the abandoned school . . . the trail was just behind the community college, where I was taking classes.

Paylee22: I worked at the yacht club across the street from the college. I was working on the morning that I was taken.

NightTerra: Wait, why are you telling me all this?

Paylee22: Because I really care about you. You really matter to me, Terra. And I want you to trust me.

Paylee22: He's coming back for me.

NightTerra: Or so you think.

NightTerra: Have you told anybody yet?

Paylee22: Would you even believe me if I said yes? Or have I completely lost your trust?

NightTerra: If you haven't already told someone about the book page in your mailbox, you really should.

Paylee22: I'm so sorry, Terra.

NightTerra: Don't worry about me. Worry about yourself right now. Ok?

NightTerra: Why don't we talk later?

Paylee22: You have to go already?

NightTerra: You should too. You need to show your parents the message you found.

Paylee22: Ok.

Paylee22: Bye, Terra. Love you.

She logs out, before I can say goodbye. Part of me feels bad if it seems I'm erecting a wall between us. But I guess that's how I felt too, when she told me she'd lied. So, maybe that makes us even.

Or maybe it just makes us hurt.

31

My aunt knocks on my open bedroom door. *"Terra?"*

I look up from my laptop.

Aunt Dessa is standing in the doorway, dressed in the pale green hospital scrubs that make me squirm. Her arms are folded. Her mouth forms a straight, tense line. "Care to explain where you were today?"

Where I was . . .

"Is that a difficult question?"

"I was here," I tell her. "Catching up on homework." I nod toward the calculus book on my desk as if it contains any relevant answers.

"And the reason you missed your appointment today?"

Appointment?

"You were supposed to meet with Dr. Bridges."

Who? "I was?"

"I told you . . ." Her jaw clenches. "Cecelia Bridges, the woman who does hypnotherapy."

Oh, right. I remember: Dr. Bridges, the specialty in false memories, the agreement I made to go for an appointment . . .

But did we actually make one?

"I pulled some major strings to get you in today," Aunt Dessa says. "How do you think it looks for me when you don't show up?"

"I'm sorry. I didn't know about an appointment."

"I told you. This morning. Cecelia texted me late last night. *Remember?*"

I really don't. My aunt and I passed in the hallway this morning. She mentioned coffee and something about fruit, but I don't recall anything else. I'd been so tired, not having gotten much sleep. I grab my phone and check the screen, but I have no missed messages. "Did you try to call me?"

"Why should I have to call?" Aunt Dessa's face wilts like a rose in the heat.

"I'm really sorry." I wilt too.

Her gaze lands on the syrup bottle clenched in my hands before continuing to travel around the room as though searching for other things:

The yoga blanket . . . Check.

My mom's sweater . . . Check.

The starry doorknob, my basket of troll items, and the collection of fire extinguishers . . . Check, check, check . . .

"I'm sorry," I say for a third time, hoping the tension in her face will break.

But she remains as rigid as steel with her lips screwed tight. Eventually, she starts to turn away, but I stop her before she can.

"Did you buy a garden gnome?" I ask.

She moves closer as though to hear me better. "A *what*?"

"A garden gnome—one of those ceramic ones . . . about a foot tall? I saw one on the back deck."

Her face furrows. "I'm not sure what you mean."

"A garden gnome," I say once again, getting up from the bed. "I can show you." I lead Aunt Dessa downstairs and through the dining area. I flick on the outside lights and peel open the sliding glass door.

The outdoor table sits in direct view. But the garden gnome is no longer there. In its place is one of my aunt's ceramic planters—a red-and-green one with flecks of gold and black.

I close my eyes. My stomach twists.

"Terra?"

"Did you put this here?" I ask.

"The planter? No. Did you?"

Did I? Is this what I picked up and moved? Was my mind playing tricks? Are my meds screwing with my brain?

Or is it possible I dreamed up the gnome? Had I somehow fallen asleep on the deck? Did I ever leave my bedroom?

"Terra?"

"It was here," I say, searching anyway, beneath the table, behind the potted plants . . . I pull out every chair.

"When did you see it?"

"Late last night. I came out here in the rain."

"What were you doing in the rain?"

Panic fills my mouth: a sickly, sour taste. Sometimes I forget to lie. "I just wanted to sit," I tell her as if sitting in the rain is normal.

Aunt Dessa clasps her hand over her mouth.

"I mean, I thought I heard something. There was a clanking sound, so I came out here . . . But maybe what I saw was this planter."

"And you think the planter made a clanking noise?" She looks toward the row of potted plants. "Nothing appears broken or disturbed."

"So, maybe what I saw—and heard—was an owl."

And maybe the owl was a ceramic planter.

And maybe the planter was a garden gnome.

And maybe the garden gnome is a big red flag that I can no longer trust myself, that I'm truly going crazy.

32

Back in my room, I change into my mom's old sweater and burrow beneath the covers. I need to sleep, but thoughts spin like hamsters on a wheel, inside my head, keeping me up. What are the odds that someone who knew about my case placed the gnome on the back deck—only temporarily—as a joke or to make me feel crazy?

Or what if the guy who took me left it? Could it have been a warning that he's somewhere nearby, waiting to take me again, just as Peyton fears with her captor too? Do either of those scenarios even make sense when the person would've had no way to predict I'd ever see it?

And what if the gnome was never really there? If I'd only imagined it? My heart races at the mere possibility; somehow, it's the most terrifying option of all.

I rub my cheek with the cuff of the sweater, thinking how Mom used to tell me how strong she thought I was. But I don't feel strong. I feel more like the way she sometimes got, when she'd curl up into her shell like a hermit crab—like the time I came home from school and found her on the living room sofa staring out into space. The TV wasn't on. There was no book in her hand. I stood in the doorway waiting for her to acknowledge my presence, but it was only when I scooted down and touched her bony fingers that she finally noticed I was there.

"Terra?" Her eyes met mine. "You're home early. Was it a half day?" She was still in her pajamas from the morning. The coffee Dad had made her—and poured into the smiling heart mug—still lingered on the table beside an untouched breakfast cookie. She obviously hadn't gone to work.

"Having one of those days?" I asked her.

Mom faked a smile, but her eyes filled up, which was my cue. I turned away to allow her to cry in peace.

With my back to her, I asked, "Are you coming to my belt ceremony?" For tae kwon do.

"Would it upset you if I had to miss?"

"No," I lied.

"I'm so proud of you." Her voice crumbled like cake. "You're so strong, so resilient. You'll always be just fine—no matter what happens."

If only she could see me now.

I stare at the window, half wishing the rainbow bird would visit me again. Somehow the bird, with its unicorn stripes and sparerib gift, seemed so much clearer than this.

Sometime later, my aunt comes into my room again. "Terra?" She sits down on the edge of my bed, no longer wearing the pale green scrubs. "Is there something you want to tell me?"

I roll onto my back to meet her eyes. "What do you mean?"

"I mean, what *was* all of that about downstairs, earlier?"

Where do I begin? And do I even know?

She takes my hand and pats it like a wounded animal—*stroke, stroke, stroke*. The gesture takes me aback, and I can feel it in my chest—a churning sensation inside my heart. I pinch my leg beneath the blanket to make sure I'm fully awake.

"Are you feeling confused again?" she asks.

Did the confusion ever stop? *Pinch, pinch, pinch*. My lids feel heavy. My brain is fuzzy.

"Terra?"

What does she want to hear? That I'm questioning my reality? That I lied about the well? Sometimes I'm tempted to tell her I did. Would it bring us closer, make things better? *I was so screwed up from the fire,* I could say. *I ran away, just like I did those other times. I'm not sure why. The need for escape? The desire for attention? I'm so sorry. Will you ever be able to forgive me?*

Would she understand?

Could we start anew?

"I'm sorry," I say, at a complete loss for words.

Aunt Dessa is standing now, wearing a long blue T-shirt that looks like Mom's. She brings the covers up to my chin and kisses my forehead: a soft, warm peck. The letter *M* dangles toward my mouth. "Thank you for saying that, sweetie."

What did I say? What does she think it means? I want to ask her, but I almost don't care—at least not for now. Because right now, though I might be on the verge of sleeping, I'm *sweetie* once again.

33

I wake up, hours later, and check the chat feed for Peyton's name, unable to find it. I stay in the chat room anyway, hoping she'll show up. But two hours go by and she still doesn't.

To keep my mind occupied, I open up a search box and type the words *homeschool group, bridge project,* and *Hayberry Park* into the search engine. I end up finding an article from two years ago. A local newspaper featured the footbridge donation. The group of students, called the Mighty Mindbenders, uses the park to do nature-based activities.

I click on the link for the group's website. Several of the photos show the students hiking the Hayberry trails, building stick houses from fallen branches, and doing science experiments by the creek. The online calendar says the group is meeting at the park's main entrance first thing in the morning. I plan accordingly, setting my alarm. When it goes off, I change my clothes and go downstairs.

My aunt is sitting at the kitchen island with a shoebox full of photos.

"What's that?" I ask.

"It's my sorry excuse for a photo album. I thought it was time I sorted it out." She sets a few of the photos in front of me, those of her and my mother, when she and Mom were teenagers (sunning on the beach, hugging in a park, and huddled up by a campfire).

"You two looked so close."

"We *were* close—at one time, that is." She flips another

photo—one that shows the two of them at a restaurant. My mother's expression is vacant; she looks present but absent. She's like that in another photo too, what appears to be a family cookout. While everyone else looks straight ahead cheesing it up for the camera, my mother gazes downward at her hands, seemingly lost in thought.

"How old is she in that one?" I ask, pointing at the restaurant pic.

"High school. The summer after her sophomore year."

"And these other ones?" I nod to a picture of Mom and Aunt Dessa sitting at a park caught in a laugh, both of them wearing matching necklaces with the initial pendants.

"*Before* sophomore year."

An invisible light clicks on above my head. Obviously, I knew about the attack, but I never knew how much it framed their lives, compartmentalizing events into *before* and *after* (like *before and after the fire* and *before and after the well*).

"I wanted your mom and me to be close like that again," she says.

"Why do you think that didn't happen?"

She gives a slight shrug. "That's life sometimes, I guess."

"*What* is?"

"Not getting to do the things you want because you think you have so much time. But sometimes you don't. Sometimes you wind up living with regret, elbow-deep in old photos that act like ghosts."

"What didn't you get to do?"

She touches the letter *M* around her neck. "Remember this: Life is short. And time is limited."

I nod and look away, having learned that lesson all too well.

"We need to have a talk."

Unlike the way we're talking now? "Okay." I brace myself for her words by grabbing a fork and pressing the prongs into the flesh of my thumb.

"You seemed really confused last night. You said some things."

Is she referring to my confusion over the garden gnome? Or to what I said after that, when she came back to my room, when I'd been on the verge of falling asleep?

"We're not going to talk about it now," she says.

"Why?" I ask.

She delves back into the box and starts to hum, flipping through photos, sorting them into before-and-after stacks, evidently done talking.

I'm done too. I head out the door, eager to lose myself in research. The #22 bus is about a ten-minute walk. It'll take me into the city of Crestwood, to Hayberry Pond, which isn't so far from the main entrance of the park. I begin in that direction. The neighbor's dog barks as I pass by. I grab the wasp spray in my pocket—not for the dog but to help calm my nerves—and continue forward, eventually turning a corner.

A dark gray pickup crosses the intersection, headed in my direction. The truck passed me once already. I swivel to look as it passes by again. It stops and turns into someone's driveway, then backs out onto the street. It comes this way again, and I take a mental snapshot: Ford, older model, dented fender. I reach for my phone, wanting to get a photo.

The truck drives by before making a U-turn and heading straight for me. It pulls over to the side of the road. I look toward the driver, but the windows are blacked out.

The driver's-side door whips wide open.

Without even thinking, I start to cross the street in front of the truck just as I hear my name, the familiar male voice. It stops me in my tracks.

Garret's voice. He exits the truck. It's only then I realize: I'm standing in the middle of the street, trying to breathe at a normal rate, despite the knot inside my chest.

"Terra? Is everything okay? I saw you," he continues, when I don't respond. "I hope this is okay—that I stopped, I mean. I promise I have no library books." He smiles.

I move back to the sidewalk. He joins me, and I take a deep breath.

The sun is too bright.

·

The air feels so warm.

"Where are you headed?" he asks.

My mind won't stop reeling. "You just happened to be driving by?"

"Yeah, on my way downtown. Critter's has the best coffee. Want to be the judge?"

"No. Thanks. I have to be someplace."

"Where? I'll drive you."

"Thanks, but I'm fine walking."

"Why do I feel I've heard that before?" He grins.

"Excuse me?"

"Come on." He smiles wider. "Where are you headed?"

"Why do you want to know so badly?"

"Basic conversation. Trust me, I come in peace."

"I'm going to Hayberry Park."

"*Really?*" He eyes the phone in my grip. "That's a long walk, don't you think?"

"I was going to take a bus."

"When you could have a personal escort?" He motions to his truck. "Seriously, let me drive you. Or, at least, let me walk with you. Contrary to what you must be thinking because of the tautness of my muscles, I haven't gotten in my daily workout yet. A walk would do me good."

I set my phone to camera mode and take a photo of Garret's license plate when he isn't looking. I text the pic to my aunt, along with a message: *I bumped into Garret, the guy from the sorority party, and he offered to give me a ride. Just keeping you informed.*

Just leaving a trail of clues.

"Okay, thanks," I say, agreeing to the ride.

Garret opens the passenger-side door, and I climb in. He gets in right after (on the driver's side), readjusting his seat—back, forth, back, forth; it doesn't seem to lock. Still, he starts the engine. A big rumble sounds as though the truck might come apart.

"So, how have you been?" he asks, steering the conversation elsewhere.

"Okay, I guess."

He pulls away from the curb. "Can I ask why you're going to Hayberry Park?"

"There's a homeschooling group I'd like to meet."

"A homeschooling group you want to join?"

I peer out the window. "I just want to talk to the teacher."

Garret must get the message—that I'm not much into talking—because he turns on the radio, then apologizes for not getting FM stations. "She's an old-fashioned lady, but my grandfather's pride and joy. He passed away last year."

"Sorry."

"It's okay." He pats the dashboard. "My grandfather wanted me to have the truck but said I'd have to treat it—her—with utmost respect, which means no using my cell for music either. Can't make a lady feel as though she's not enough, right?"

"You're joking." I smirk.

He smirks back. "Maybe a little."

About twenty-five minutes later, he turns into the east entrance of Hayberry Park, as directed.

"Thanks for the ride," I tell him.

"Anytime. But, hey, wait. You don't seriously think I'm going to let you disappear—alone—into the very same park you spent what must've been the worst, most horrifying days of your life, do you?"

"Do you honestly believe that?"

"That I'm not going to let you go into the park alone?"

"I'll be fine," I tell him. "I have my phone." As well as the wasp spray and a pocketknife.

"This is nonnegotiable. I'm coming with you." He exits the car.

I do as well, just as my phone buzzes. There's a text from my aunt:

Ok. Thanks for letting me know.

Also, are you working Sunday?

Sunday night. I go in at 9.

Can you make sure you're home
around 5?

Is this about the talk you
mentioned?

Can you be home?

I guess.

Great, thanks.

"Is everything okay?" Garret asks.

"It's fine," I say, pocketing the phone, wondering what Aunt Dessa has to say. Why does she need to make an appointment? What else might she be planning? Does it have anything to do with the photos of her and my mom?

We begin down the path that cuts through the woods and walk for several minutes, through a clearing, passing by a tall elm tree with what appears to be hundreds of initials carved into the bark. We cross a bike path that's bordered by maple trees on both sides.

"It's pretty here," Garret says.

Admittedly, it is, especially with the sun shining down through the maple tree limbs, making the red leaves glow.

"How often do you come here?" he asks.

"You don't want to know."

"It's pretty brave of you. I mean, returning to the place where you were being kept like a prisoner, against your will . . . Why would you want that?"

"Do you even believe that I was taken?"

"Why wouldn't I believe it?"

Because not many people do. Because I was publicly called out.

So, is he acting? Does he not follow the news? Or does he have his own personal agenda?

"Actually, part of the problem is that I *can't* return to the place," I tell him. "I don't know where it is."

"And you think this homeschooling group could help?"

I pull the paper map from the back pocket of my jeans and place my thumb below the spot where I've drawn in the footbridge. "It should be just past these evergreens."

We proceed in that direction, rounding a corner and passing by a creek. I brush a tree bough from in front of my eyes, able to see the bridge's dedication plaque; it faces us, beneath the first step. As I proceed across, I can hear the group's voices.

The students stand scattered about the clearing—all of them with easels, painting the scene around them. An older woman—likely the teacher—moves among the group, stopping to observe and comment.

I approach her slowly, waving when she spots me. "I'll be right back," I tell Garret.

Still, he follows for several footsteps, staying within earshot.

I introduce myself as Addie Singer. "I'm a student at Dayton University."

"It's nice to meet you, Addie." The woman smiles. Bright white teeth. "Have we met before?"

"No. I mean, I don't think so. But I understand that you and your group use this park for some of your homeschool studies."

"That's right."

"A friend of mine is a homeschool teacher as well. She'd like to use this clearing for a science activity, and the park ranger said that she should come and check with you."

"With *me*?" The lines across her forehead form a map of their own. "I don't *own* these woods."

"Oh, right. Sorry. I'm afraid I'm not explaining myself very well. She's hoping to do a collaborative project with you, something with STEM . . . Her group is small—just three middle-schoolers . . ."

"STEM?"

"Yes, the whole science, technology, engineering, and math initiative."

"I know what STEM is, but what is the project? And who's your friend?" She peers over my shoulder, just noticing Garret maybe.

"Her name is Kelsie," I say. "She's pretty new to homeschooling, but she has her teacher's license. Anyway, the project is based on water systems and environmental engineering. She wants to investigate the park's water well."

Her face scrunches up, reminding me of William's. "I didn't even know the park *had* a water well."

"Apparently, it does. I'm assuming you haven't seen it, then? My friend didn't specify the location, but maybe one of your students knows about it."

"Okay, well, does your friend have a card? I can reach out to her. There's another homeschool group in the area that we sometimes get together with."

"Perfect. And, yes, she does have a card. But I'm not sure I brought it." I search my pockets as panic rushes my face, heating my cheeks. "Maybe I could give her *your* card instead?"

"We're online, under the Mighty Mindbenders Group. Tell your friend to look us up." She takes a step back as though finished with our talk.

But I'm not nearly done. "Could I ask your students if any of them have seen a water well?"

The woman turns away, moving back toward her students.

I follow along. "Please," I insist.

She stands in the clearing. Her face goes stern. At the same moment, something touches my shoulder, making me flinch. I turn to look.

Garret's there. "We should probably go."

Not yet. I move closer to the group. "I have a few more questions," I tell her.

"Well, I'm done answering." The woman grips her phone as

though making a threat, but she knows as well as I do that the reception in these woods is patchy at best.

"Have any of you Mighty Mindbenders seen a water well in Hayberry Park?" I shout out to the kids.

The children stop painting. A few of them gawk. Others exchange looks.

No one says a word—until a boy comes forward, from behind his easel. He's ten years old maybe, with round eyeglasses and dark red hair. "I've seen it," he says.

My heart clenches.

"Mitchell, *no*." The teacher scurries to his side, places her arm around his back, as if protecting him from me.

Still, I ask him, "Where did you see it?"

Mitchell looks to the right, then to the left, his face puzzling over. "It was behind some bushes. My ball fell inside it."

"When?" My pulse races.

"I'm not really sure." His face goes twisty. "Six months ago, maybe. Or last year . . ."

"*Which was it?*"

"You need to leave now," the teacher orders, pulling the boy closer.

"Let's go," Garret says.

"*No!*" I shout, still focused on the boy. "Who were you with? What were you doing? Which entrance did you use to get into the park that day?"

"I don't remember," he says.

"*Think,*" I insist, hearing the urgency in my voice.

"Is she crazy?" a girl asks.

"I think she's probably crazy." Another voice.

Snickering follows.

"I'm calling the police," the teacher says.

"No!" I shout, moving even closer, wanting to fix this.

But Garret takes my forearm. "It's time to go."

I look back at the group—at the little girl tucked behind the teacher's leg—and reluctantly let Garret lead me away, over the footbridge, and through a grove of trees. But after several minutes of walking, I stop short.

My chest retightens.

How can I leave without talking to that boy some more, without trying to elicit as much information as possible?

"Terra?" Garret asks.

"You should go."

"Go, *where*? I'm not just going to leave you here."

"Didn't you hear her? She's calling the police."

"So, let her. We haven't done anything wrong. Not really." Garret places his hands on my shoulders and levels his gaze, forcing me to look into his dark blue eyes. "You're not going to find your answers here."

"Then where will I find them?"

"I wish I knew."

"They think I'm crazy."

"Let them think whatever they want. It doesn't make it true."

I close my eyes and see an inferno all around me. And picture the ceramic garden gnome. And envision climbing down a ladder from my bedroom window on Bailey Road.

"That night at the party," he begins, "when we were talking about how the people who cross our paths—the good ones, the bad ones, and the everything-in-between ones . . . how they do so for a reason . . . That was honestly one of the sanest conversations I've ever had."

"Too bad it was bullshit."

"You know it wasn't."

I suck back tears. He's way too nice. I'm way too emotional.

"Look, I know you've been through a lot," he says.

"You *don't* know," I snap.

"What it's like to lose my parents? No, I don't. Or how it feels to survive something and have no one believe that it happened to begin with? You've got me there too. But that doesn't mean I can't at least try to understand."

"Why would you even want to?"

"Believe it or not, there are lots of people who'd love to know and understand you more."

I reach into my pocket for my troll key chain and squeeze the belly and stroke the long rainbow hair. "There's so much that you don't know about me."

"I'm sure there is. And, likewise, there's so much that you don't know about me either." He takes off his sweatshirt and drapes it over my shoulders.

It's only then I notice how hard I'm shivering, how cold I feel.

"You just have to be open to giving people a chance," he says.

"Opening up hasn't really worked well for me so far."

"Sometimes it won't, and sometimes you'll open up to the wrong people. But that doesn't mean you should stop looking for the right people."

His words create a riptide inside my body; all currents flow through my veins, heating up my face.

Garret's gaze travels from my eyes to my mouth, before he looks away and takes a step back. "So, what do you say?" he asks. "Shall we get out of here?"

I nod, knowing it's the right thing to do, but not quite ready to let the moment go. As we exit the park, there are things I want to tell him—like that one day, maybe, I *will* trust again and that possibly, yes, I'd like to open up. But instead I picture the self-portrait in my room with its soot-stained face and wax-sealed lips.

And I hear my father calling my name from outside my bedroom door.

And I think of my last stint in the hospital, when Dr. Mary told me, emphatically—with no room for argument—that what happened in the well was a story my mind created.

And I burn a little crisper.

And I feel a little lonelier.

And I remain as silent as snow.

34

It's quiet between Garret and me on the ride home. His fingers are tense on the wheel, like a cat hanging on to a ledge.

I gaze out the window, rubbing the sleeve of his sweatshirt against my cheek. "I'm sorry if I freaked you out back there."

"Are you kidding? You didn't freak me out."

"So, you didn't mind nearly getting arrested in front of a bunch of homeschoolers?"

"*Nearly,* not really." He winks.

"You're crazy."

"Isn't that precisely what you called yourself?"

"It is."

"So, it would seem we have something in common." He turns onto my street and pulls up in front of my aunt's house. "Let's do this again sometime, shall we?"

"Harassing schoolteachers?"

"Unless you'd rather we target some other selfless member of our community, like one of the nurses at the public health clinic, maybe? Or a volunteer at the Red Cross?"

I let out a laugh—the first one in I can't even remember when. I look back at the house, not really wanting to go in. "Thank you for everything." I start to hand him back his sweatshirt.

"Keep it," he says, pushing it toward me. "At least until the chill wears off. Also, before you leave, I want to give you my number. Just in case of anything. You can feel free to contact me if and when you ever need to. And don't feel like you have to give me your number too; I'll just give you mine—not that I don't want your number, that is. I mean, you can give it to me if you want." He flashes a sheepish grin.

I open up the address book on my phone. Garret tells me his number. I save the contact, then press to dial it. Garret's phone buzzes with the call.

"Now you have my number too," I tell him.

"Hopefully, that's not something you'll regret."

"I won't regret it." My face reheats. I cover it with the sweat-shirt, pressing the sleeve against my mouth, noticing for the first time how much it smells like him—a mix of tangerine and musk. "Thanks again."

"No problem at all. I'm really glad I ran into you today."

I start to exit the truck, knowing full well what I'm leaving be-hind: a taste of what life felt like before I was taken. The last thing I want is to leave it again. But I tell him goodbye anyway.

35

In my room, I log on to Jane and check the chat feed for Peyton's name, but she isn't on, once again, leaving a sickly feeling in the pit of my stomach.

JA Admin: Welcome, NightTerra. Remember the rules: no judgments, no swearing, no inappropriate remarks. This is a safe space for honesty and support.

TulipPrincess: She thinks it's ok, that this is what's normal.

Cobra-head43: Did you meet him yet?

TulipPrincess: Unfortunately. She brought him home last night. She was all flirty with him too, touching his shoulder and giggling about stupid stuff. It made me want to yack.

NightTerra: What did I miss?

TulipPrincess: My mother found herself a new leech (boyfriend). They met at her support group, even though hooking up with fellow victims is supposedly against the rules.

Cobra-head43: Maybe he'll be different.

TulipPrincess: And maybe I'll shit roses. They're always the same. Trust me. He's just a newer, shinier version of the same old asshole.

JA Admin: Remember the rules. No swearing, please.

TulipPrincess: Oops, sorry.

TulipPrincess: Am I the only one who constantly breaks this rule? Lol!

TulipPrincess: Anyway, the leech kept telling me how lucky I am, that my mother is such a warrior woman, fighting for me.

TulipPrincess: If I wanted everyone to know my business, I'd wear a T-shirt to announce it.

Cobra-head43: I guess that makes sense, though, right? That he knows stuff, I mean. Since they met at a support group . . .

TulipPrincess: I feel like it should be my story to tell, not hers—and especially not as a way to pick up guys. Seriously, she can't handle being single for more than five minutes. T-minus 52 days until I'm legal and can move out. #buh-bye

NightTerra: I'm so sorry.

TulipPrincess: And I'm so done. Can we talk about something else now? I'm kind of over my shitty drama. I want to hear about someone else's. Lol.

Cobra-head43: Not exactly dramatic, but def shitty . . . I haven't slept in three days.

NightTerra: Has Paylee22 been on here today?

NightTerra: Sorry, Cobra-head43. We must've typed at the same time.

JA Admin: One more time, watch the language, please. No swearing.

TulipPrincess: Not that I've seen so far.

Cobra-head43: NightTerra, Np.

Cobra-head43: JA Admin, Sorry for swearing. :(

TulipPrincess: Me too. #pottymouth #multipleoffenser

Cobra-head43: Paylee was on yesterday, I think.

Cobra-head43: She seemed quiet, not her usual chatty self. I asked her what was up and she said she had a lot on her plate.

SugarRush911: Who on here doesn't?!?

Cobra-head43: Right, but she didn't really want to talk about it.

SugarRush911: Then why come on a chat site?

NightTerra: What time was that?

Cobra-head43: Late, like 2AM, my time. West Coast.

Cobra-head43: What time is that for Paylee?

NightTerra: Five maybe. This morning. ???

TulipPrincess: She was probably looking for you, NightTerra. You guys are always disappearing from the "public" chat to go into private chat rooms.

Cobra-head43: Actually, now that you mention it, I kind of remember her asking about NightTerra.

TulipPrincess: She'll probably be on later. That girl doesn't stay away for long.

Cobra-head43: Paylee doesn't seem to sleep much. Like me. Lol.

I remain lurking in the chat room for another full hour, waiting for Peyton. But she doesn't show up. Might she be purposely staying away? Has she told anyone about the book page in her mailbox? Was that what she was referring to when she said she had a lot on her plate? Could *I* have been on her plate too—because of how cold I was to her? Is that why she was asking about me?

I hate that I don't know the answers. Hate that people say she seemed quiet on the chat. And hate, most of all, that I consciously chose to push her away, ignoring her cries for help, as though I haven't learned a thing.

36

I search the chat room feed for Peyton's name at various times throughout the following day. But still no luck, and so I draft her a message:

> Dear Peyton,
> I'd really like to talk to you. I'm sorry about our last chat. You were right about protecting your privacy. Maybe part of me feels stupid for not doing the same. I'm not perfect—nowhere close—which you probably know better than anyone else. When you have a moment, could you please let me know that you're okay? I miss you.
> Xoxoxo!
> Love,
> Terra
> P.S. I've been watching more of Summer's Story.

I hit Send and join the chat:

JennaIsDead: No, my brother told me. It's totally fine.

TulipPrincess: Well, at least, now you know.

NightTerra: Hey, everyone!

TulipPrincess: Hey, NT! When did you sneak in?

NightTerra: Any Paylee22 sightings?

JennaIsDead: Who????

TulipPrincess: Nope.

Cobra-head43: Nada.

JennaIsDead: Sorry, I'm new here.

TulipPrincess: Paylee22 is a girl who practically lives on this site. Aside from the past few days, I'm not sure I've ever come online and not found her on here. But you could probably say the same about me. Lol.

Cobra-head43: Ditto.

CityGirlSal: Maybe she got blocked.

NightTerra: Blocked for what?

CityGirlSal: I don't know. Trying to share her cell number or something.

NightTerra: Share it with whom??

CityGirlSal: I don't know. It's just a guess.

TulipPrincess: She's probably just busy.

CityGirlSal: Maybe she got a job. Is she still in school?

CityGirlSal: Why not ask one of the Jane administrators about her? Maybe they know something. They'd at least know if she were blocked.

CityGirlSal: Isn't that right, JA Admin? Are you guys listening??? #ThisIsATest

TulipPrincess: If you click on the About Jane page, you can find the contact link. They'll answer you too. I once got a response from "Jane Anonymous" herself.

CityGirlSal: What did you contact "JA" about?

NightTerra: Good idea. I'll try that.

TulipPrincess: Wouldn't you like to know? Lol.

CityGirlSal: Be sure to report back, NightTerra. You've got me wondering about Paylee now.

NightTerra: Will do. 'Night, everyone. Thanks for your help.

NightTerra has left the chat room. There are currently 6 people in the chat room.

37

The next morning, after a mostly sleepless night spent checking and rechecking the chat room for Peyton, with still no luck or any messages in my JaneBox, I click Contact and choose the option to chat with one of the administrators.

> **JA Admin:** Hey there, NightTerra. What can I help you with?

> **NightTerra:** I'm worried about one of the members on the site. Her name is Peyton (chat name, Paylee22). She's usually in the chat room, but she hasn't been on in days.

> **JA Admin:** How many days?

> **NightTerra:** Two, maybe. I'm not really sure. Some people said they saw her on, but it's a little iffy.

> **JA Admin:** Ok, well, two days is not so many. Maybe she's on vacation.

> **NightTerra:** She would've mentioned if she were going away someplace.

JA Admin: Maybe . . . Does she have a job?

NightTerra: Not anymore.

JA Admin: Are you sure about that? Maybe it's a new job.

NightTerra: I don't think that's it. She has a hard time even leaving her house.

JA Admin: Did something happen in the chat room?

NightTerra: What do you mean?

JA Admin: I mean, was she involved in a recent disagreement or argument with anyone?

NightTerra: Why would that matter?

JA Admin: Sometimes disagreements or altercations of any kind can make it harder to come back to a chat room.

JA Admin: The person may feel anxious that things could get heated again. They might also regret something they said.

JA Admin: Remember the whole reason people enter a chat room to begin with is so they can release their stressors, not create new ones. :)

NightTerra: Ok, but Peyton is always on. Do you know who she is—her real name, I mean? First and last? And where she lives? Is there any way you can check up on her somehow?

JA Admin: You want us to check up on someone because she hasn't logged in to a chat room for two days?

NightTerra: I think she might be in trouble.

JA Admin: What makes you think that?

NightTerra: Because she thought the guy who abducted her before—eight months ago—was watching her, tracking her movements . . . She recently got a message . . . It was in her mailbox.

JA Admin: Ok. Let's start from the beginning.

I spend the next several minutes telling the Jane administrator everything I know about Peyton's recent trip to the pharmacy; the page left in her mailbox, including the highlighted message; and the constant fear she has that her abductor is going to come back for her. At the end of it, the administrator reminds me that when I registered on the site, I had to fill out a security form that included my name, date of birth, zip code, and private email address.

"So, we'll have that information on Peyton too," she says. "I'll discuss the situation with the people here and see what I can find out on my end. I'll also look up the last time Peyton logged in. In the meantime, try not to worry. Often the people that engage on chat sites engage in several of them at once. Sometimes they just naturally gravitate toward the ones they find most helpful or enjoyable. Try not to take it personally."

"This isn't about me. I just want to know that she's okay."

"I can understand that, and I'll see what I can do, okay?"

"Okay," I say, less than convinced.

I click the chat room link and post a message:

NightTerra: Hey, everyone. I'm looking for Paylee22. She hasn't been on here in a couple of days (at least not that I've seen), and I just want to make sure that she's ok. If you've recently seen her on here (or on other chat sites), or if you know anything about her or where she might be, please send me a private message. I've already alerted the Jane Anonymous administrators. Thank you in advance.

TulipPrincess: Omg, you still haven't seen her on here???

RainyDayFever: Where is that girl???

CityGirlSal: So weird. But, um, Paylee22 is a little weird too, right? #JustSayin' #NotSoSurprised

Cobra-head43: Paylee is always super paranoid. #ButSoAmI

CityGirlSal: So, maybe she checked herself in.

Cobra-head43: In where?

Darwin12: I'll bet you anything she's taking a break by getting unplugged. We should all get unplugged . . . spend some time in nature, away from all things materialistic.

Darwin12: We spend too much time trying to acquire, not taking advantage of what already exists.

CityGirlSal: Um, ok? "No comment." #IHaveComments !!!

Cobra-head 43: I kinda like acquiring. It's fun to buy. $$$$$ #ShitCollector4Life #GluttonyRules

CityGirlSal: Omg. Lmao!!!

While they continue chattering, I grab a notebook and write down all the personal details Peyton has shared, hoping at least a few of them are true.

Name: Peyton
Age: 22
Location: Maine (a coastal town, known for having one of the oldest lighthouses)
School: used to go to a community college (not sure where)
Work: used to work at a yacht club across the street from the community college
Homelife: lives with parents; younger brother Max died from heart issues when he was eight years old; doesn't like to leave the house but goes out occasionally; sees a therapist weekly
Taken: while on a hike (on a trail behind the community college). She'd been searching for an abandoned school when someone impersonating an officer approached her and put her in his car.

I begin an online search for community colleges in coastal towns in Maine, where there's also a yacht club across the street. Oddly enough, it doesn't take long to narrow things down. Pineport, Maine, is known for having one of the oldest and most well-preserved lighthouses in the country. Pictures show it standing at the tip of a peninsula and painted with blue and white stripes. There's also a community college in Pineport, located across the street from the Meridian Yacht Club.

Bingo.

I click on a link for the yacht club and search a staff photo for Peyton's name. No luck. But maybe she no longer works there. All the times I've chatted about my shifts at the library . . . She's never mentioned currently holding a job herself.

I check the yacht club's hours, then grab my cell phone to call the main number. A woman picks up right away. She sounds around my age.

"Hi," I say, wishing I'd rehearsed. "I'm hoping you can help me. I'm looking for someone who works there. Her name is Peyton."

There's silence for several seconds, then, "I'm really sorry, but no one by the name of Peyton works at this yacht club."

"Maybe she *no longer* works there, but I'm pretty sure she did at one time—maybe eight or nine months ago. She is—or she *was*—a student at the community college across the street from your yacht club. I'm not exactly sure if she's currently enrolled in classes."

"Is there something specific I can help you with?"

"Do you know who I mean? *Peyton*," I repeat. "She's twenty-two. She went missing for a few days. Does any of this sound remotely familiar?"

"*Who* did you say you were?"

"My name is Terra, and I'm a friend of Peyton's. I'm looking for her."

"Okay, well, obviously Peyton doesn't work here anymore."

"Wait, so, you know who I mean, then? You *know* Peyton? Do you also know her famil—"

"I don't think I can help you," she says, cutting me off. "Please don't call back here." She hangs up.

My heart tightens.

I look back at the chat room screen and scroll upward to read the feed of posts. Most don't seem alarmed by Peyton's inactivity, especially since it's only been a couple of days. The chat quickly branches off in another direction: Cobra-head43's issues with insomnia. But then Darwin12 brings up Peyton's name again:

Darwin12: Paylee22 has snoozing issues too. What are the odds that it finally caught up with her and she's been sleeping for days?

NightTerra: Who says she has sleep issues?

Darwin12: I do. I say.

NightTerra: And how do you know? Did she tell you she has sleep issues?

Darwin12: Do I sense a little tension?

Darwin12: I'm surprised she didn't tell you, esp. since you two are supposedly so close. #MaybeNotAsCloseAsYouThink

NightTerra: We are close.

CityGirlSal: It's true. Paylee's always on . . . Even when I've come on at 2 and 3 a.m. I don't think she sleeps.

Cobra-head43: Maybe she's a vampire. Lol.

CityGirlSal: Remind me . . . Was she in school?

Darwin12: Am I allowed to answer that? Or is NightTerra the only one who's supposed to know anything about Peyton?

TulipPrincess: Defensive much?

TulipPrincess: Peyton's taking a year off from school. Isn't she???

NightTerra: She told you that?

TulipPrincess: Yeah. She said she couldn't imagine sitting in classes, trying to focus. I can't say I blame her. I'm not focusing much these days either.

RainyDayFever: I think Paylee wanted to be a vet. But didn't she also work at a yacht club—just a part-time thing?

Cobra-head43: Where is she from again?

NightTerra: She doesn't work at the yacht club anymore.

TulipPrincess: I'm sure she'll come back on soon.

Darwin12: She seemed kind of upset the last time I chatted with her.

NightTerra: When was that?

Darwin12: Not sure. A couple of nights ago? She said she lost someone close to her.

Darwin12: At first, I thought she was talking about a death. But then she said she wanted the person to forgive her.

Darwin12: I asked her more about it but she had to go.

CityGirlSal: Try not to worry too much. She'll come back on soon.

TulipPrincess: Team Paylee!

NightTerra: Thanks, everyone. I'll keep you posted.

TulipPrincess: We will too.

I exit out of the chat, wishing I could rewind the last few days. Am I the one Peyton hoped would forgive her? The person she described as having lost? I close my eyes, thinking how scared she seemed the last time we chatted. And still I felt the need to make her feel worse.

My cell phone chimes. A reminder to take my meds. I swallow one down, hoping to get some sleep. But first, just a little more journaling.

38

Somehow, I managed to climb back up, onto the wall of the well. Miraculously, I was able to swing out and grab the chain again. Keeping a solid grip, I kicked outward. My feet met the cold brick surface.

I scaled the wall—right, left, right—refusing to look down, even when my hip froze up. From the fall? From too much straining? A stabbing pain shot down the length of my leg to the back of my knee.

Part of me wanted to quit. Another part feared getting to the top and what I would find. Would he be there waiting? Would he slide the lid closed just as my head crested the surface?

No, said the storyteller inside my head. *Your parents will be up there. They're already waiting. Just you wait and see.*

What was that?

A squeaking sound.

I peered upward. A glimmer of light shone at the top of the well. Was it daytime again? How long had I been climbing?

Birds chirped from somewhere above. I was getting closer. I moved quicker, repeating a chant: *Left, right, left; one, two, three. You're almost there, then you'll be free.*

My palms singed. Meanwhile, a cooling sensation crawled at the back of my neck. At first, I thought it was the sprinkle of rain. But soon I realized what it really was. I tilted my face upward, able to feel the cool, fresh air hitting my skin and able to see that the sky above had brightened to a silver color that reminded me of doves, light enough to peep the overgrown bushes that branched over the well's edge.

I breathed them in. It was almost too much, like sensory overload—the smells, the sounds . . .

My pulse raced. My arms wouldn't stop shaking. Still, I took a few more steps, having finally reached the opening. I hooked my foot over the rim of the well and drew myself closer, kicking outward, maneuvering my body onto the ledge, then over the side.

My feet hit the ground. The sensation of tall grass, like crawling spiders, nibbled at my skin. I looked all around, my eyes struggling to take in the landscape that surrounded me: the trees, the brush, the bushes and blooms . . .

Too much to see.

Way too much to hear.

Were those sticks breaking? Was that someone whistling? Was that the peck-peck-pecking of a bird?

Peck.

Peck.

Peck.

Swish, swish.

My head hurt. My ears wouldn't stop ringing. The fresh air in my lungs seemed suffocating somehow. I began forward, gasping for breath, searching for a path.

Where was I? Where was the guy who'd taken me? Still in these woods? Watching from afar?

I began down a trail, swiping branches and brush from in front of my eyes.

It was so cold. I felt so chilled.

My eyes ran raw. My skin had turned to gooseflesh. Where was the fairy-tale book? Why hadn't I thought to take it with me somehow? Or the troll doll?

My muscles tremored. I'd never felt so tired: an all-encompassing fatigue that distorted my judgment. The pine trees I could've sworn were still a few feet away were suddenly in my face; I collided with one. The dirt-laden path that seemed to bend to the left really went right; I stepped on a burr.

Sticks broke somewhere behind me. The sound of footsteps?

The caw of an overhead bird?

The screech of a wild animal?

The panting of my breath as I arrived at a fork.

I went right, stepping on something sharp. I let out a yelp. Meanwhile, the landscape dimmed, as though a veil had dropped down in front of my face. Was it approaching dusk? Or was the darkening inside my head?

How long had I been running? Four hours? Forty minutes? Did I ever take a break? I'm pretty sure I did. I remember the sensation of tall grass and weeds brushing against my face, poking into my eyes, making me sneeze, as I leaned back on a fresh bed of soil, imagining myself like a snake, camouflaged by nature.

Unless maybe I didn't stop. Maybe that was just a fantasy inside my head, as I continued on the path, trying to get away. One thing I know for sure: The bottoms of my feet were raw and burning. My side ached, below my ribs, a jolting pain that caused me to hobble.

Moments later, I heard it: a high-pitched voice. A happy sound. A girl's laughter?

Someone let out a crying-moaning wail. It took me a beat to realize it was me. *My* cry. My tears. Something in my heart burst. I pictured confetti shooting out from my chest.

I'd reached a clearing: a carpet of grass, a rock sofa, a pit for a fire. And a water fountain, where I drank and drank, as my jaw ached and my shirt got wet. Meanwhile, two girls stopped doing cartwheels. And a woman with her dog turned in my direction.

Beyond them, the path continued. I hobbled forward, past the woman with a baby carriage and the tourists taking pictures. Past the old man reading a book. And the lady picking soda cans from the trash.

"Are you okay?" someone called, a high-pitched voice.

"She isn't wearing any shoes!" another voice shouted.

The sun was setting. Eventually, it turned dark. I ran under lights and tore across streets. I was still miles from home and should've stopped along the way—to call my aunt, to phone the police. But I didn't stop, even though I told myself I would at nearly every corner. My body kept on moving—until I found my way "home."

NOW

39

I roll over in bed, able to smell something. The scent of burning chemicals hangs heavily in the air. I sit up and click on my night table light. The smoke detector by the door remains in neutral. It isn't flashing. There is no beeping.

Where are the extinguishers? Did Aunt Dessa move them again and rearrange my things? My art supplies are gone now too—my easel, my side table, my crate of paints and sprays . . .

I get up, noticing the carpeting beneath my feet, as well as the pajamas I'm wearing—the pink ones with the yellow daisies, just like the night of the fire. Somehow, I'm back in my room on Bailey Road. My fuzzy green chair sits opposite my bed. I look up just as a spotlight blinks above my head. The light shines down from a rusted chain, like the one in the well.

Terra? a female voice calls from behind my bedroom door. *Can you open up?*

"Peyton?" I try the knob, then snatch my hand back. It's too hot. The metal burns. I turn my hand over to look at my palm. The words *To Be Continued* are seared into my skin.

Please! Peyton cries. *You're like a sister to me. You have to believe me when I say that your friendship has been the one thing that's kept me going these past couple of months.*

I search for something to use as a buffer, spotting a strewn sock. I slip it on like a glove and grab the knob, aiming for the star. Finally, I'm able to handle it, but the knob falls off in my grip and topples to the floor, shattering like glass. A spill of water surrounds my feet.

The spotlight blinks—*one, two, three*—before going out completely. And meanwhile, the burning rubber scent fills the room, constricting my breath.

I go for the window, just as my phone chimes. A reminder to take my meds. My doorbell ringtone startles me awake.

I sit up in bed, only to discover I'm in my room, in my aunt's house. There is no spotlight, no carpeted floors. "It was just a dream," I mutter to myself.

Crazy Sally used to mutter too, used to talk in her sleep, used to tell herself stories.

I take a deep breath. What is that smell? The burning scent . . . I get up and check the hallway.

Check the kitchen.

Check the living room.

Check outside.

Nothing.

No flames.

But the bathroom window, across the hall, is open a crack. Is something burning outside? I inhale through the screen, unable to tell.

Meanwhile, my phone continues to chime. I cross back to my room to grab it. It's not a reminder. Garret's name flashes across the screen. "Hello?" I answer.

"Hey."

I stare at my palm. The words from my dream—from the message Peyton received—*To Be Continued*—appear in blistered red letters. I press my eyes shut and count to three before looking again. The words have vanished. In their place is the phantom burn mark from five years ago, the patch of skin without any lines.

"Terra?" Garret asks. "Are you okay?"

"Yes," I lie, stretching the truth like bubble gum.

"So, I'm doing research," he says. "About water wells . . . I know you've been searching for the one in Hayberry Park. I also know it doesn't seem to exist."

"You heard that kid in the homeschool class. He saw it too."

"Or at least he claims he saw it. What if he saw something that *appeared* to be a well—with a brick base, a wide opening, and that burrowed deep into the ground? But what if it was something else entirely?"

"What are you saying?"

"Ever consider the possibility that maybe you weren't inside a well?"

"Wait, *what*? What else could it have been?"

"Well, as I said, I've been doing some research, specifically about mining tunnels. I found evidence of salt mines located about a mile from Hayberry. Maybe some of those mines were even closer; maybe they just weren't documented. From what I've seen, some of those underground tunnels went on for miles, branching off in different directions. A lot of them caved in over the years, restricting passageways and creating new crevices. Anyway, it was just a thought."

Just a thought.

I bite my lip.

What are the odds that I've been looking for the wrong thing all this time, assuming the water-well book was indicative of the location? "But don't you think the park rangers would know if there were an opening to an underground mine? There's nothing to indicate one on the park map."

"Right, but the space you were in . . . it didn't go anywhere, right? Wasn't it just a pit? So, maybe it'd been created after the fact—from one of those cave-in situations. Or could it have once been used for storage?"

"Still, don't you think the rangers would know about it?"

"I guess that depends. Where was it? Hayberry Park spans, like, a bazillion acres. Do you really think the rangers know every inch?"

The hairs at the back of my neck stand on end, as though charged by possibility, like an animated cartoon. "I can't believe you did all this research."

"Don't worry about it. It was fun for me."

"You can't be serious. But thank you. So much."

"No problem. We'll find the answers. But right now, how about we find ourselves some coffee? Care for a cup of Critter's?"

"That sounds a little gross."

"But it'll taste so good. Can I pick you up?"

There's so much research I need to do. Plus, I'm supposed to work later. But I tell him okay anyway. "I could use the caffeine."

"Say no more. I'll be by in a bit."

I hang up and look back at my computer screen. My mailbox shows one private message—from Darwin12. I click to open it.

Dear Terra:
I hope I didn't offend you before. I'm dealing with my own inner gremlins and sometimes I have a hard time knowing boundaries. Anyway, it's true that Paylee22 and I used to chat a bunch, especially late at night when neither of us could sleep. If I can be at all helpful, just let me know. Believe me, if I could make one wish, it'd be for Paylee22 to log on. I'm worried about her too. I messaged the Jane administrators to see if they know anything. If I hear something, I'll definitely keep you informed. Here's wishing us both luck. Talk to you very soon.
—Darwin

I type back a quick thank-you and close the lid of my laptop, curious as to why Peyton never mentioned chatting with Darwin before. Was he a new friend? Or someone she'd been chatting with for a while? Was there a specific reason she never brought him up? I'll try to find out later. Right now, I need to get ready.

40

Garret picks me up and drives us over to Critter's. The place is named after the owner's pet ferret. There's a picture of the two of them hanging on the wall, beside an ample array of Critter merchandise: T-shirts, thermoses, water bottles, baseball caps.

We stand in line. A stack of newspapers faces me on a rack. The front page shows a cute little boy with curly black hair. The headline reads, TEN-YEAR-OLD SAVES ENTIRE FAMILY OF SIX FROM A HOUSE FIRE.

I read the headline again, making sure I got it right.

"Excuse me," someone says, bumping me from behind.

I get out of the way, moving closer to the paper. I start to scan the article for details. How big was the fire, and how did it start? An accident? Negligence? Or something else? Did it happen in the daytime? Did smoke detectors go off?

"Terra?" Garret's voice.

The fire must've been smaller than the one on Bailey Road. The family members were probably already awake. The boy likely smelled smoke long before the flames.

"Terra?"

I look up, reminding myself: *This is just another trigger. I did the best I could. (Is that really, really true?)*

Garret: "I ordered you a café mocha. I hope that's okay." He's holding two cups.

How long have I been standing here? I move away from the news rack, noticing a couple looking in my direction, exchanging words in hushed tones. Do they recognize me? Or are their stares because I can't seem to catch my breath?

Garret and I sit on barstools, facing the street.

"I'm really glad you agreed to come out," he says.

I take a sip. The drink reminds me of Aunt Dessa's mochaccinos. "This is perfect."

"Good. I'm glad. It's my favorite too. Everything else okay?"

Okay? The word no longer has meaning. I use it too much. It's used on me too often. "Thanks again for all your research," I segue.

"Sure. It's been interesting. But I have to ask: What made you think you were being kept in a water well to begin with? As opposed to an underground tunnel or cellar of some sort?"

"It's a long story."

"Try me."

"A book," I say, proceeding to tell him about *The Forest Girl and the Wishy Water Well.* "I haven't been able to find a copy of the book anywhere, so I've been writing some of it down, what I remember, at least—to see if there might be a message I'm missing."

"That's really smart."

"Depends who you ask. No one really believes the book exists."

"What *do* they believe?"

"That I made it up."

"Including what you're writing?"

"No one really knows I'm writing the story. When I originally told people about the book—and no one could find any evidence of its existence, including an author—it got dismissed pretty quickly, right along with my sanity."

"Did you try the Library of Congress?"

"I tried everywhere. I think it must've been self-published and never registered."

"As though written just for you?"

"Or rather my abduction was inspired by it."

"Any chance you'd let me see what you've written?"

"Why would you even want to?"

"I think you're forgetting who you're talking to. Need I remind you that in addition to my status as a criminal justice and forensic psych major, I'm a two-time trivia champion, American Crime Story edition? And, though I don't typically like to brag, I also play a mean game of Clue. Come on." He smirks. "It'd be fun for me."

"Sounds like you have a pretty wacko idea of fun."

"And that's only part of my charm."

"What's the other part?"

"My outstanding wit, my dashing good looks, my ability to make origami roses out of paper napkins." He grabs a napkin and begins making folds, producing a flower, complete with a leaf and stem. The buds are printed with Critter's furry body.

"That's kind of amazing."

"And it's only one of my tricks."

"I thought it was part of your charm."

"I'm glad you're paying attention. So, what do you say? Can I read the story?"

I open up my phone and log on to the Jane website, noticing another private message from Darwin. The subject line reads, "One more thing . . ." I click on it:

Hey, Terra,
Sorry to keep bothering you, but when you get a chance,
come find me on here. We need to talk.
—Darwin

"Everything okay?" Garret gives me the paper rose.

"It is," I say, unsure where to begin. I start by telling him about Peyton, about how she dropped off the chat site, and how it seems she'd recently been chatting with some guy named Darwin12. "Which is really kind of weird," I add, "because she never mentioned him."

"But isn't the whole idea of a chat room that you talk to whoever happens to be online?"

"Yes, but you're missing the point."

"I'm not. Really. It sounds like your friend Peyton might've had some secrets, which is kind of expected. I mean, it's a chat site, after all. You're taking everyone's word for granted."

"I know. Totally stupid."

"It's fine if you know going in that people could be stretching the truth or misrepresenting themselves."

"I meant me. *I'm* stupid."

"Stupid people don't rewrite a book from memory. They also don't manage to escape their abductor with no help whatsoever. So, let's see it." He nods to the screen.

I click on the journaling tag for *The Forest Girl and the Wishy Water Well* and give him my phone.

He takes several minutes to read what I've written. When he's finally done, he looks up at me, his eyes gaping. "Have you gone to the police?"

"They know the book exists. At least, I told them about it. But I haven't gone to them with this—not yet, at least."

"What do you think the story means—in the whole scheme of things, that is? With the abduction and with your captivity."

I shake my head. "I've racked my brain about it. It's one of the major reasons I'm writing the story myself—to understand it more, to see if an idea clicks. I'm wondering if my being taken has something to do with wishes."

"That's definitely a possibility. The story also seems to be about trusting the wrong people, making assumptions, being insecure, feeling isolated."

"When you put it that way, it sounds like he had me pegged."

"Not necessarily. Most people experience all of the above at least at some point in their lives. Do you think it might've had something to do with the theme of not going with your gut?"

"I *didn't* go with my gut. I knew I shouldn't have been walking home alone that night. But that can't be it."

"How about the value of a day—like who's to say what a day is worth . . ."

"Do you also major in English lit?" I ask him.

"Seriously. That's probably the biggest theme to the story."

"I know. And it's something I've thought about too. But I already know the value of a day." I'd give almost anything to have another day with my parents.

"So, maybe the story isn't about *you* specifically. Maybe it's more about the guy who took you and what *he's* figuring out. Do you think he might've known you from someplace?"

"Honestly, I'm not really sure, but I don't think so; at least, I didn't recognize his eyes that night."

"And you didn't see his face."

"No." I shake my head. "And, before you ask, *no,* he didn't touch me; and, *no,* I wasn't tortured. My battle wounds are inside my head." Burned through my heart.

"Good to know."

I look down into the black hole of my coffee. "Aren't you glad you asked me to come out?"

"Absolutely."

"You're very kind."

"Is talking about this stuff a little too intense?"

"It *is* intense, but it's nice to be taken seriously."

Garret taps his cup against mine. "I'll always take you seriously—unless, of course, you're joking." He grins. "Don't worry, we'll figure the story out. But, in the meantime, you really do need to show the story to the police."

"There's more," I say, proceeding to fill him in about the book in Peyton's captivity quarters and the page she found in her mailbox.

"Some of the letters on the page were highlighted; they spelled out the words *To Be Continued*."

"Did she tell anyone?"

"Aside from me? I'm not really sure."

"You definitely need to share all of this with the police," he says. "What if there's a connection? Books that potentially mirror the victims' captivity situations . . ."

"I know." I sigh.

"Okay, well, *they* need to know."

"Except I can't find news of Peyton's case anywhere. I don't even know if Peyton is her real name, though I called a yacht club where she might've worked. It seemed the person who picked up may've recognized her name."

"The police should be able to identify the case, just based on the details. Do you want to go talk to them now?"

"Seriously?"

"Why not?" He gets up from his seat.

"You don't have to do this." I get up as well.

"Are you kidding? This is the most fun I've had in months."

"Well, if that's the truth, then maybe *you* are crazy."

NOW

41

At the police station, the woman at the front desk tells us that Detective Marshall is already with someone. "Do you want to leave her a message?" she asks.

I shake my head. "We'll wait."

We head for a wooden bench. There's a bulletin board across from it; it's loaded with most-wanted pictures and crime-watch posters. I've studied the faces before, desperate for even a hint of recognition. I study it now too, but still with no luck. Finally, Detective Marshall appears behind the main desk. She couldn't look more deflated to see me: straight face, tired eyes, zero expression.

"Would you like to come into my office?" she asks.

Garret and I get buzzed through a security door. We follow Detective Marshall down a long narrow hallway, into a small office with a round table. This isn't the usual space. Normally, she brings me into one of the private conference rooms. Is she not taking me as seriously now?

We sit at the table. Garret reintroduces himself, reminding Detective Marshall that they've met before.

"I was the guy from the sorority party," he says. "I met Terra on the night that she was taken."

Detective Marshall doesn't let on whether she remembers him or not. She just sits back in her seat with a smallish notebook in her lap. "So, what can I do for you both?"

I get right down to business by taking out my phone and opening up to the Jane Anonymous website. I click on the link for my version of the water-well story, then set the phone in front of her. "As you know, I wasn't able to find the book."

"The *book*?" she asks.

"From when I was in captivity . . . ?"

Detective Marshall's face furrows, as though she doesn't remember, but she takes the phone anyway and reads through the first few paragraphs. "What is this?"

"It's the book," I say one more time. "The story, that is—*The Forest Girl and the Wishy Water Well,* the one I talked about before that was in the water well with me."

"Actually," Garret interjects, "it may not have been a water well, after all. I've been doing some research, and . . . Are you aware of the mining tunnels located about a mile outside Hayberry Park? They seem pretty extensive."

Detective Marshall slides the phone back toward me, across the table. "People don't mine around here anymore."

"They may not," he says. "But that doesn't mean those tunnels don't still exist. Maybe what Terra thought was a well was instead an underground storage area."

"Then why is she showing me a story about a water well?"

"What difference does it make what the storybook says?" Garret asks.

"*You* tell *me*. You're the ones wanting me to read said storybook."

"What if the person who abducted me just wanted me to *think* I was in a water well?" I ask. "What if that's what worked best for his story?"

"Don't you mean *your* story?" she says. "Didn't *you* write this?"

"I wrote it from memory," I say, knowing she doesn't believe my memories. "I can also describe some of the illustrations, if that's helpful."

"We figured you'd want to read the whole book, or as close to a whole book as we currently have," Garret explains.

"Why don't you email me a copy?" She sets a business card down in front of me as if I don't already have a stack sitting on my night table. "Is there anything else?"

"Yes. There is." I tell her more about the Jane Anonymous website and what I know about Peyton's case. "Peyton feared her abductor was going to come back for her, and now she's gone."

"Gone from the chat site, you mean."

"Yes, but just out of the blue, after she received what she thought was a warning."

"Just to clarify: When you say *warning,* do you mean the torn page from the book about junkyards?"

"The page with the shaded-in message," I say to correct her. "I think *To Be Continued* should count as a warning, don't you?"

"Okay, but if she were *really* missing, authorities would've been alerted. A missing-persons case would've been filed in her city or town."

"The same way one was filed on me?" I ask. "People have to notice a person is missing in order to report it."

My aunt never noticed.

No report was ever filed.

No one ever came looking.

All the hours I spent in the well, telling myself stories about search teams and candlelight vigils . . .

"Peyton posted a picture of the torn page," I tell her. "Maybe you could ask the Jane administrators to view our chat history?"

Detective Marshall jots the details down, but I can't quite tell if she's taking them seriously or not.

"I'm pretty sure Peyton's from Maine," I continue. "From a town called Pineport. I'm not sure where she'd been kept captive—what city or state, I mean—but I remember she said she'd been in a shed, in the woods, and that it'd gotten dismantled by the time the investigators found it. She was able to escape by digging a hole beneath a loose floorboard and tunneling her way out."

"Do you know the case?" Garret asks her. "Does it sound at all familiar?"

"I'll look into it." She stands from the table.

"Peyton said that a book had been left in the shed," I continue, nowhere near ready to leave. "It was about a group of people who came together as a family. They lived in the middle of the woods, in tiny one-room shacks, with their own set of rules. I don't know the author. But think about it: the woods, the shack . . . Both of those details match Peyton's captivity situation in the shed, just like the water-well book matches mine."

"Anything else?"

"Do you think there could be a connection?" I ask. "Or maybe my crime was the result of a copycat person?"

"I'll look into it," she repeats.

"Will you really?" My face flashes hot.

She's standing in the doorway now. "How's your aunt doing? Is everything okay at home?"

"What does that have to do with this?"

"It was nice to see you again, Terra. I'll be in touch if anything comes up."

"And how about my storybook pages?"

"You have my card," she says instead of answering.

I have her card but no incentive to use it.

42

Once outside, we start across the parking lot, headed for Garret's truck. The air is chilly. Still, I breathe it in, feeling stupid for coming here, especially with Garret, especially after everything.

"Is that what it's been like?" he asks.

"What do you mean?"

He stops in front of his truck and looks back at the police station. "I mean, was that any indication of what you've had to deal with? With the investigators? With no one believing your story?"

I manage a nod, somewhat startled to see his reaction to my world. "It wasn't always that way. People believed me at first."

"What's *not* to believe? You were gone for four days."

"I know." I shrug. "But I wasn't a stranger to taking off, ditching school, disappearing for days . . . I can't really blame anyone for not noticing."

"Why not? *I* blame them."

"What do you mean?"

"I mean, you deserve to be noticed."

I look away, feeling my eyes well up. "Why are you being so kind?"

"This isn't about kindness, Terra."

"Then what *is* it about?"

He nods to his truck. "I think I told you before this was my

grandfather's old ride? He was pretty much my hero. In the last
fifteen years of his life, he worked for free as a vet just because of his
love for animals."

"And so, your grandfather's selflessness rubbed off on you?"

"This isn't about me."

"I'm not some wounded bird."

"Maybe not, but it wouldn't be a bad thing if you were. Wounded
birds deserve their time to heal. It doesn't make them any less viable.
It just means they're getting better."

"Are *you* a wounded bird?"

"In some ways, I am. We *all* are. Don't you think? Anyway, I
believe you about everything that happened. And I'm happy to help
as much as you want me to. We can be in this together."

Wouldn't that be nice? But I'm in it alone. Garret can bring me
to the station and help me with my searches. He can take me out for
coffee and make me paper napkin roses. Together, we can search for
water wells that may or may not exist. But, at the end of the day,
I'm the only one who knows the truth about my hell and what it's
like to live in it.

"Well?" he asks.

"Thank you."

"Don't thank me. Just remember I'm here, willing to listen,
whenever you want to talk." His eyes look somber and serious, as if
he really, truly means it.

I want so much to believe him. And maybe part of me even does.
But I can't help remembering: My aunt had said the same—that she
wanted to listen too. Jessie and Felix were no different, pledging
their friendship allegiance, but then taking said friendship away. Investigators fooled me too—all of them sitting across the table, telling me it was safe to say anything I wanted but then using that same
info against me to "prove" my unreliability. The only person who's
taken my word without question is the same person who also lied.

Peyton.

Where is she now? How is she doing?

"What's on your mind?" Garret asks.

"Nothing," I lie too.

"Tell me the truth. I can take it."

Can he really?

I look out at the empty lot. "Those days in the well . . . It's beyond words what that felt like, how scary and isolating, but it felt nowhere near as isolating as coming back home and having everyone I love turn their backs on me."

"I won't turn my back."

"Don't make promises you can't keep."

"I don't," he says, his eyes locked on mine.

I turn away again so he can't see the emotion heating up my face, making my eyes sting. "Like I said before, there's a lot that you don't know about me. There are things I've done that I'm not exactly proud of."

"Okay," he says slowly, carefully, as though too much sound will shatter me like glass. "Is it helpful to know that I could say the same about myself?"

"You don't understand."

"Okay, then make me understand."

"I escaped a burning house," I snap. "But my parents didn't."

"I know," he says, his face in neutral as though he doesn't hear what I'm saying.

"The house was on fire," I insist. "I fled out the window while my parents were still inside."

"And I can't even imagine what that feels like," he says, maintaining a poker face. "But I'm willing to try. No friendship starts with both people knowing everything about the other."

"Do you really consider me a friend?"

"I'd *like* to think so. Is that okay with you?"

I want to tell him yes—so unbelievably much. But I haven't exactly given him a reason to even like me, so then why is he here, when I can barely stand myself?

"Thank you so much for your help," I say, knowing the answer doesn't quite fit.

Garret musters a smile but doesn't say any more. I can tell I've probably disappointed him. I'm disappointed too. But it's better this way.

Safer.

Simpler.

A whole lot less painful.

43

Garret watches me get inside the house before driving away. As I lock the door behind me, I can hear my aunt talking in the kitchen. At first, I assume she's on the phone, but then I remember. The text she sent. The "appointment" to talk. What time is it?

I linger a moment, seeing if I can figure out who she's with.

"Terra? Is that you?" she calls. Not two seconds later, Aunt Dessa appears in the doorway, all dressed up in a blazer and dark pants.

"Who's here?" I ask.

"Well, hello to you too. How was your day?"

"You have company," I say, stating the obvious.

"Yes. It was supposed to be a surprise."

A surprise for her? For me?

"Come see," she says, turning away, expecting me to follow.

Instead, I look back at the door, tempted to bolt. I tighten my grip around the wasp spray in my pocket—my version of security—and gaze at my reflection in the entryway mirror, with my stringy golden hair and pale, slim face. There's a layer of soot crusted over my skin. I blink it away and move into the kitchen.

Dr. Mary is sitting at the table. "It's so good to see you." She pops up like toast and wraps her arms around my limp body.

"What are you doing here?" I ask.

Dr. Mary is dressed up too—in her hospital suit, with her hospital tag. She and my aunt are drinking tea out of pretty china cups I've never seen before. It appears that my aunt either bought or made muffins.

"Come sit," Aunt Dessa says.

"Your aunt is quite the baker. Have you tried her raspberry-filled scones?"

A plate has already been set for me. An empty china cup sits on my rosy placemat, along with a matching floral napkin.

"What are you doing here?" I ask once again.

"*Terra,*" my aunt scolds. "Is that very polite?"

"That's okay." Dr. Mary smiles. "Terra, your aunt just invited me to come have a chat."

"A chat about me?" I ask.

"Is that okay?"

"Is it the truth?" I sit. The air smells like blueberries.

"It is," she says, getting right to it. "Your aunt reached out to me out of concern."

"Concern," I say, processing the word.

"Would you like some tea?" Dr. Mary lifts the rosy pot, like this is her house.

I shake my head. Meanwhile, my aunt faces away from the table, her posture angled sideways.

"There was an incident," Dr. Mary continues. "You recently ran into an old neighbor."

I manage a nod, completely unprepared. But maybe they're talking about something else, some other incident.

"Tell her," Dr. Mary says, speaking to my aunt.

Aunt Dessa folds her arms, still keeping her posture angled away. "Did you recently bump into Connor Loggins?"

"Yes." I nod.

"Care to tell us what happened there?" Dr. Mary asks.

"Nothing much." I shrug. "I just hadn't seen him in a while."

"So, you *didn't* threaten him with bug spray? And he *didn't* have to pry the can out of your hands? And a little girl *didn't* go crying to her mother because you made her so afraid?"

A little girl?

My aunt shakes her head when I don't argue. "I don't know what else I'm supposed to do."

Dr. Mary responds by swiveling in my aunt's direction, handing her a tissue, reaching out to touch her forearm. There's a fresh box of Kleenex on the table. Where did it come from?

"What's happening?" I ask.

"What's happening is that I've tried to be patient," Aunt Dessa says. "But I can't do this anymore."

"Because of Connor Loggins? I thought he was someone else."

"As if that makes it okay? He said you could've blinded him."

Blinded him? I didn't even shoot. Or *did* I? Did I press the nozzle and not even realize it? Did a little come out?

Dr. Mary pats my aunt's arm like a favorite cat, as if my aunt is the wounded one. And maybe she is. Maybe I've done this too.

"Let me guess," Aunt Dessa continues, finally meeting my gaze. "You thought it was the guy who took you from your bed and put you in the ground."

When did my aunt's skin get so blotchy? Why do her eyes look so tired? I study her face, desperate to find even a trace of my mother. But I can't seem to see one now.

"There was no proof," she says.

"My hands were proof." Doesn't she remember the welts from the chain, the dirt in the tub, the mud in my hair?

"And now you're seeing things . . . statues on our back porch."

"Why don't we start over?" Dr. Mary says. "Terra, would you like some tea?" She nods at my empty cup.

It's only then that I realize I'm stirring my spoon inside it.

"I don't even feel like I know you," Aunt Dessa says.

"That's because you don't," I tell her.

"All the secrets you've been keeping—from yourself, from me . . ."

Secrets?

"I went through your room. And I saw all of *that stuff*." Her lip curls up.

What did she see?

Dr. Mary turns to my aunt. "Tell Terra what specifically bothers you about some of the things in her room."

Aunt Dessa's lip coils up farther, bearing her teeth. "I worked so hard . . . making your room look nice, doing it all over."

"Be *specific,*" Dr. Mary orders.

"The knives, the repellents, the baseball bats and bottles of insecticide," Aunt Dessa says. "I took it all—whatever I felt looked unhealthy . . ."

I stand from the table. Every inch of me feels on fire. "You took my things. Where did you put them?"

"It doesn't matter now. What matters is that you need help." Her eyes throw daggers. "I think you're a safety risk—to yourself, to others."

Dr. Mary is speaking now—her lips are moving. I can hear the sound, but I can't decipher the words. What do they mean?

What is my aunt doing?

I look above her head at the cat clock on the wall. Its shifting eyes move back and forth, back and forth to the ticking sound.

Tick.

Tick.

Tick.

Like a bomb inside my heart.

Dr. Mary says, "What do you think about taking a little break?"

The cat's tail is broken. It doesn't move in sync with the eyes.

"Your aunt wanted me to tell you about a new therapeutic program at the hospital," Dr. Mary says. "We're really excited about it; it's cutting edge and has an impressive success rate."

"New program?" Isn't that what they said before?

"That's right," she says. "And it's totally voluntary, totally tailored to the individual. Some of the participants do a full day.

Others participate in the partial program. And then some do full immersion. So, this would be your choice."

My choice.

"Your bus, remember?" she chirps.

Right. I nod. I'm driving my own bus. I'm the leader of my own pack and the strongest link in my chain.

"So, what do you say?" Dr. Mary motions to my seat. "Shall we discuss the program options a bit more?"

I shake my head, backing away, bumping into the wall from behind.

"Terra," my aunt calls once I get out of view.

I pause in front of the mirror, listening to them talking. My aunt wants me to enter the overnight program; she doesn't think I'm "safe" enough for partial placement. It's either that or I move in with my grandparents in Florida and enter a day program, after a thorough screening. She's already contacted them. My grandparents are okay with the plan but not thrilled. There isn't an extra bedroom in their condo. Plus, Grampa's heart condition is a major consideration. How much will my presence add to his level of stress?

"I think the immersion program is really the best option," Aunt Dessa says once again, making it emphatically clear. "I can't go on like this. It's affecting my health too. It's also affecting my work."

I grab my bag, noticing the door to the study is closed—a rarity at best. I open it up. My things sit in a heap on the floor—my art solvents, my scissors, my carving tools, my troll items. My most recent self-portrait sticks out at the bottom, beneath my mom's yoga blanket. A bottle of maple syrup has poured over the eyes, stealing my breath.

I take a step closer, noticing the star-studded doorknob amid the rubble, just as I did five years ago. I pull it out. It feels hot, fresh from the flames. I stuff it into my pocket, grab the yoga blanket, and bolt out the door.

44

Not knowing where else to go, I drive to the library even though my shift doesn't begin for a few more hours. Tucked away in one of the study carrels on the second floor, I hold the doorknob to my lips, feeling hot bubbling tears well up in my eyes. My phone vibrates at the corner of the desk—again and again.

A text from my aunt.

A reminder to take my meds.

A phone call from my aunt.

A phone call from Dr. Mary.

Felix's voice plays in my mind's ear: *Just finish high school and get the hell out of there.* But where would I go? And what could I do? Somehow, it seems I forgot to have dreams.

I'm not sure how long I sit before my pulse stops racing and mind stops spinning, before I'm finally able to remember that Darwin12 had something to tell me. I grab my phone and log on to Jane, still hoping to find Peyton logged on too. I enter the chat room and scroll downward, searching for her name, unable to find it.

TulipPrincess: Hey, NightTerra. Any Paylee22 sightings yet?

NightTerra: Unfortunately, no.

RainyDayFever: Wait, wasn't she on here for a second?

TulipPrincess: When???

Darwin12: Hey, NightTerra. Glad to see you. Can you go talk?

NightTerra: Wait, did someone see Paylee22 on here?

Darwin12: I saw her. Can you talk to me now?

JennaIsDead: Guys, don't leave me hanging! I need your advice!!! What should I tell my stepmom???

A link from Darwin12 pops up on my screen. He wants me to go into a private chat room. I click on it.

Darwin12: Hey.

NightTerra: You heard from Peyton?

Darwin12: Yeah. About an hour ago. She logged on, saw me in the chat room, then sent me a link right away to go chat in private.

NightTerra: So, she's ok then.

Darwin12: I wouldn't go that far. She def wasn't herself.

NightTerra: What do you mean?

Darwin12: I asked her why she hasn't been online, but she wouldn't tell me.

Darwin12: She did say that you and she had gotten into an argument and that you don't trust her anymore. Something about her not being 100% honest about stuff she shared online . . .

Darwin12: I don't know . . . It sounded pretty stupid, but she was def upset.

NightTerra: Did she mention the message I sent her?

Darwin12: No, when did you send it?

NightTerra: Yesterday. Or the day before? The days are blurring together.

Darwin12: You sound like me.

Darwin12: Anyway, she asked me to come get her, like that's even an option, right?! I live in Oregon, all the way across the country. She knows that too.

NightTerra: She told you where she lives.

Darwin12: Yeah. Maine.

Darwin12: Pinecliff or something like that.

NightTerra: Pineport.

Darwin12: Yeah, that's prob it. I asked if she was ok because that seemed totally weird and really random. I mean, why ask me to come, of all people? Why not ask her parents or a friend that lives closer?

Darwin12: Or maybe she's in some kind of trouble and doesn't feel she can tell anyone—except for the faceless guy in the chat room who's prob just as screwed up as she is . . . Lol.

NightTerra: Is she in trouble?

Darwin12: That's just it. I don't know. She just kept telling me she was inside a phone booth, like the kind you see in old movies. I didn't even think they still existed, but I guess they do because, apparently, she was in one.

NightTerra: What???

Darwin12: I know. Definitely weird.

Darwin12: She said she was staring out at a blue-and-white-striped lighthouse.

NightTerra: Why was she telling you all that?

Darwin12: Exactly. Why? I have no idea. But it seemed she wanted me to know, as if she was giving me landmarks.

NightTerra: Do you think she was drunk or something?

Darwin12: I don't know. She couldn't really talk. It was almost as if everything was in code. Plus, I think her cell reception must've been bad because her messages kept getting delayed and some of them seemed out of order, like not in sync with mine.

Darwin12: The only thing for sure was that she wanted me to drop everything and come get her.

NightTerra: In Maine?

Darwin12: Yep. At that phone booth.

Darwin12: Totally messed up. So, I've been staying online, just to see if she might come back and explain herself.

Darwin12: But, of course, she hasn't.

NightTerra: How long was the chat?

Darwin12: I don't know. Maybe 5 min tops. The chat cut off in the middle of things.

NightTerra: Are you sure that's all you remember?

Darwin12: There was one more thing. She said she was scared. I asked her why—more than once. But either she wouldn't tell me or she wasn't getting the question, like maybe it wasn't coming through. I don't know.

NightTerra: Was she alone?

Darwin12: Probably not completely alone, since she was being all cryptic. Maybe someone was nearby. Again, not sure.

NightTerra: Do you think we should tell someone? Maybe the Jane administrators . . .

Darwin12: I already did. I'm just waiting to hear back.

NightTerra: Is there anything I can do?

Darwin12: No chance you live in Maine and know where

there's an old-fashioned phone booth that looks out at a blue-and-white-striped lighthouse, is there?

NightTerra: I have to think a bit.

Darwin12: Well, don't think too long. I'm worried about her. And I'm almost ready to cash in my frequent-flyer miles and hop on a plane.

Darwin12: I feel partially responsible because it's me she's confiding in. I have this info. I need to do something with it.

NightTerra: Sounds like you're already doing something.

Darwin12: I guess. Anyway, let me know if you think of anything else.

NightTerra: I will. Talk to you soon.

I log out, then check my JaneBox. There's a message from the Jane administrators.

Dear NightTerra:
We hope you're having an empowering day! We just wanted to let you know that Paylee22 logged on to the Jane Anonymous website at 4:22PM EST this afternoon. We're still looking into things, but we know you were worried about her and hope this news helps to ease some of your concern. Hopefully, you'll see her around the chat room very soon. In the meantime, please let us know if we can be of further assistance.
Yours,
"Jane"

I hit Reply and send a message back, asking what "other things" they're looking into and to send me a response as soon as they know anything more.

In my search box, under Images, I type in *Pineport Community College*. Several of the pictures feature the campus and buildings. Others show glimpses of a blue-and-white-striped lighthouse. I try another search, using Peyton's name and the name of the community college. A photo of a group of students pops up. They're all sitting on the campus lawn in front of a brick building. The caption reads *Back to the Books* and lists the students' names. The second person from the left is a girl named Peyton Bright. Could that be her?

I do a search on Peyton Bright. A series of options comes up: Peyton Bright, the marine biologist; Peyton Bright, the photographer; an obituary for Peyton Bright, who died at eighty-four.

On and on.

Nothing that fits.

My head aches.

I shut my phone off and close my eyes; they feel scratchy and dry. Do I have any eye drops? Or a rubber band to tie back my hair? I should really splash some water onto my face.

Also, when was the last time I ate?

Or had anything to drink?

Or took my meds?

My throat feels parched. My stomach is queasy.

Has the water cooler been refilled? What are the odds that Miguel left his stash of butter cookies behind in the break room? I need to check, but the visual of the girl in the campus photo burns inside my brain. Peyton Bright, with her long dark braid and cheeky smile. I picture her huddled up inside an old and rusted phone booth.

"Hey, you're here early," a voice says from behind, making me jump.

There's a clamoring sound; I did that, dropped something on the floor. The doorknob rolls across the ceramic tile.

I'm in the bathroom. How did this happen? When did I come in here?

Katherine's standing in front of a stall. "Sorry I scared you. Is everything okay?" She looks at the knob and then at the sink.

The faucet's running. It seems I've done that too. "Yeah," I lie, shutting the faucet off. *When did I come in here?*

"Feel like getting in a couple of extra hours of work? I could really use you at the circulation desk."

"Yeah," I repeat. "Sure. No problem."

"Great." She smiles. "Anytime you're ready, just clock in."

Once she leaves, I stuff the knob back into my bag and peek in the mirror, trying to get a grip. The skin beneath my eyes looks swollen and gray. When was the last time I got a solid four hours of sleep? Days? Weeks? I douse my face with water and search my bag for eye drops or a rubber band. No dice.

Downstairs, the clock-in room is just past the reference desk. I head straight for it, but on impulse, instead of going in, I make a beeline outside as my phone continues to buzz.

It's a text from Aunt Dessa: *Where are you? Come home. We need to talk.*

And another text from Dr. Mary: *Please let us know that you're okay. We're worried about you.*

Plus, one more from Garret: *Just FYI, I could be playing basketball, but instead I'm researching salt mines and can't seem to stop. Please send help.*

Once again, he manages to make me smile—despite the racing sensation inside my heart and my continuous efforts to push him away. I climb into my car and start the engine—*Just while I think,* I tell myself.

I'm not going anywhere.

Katherine is expecting me to work early.

I just need a moment to pull myself together—not to mention that Pineport, Maine, is way too far. It must be a two-hour drive, at best—in the dark, on a highway . . . The mere idea of going such a distance makes my heart pound and my insides squirm. It wouldn't be smart for more reasons than I can count, including my lack of sleep.

But what if I stop for a coffee en route? I could also pick up something to eat. That's what I should do: get myself a bite before I head to work. Katherine will understand if I don't start right way.

I put the car in drive, proceed out of the parking lot, and turn onto the main road. My gas gauge says full. A sign for the highway points me to the right. What would happen if I took it? The traffic will be minimal, going north, at this late hour . . .

My palms slick with perspiration, I clench the wheel, telling myself I'm not going anywhere; I'll simply turn back around and return to the library. But I take the ramp for the highway anyway.

45

It's not until after about an hour on the road that my hands ease from clenching and I'm finally able to believe I can actually do this: drive to Pineport, taking the slow lane of the highway. There aren't many cars out tonight. I pass by signs for rest stops and gas stations, telling myself that if anything bad were to happen, like blowing a tire, I could always find help. Plus, I have my phone and money if I need it. Everything will be fine. *Everything is going to be just great.*

My phone rings. It's Aunt Dessa again. This time, I pick up.

"Where are you?" she asks.

"I'm in my car, driving."

"Driving *where*?"

"I'm not going to be home for a bit."

"That doesn't answer the question. *Where are you?*"

"Hold on." I set the phone down, click on my hazard lights, and check in the rearview mirror to make sure that all is clear. There are only two other cars behind me, both of them in the distance—one in the middle lane, the other in the speed zone.

I pull over to the side of the road, where I put the car in park and pick up the phone again. "I'm going to look for a friend," I tell her.

"What friend? *Where?*"

"It doesn't really matter."

"Terra, why do we have to do this?"

I press my eyes shut, picturing my self-portrait at the bottom of a heap, drizzled with glue.

"You need to come back here," she says.

I peek over at the starry doorknob and my mom's yoga blanket on the passenger seat. Like faithful friends.

"You need to get some help," she continues. "Your parents would want that too."

"My parents would never give up on me."

"And I haven't either. Now, tell me where you are. Do you want me to come get you?"

"You keep secrets too, you know."

"*Excuse me?*"

"I have to go." I click the phone off, half expecting her to call right back. When she doesn't, I grind my head against the window glass and stare into the darkness, where the highway lights illuminate the pavement. My eyes fill with hot-wax tears. I scrunch up in my seat, wishing I were in the back, listening to *Star Up* and telling myself stories about rest stops and road trips.

What am I doing? Where am I going? Is it even worth going "home" when there's nothing for me there?

I begin on the road again. Like in the well, my eyes eventually dry up. I tell myself, *I'm in control. I always have choices. I can just go see.*

More stories.

How many more miles?

When my phone rings again, about forty-five minutes later, it's Katherine, likely wondering where I am. I let it go to voice mail.

The navigation app has me turn off the highway. A sign for Pineport points me to the right. I follow the directions through the center of what appears to be a cute, quaint town. Streetlamps shine over cobblestone streets, brick-front buildings, and pastel-colored storefronts.

I pull over again and try logging on to Jane. An error message comes up on the screen, alerting me that the site is down. I try again, using another search engine. Still down. Might it be down because of what I told Detective Marshall—because of the possible threat

Peyton got? What are the chances that Marshall searched my chat history with Peyton and found something? Did she also read my journal? And the water-well story in its entirety?

I go into my email and retrieve the message from the Jane Anonymous administrator. I hit Reply and type a response asking if the site is down because of a temporary maintenance thing.

My phone chimes. An incoming call. Garret. I pick it up.

"Hey," he says. "I have some pictures I want to show you—photos of the salt mines, both before and after a couple of them caved in. I have a picture of a root cellar too. Have you ever heard of a place called Chester Farm?"

Wait, *what*? My chest feels tight. Why has he been doing all this research?

"Terra? Are you still there?"

"Yes. I'm here."

"And is everything okay?"

"What did you say about a farm?"

"Chester Farm. Apparently, it was pretty popular a couple of hundred years ago. The owners are the ones that had the root cellars. Their property seemed to back right up to Hayberry—at least as far as I can tell. I'm thinking the farm might've been using part of Hayberry at one point and that's why it closed down. I need to do more research and consult a town historian or surveyor; the online maps don't show too much detail, and I'd really li—"

"Garret," I say, cutting him off.

"Yeah? Are you okay?"

I take a deep breath; my hot-wax tears return. "You really don't have to do all that."

"I know I don't have to."

"So, then why *are* you?"

"Researching?" he asks.

"Because you want to?"

"Well, that's one reason."

"What's the other?"

"I care about you. Is that okay?"

More tears come, making it too hard to speak.

"Terra? Are you still there?"

"I'm here," I utter, pulling the yoga blanket close.

"And where *is* there?"

"I'm fine," I tell him.

"That's not a location."

I wipe my face. "I just went for a ride."

"I thought you had to work."

"I did."

"Okay, then . . ."

"I didn't go in." I take another deep breath. "I just really need to find Peyton. That guy I was telling you about, from the chat site, he said that Peyton came back online and that she asked him to come get her."

"To come get her *where*?"

"Someplace in Maine. But he lives across the country."

"So that makes no sense."

"I think Peyton's just really scared. I think she probably didn't know where else to turn or who else to turn to."

"So, is she a little like you then?"

I bite my lip, still startled that he gets it. "You don't understand," I say anyway.

"Why wouldn't she turn to the police or her parents?" he asks. "Why ask some guy on a chat site, who doesn't live anywhere close to her, to come pick her up?"

"She must've had her reasons."

"You need to think this through."

"I need to *do* something."

"Okay, but what if this isn't the *right* something? I mean, you don't even really know her."

"I know she wouldn't have asked for help unless she really, truly needed it. I can't just sit back knowing she's scared and alone and that I did nothing to try and help her."

"Is this really about Peyton at all?"

"What do you mean?"

"Maybe it's more about that trust thing we were talking about before. Peyton trusts you, and you don't want to let her down the same way people have let you down."

I swallow hard, hearing a hitch in my throat. "I've let people down too. You just don't know it."

"Are you talking about your parents?"

I stare at my reflection in the mirror, still able to see the self-portrait I painted—my dirty face, my ashen cheeks, my soot-covered lids.

"You can't blame yourself for running from a burning building," Garret says.

"Okay, but I do."

"And you think helping Peyton will take away the guilt?"

"It won't bring my parents back, but it's still something. Plus, what if our cases are somehow connected? Don't you think I should try to figure that out?"

"Not on your own. Plus, what would a connection really change, as far as you're concerned?"

"The possibility that others might believe my story."

"*Terra* . . ."

"What?" My voice quivers.

"Where are you? Let me help."

"There isn't time."

"Why not? Please tell me you're not in Pineport already?"

I recheck the clock. "I should probably go." The yacht club closes at ten.

"Tell me where you are."

"I'll call you a little later. Thank you again for everything."

"*Terra* . . ."

I hang up and begin on the road again. When Garret calls back, not ten seconds later, I let it go to voice mail.

46

I head for the lighthouse. The directions take me past a fire station, along a public beach, and down a long, winding road with mansions bordering both sides. It'd be strange to find a phone booth anywhere around here, but still I look, driving slowly with my high beams on. A sign for the lighthouse points me down a narrow road. I take it and drive for several minutes, eventually coming to a parking lot.

The lighthouse stands in full open view, on the edge of a grassy area that slopes downward toward the sea. I recognize the blue and white stripes from online pictures. There are no other structures around it.

I park and recheck the Jane website. It's still down. I go into my email. The reply I sent to the Jane administrators sits flagged in my inbox as undeliverable. I set my nav to the Meridian Yacht Club and pull out of the lot, onto the main road. It's started sprinkling out. The rain patters down against my windshield, making the streets glisten. The town of Pineport is small. It doesn't take more than fifteen minutes to get to the other side.

Just as expected, the yacht club sits across the street from Pineport Community College. I park in the lot, noticing only a handful of other cars scattered about. I grab a mini-can of wasp spray from the glove box and shove it into my pocket before getting out.

The front entrance is decorated for fall with a leafy wreath. I go inside, with just twenty minutes to spare before the club is due to close. The interior smells like burning wood. A book group sits in a living room area, in front of a fireplace. One of the staff members uses a shovel to reposition the logs, making the flames sizzle and hiss.

"*Helloooo,*" says a voice from behind.

I turn to look. A girl around my age is seated behind a desk. Her eyebrows are raised. Her arms are folded. How long has she been trying to get my attention?

"Sorry, I just . . ." I peek back at the fire.

The man closes the fireplace screens with a *thwack*.

"Can I help you?" the girl asks.

"I'm looking for a friend," I tell her, wondering if she's the same person I spoke to on the phone. "She used to work here. Her name is Peyton."

"Peyton McNally?"

"Or Peyton Bright . . . I'm not really sure."

"The only Peyton I knew who worked here was Peyton McNally."

"Did she take classes at the community college across the street?"

"A couple of years ago, maybe. I haven't exactly seen her in a bit. She stopped working here a while ago."

"For any particular reason?"

"For the reason that the manager here is an absolute ass." The girl—named Stacey, according to her name tag—stands from the desk and peers around to make sure that no one's listening in. "Peyton ended up telling him off when he *accidentally* screwed up her paycheck for the bajillionth time."

"So, it had nothing to do with something more traumatic?"

"Does it get more traumatic than someone trying to rip you off? On second thought, maybe it does." She laughs. "But I heard he scammed her hundreds altogether."

"How well do you know Peyton?" I ask. "Does she live around here? Does she have family close by?"

"Sorry." She shrugs. "I don't know her well. She used to talk about her grandma a lot; that's who she lived with, I think. And I can sort of picture her boyfriend. He sometimes came to pick her up. Like I said, it's been a while."

"Did you know about her case?"

Her face furrows. "What case?"

"The Peyton I knew had gone missing."

"Wait, *what*?"

"Eight or nine months ago," I say. "But she escaped. She's home now. At least, she *was* home. I'm looking for her." I spend the next several moments filling her in on some of the major details, including about the shed in the woods and how Peyton burrowed her way free.

Stacey listens with her mouth parted open, clearly startled by the news. "It's obvious we're talking about two different people. I would've known if Peyton McNally had been abducted. For one, because we have mutual friends. For another, because I don't think you understand how small Pineport is. Everybody knows *everybody* around here. Last year, a boy went missing while out on his kayak, and pretty much everyone in town stopped what they were doing and went out to look. Luckily, the boy was found safe. I hope your friend is too."

The women from the book group begin to file out. I check the time. It's almost ten.

"I really need to lock up." Stacey's tone has shifted; she seems irritated now. She moves from around the desk and lingers by the door, waiting for me to leave.

"Can I ask you one more thing?"

"What?" She sighs.

"I know this is going to sound a little weird, but do you know where I might be able to find a phone booth? I mean, I know they're pretty much no longer in existence, but—"

"There's an ancient one located at Harborview Park, behind the creepy swing set and the disgusting water fountain, though I don't think it actually works—the pay phone, that is. Most people just use it for a photo op. The whole place is pretty circa 1980-something. Don't even think about going there unless you've had your tetanus shot."

"And Harborview Park . . . Do you know where it is?"

"It's by Smitherton's Salvage, not far from Evans conservation land."

"I'm sorry. I'm not from around here."

"You need a tourist map?" She fakes a smile and points to a rack of brochures and maps.

"Thank you," I tell her, forgoing the rack. I can use my nav. "You've been a huge help."

I linger a moment, taking one last look at the fireplace before exiting the building and crossing the parking lot. The sign for Pineport Community College faces out toward the street. I picture Peyton (as the girl from the online photo), sitting on the lawn under the spotlights, mouthing the words *Just, please, don't give up on me.*

I blink the image away and get into my car. According to my nav, Harborview Park appears to be a ten-minute drive. I press Start and begin on my way.

47

I pull into the lot of Harborview Park and spot the phone booth right away; my high beams shine over it. The booth stands on a cement slab, on the far end of a grassy field littered with old and rusted gang-tagged play structures: a metal slide, a lopsided swing set, and a handful of bouncy toys.

No one else is around. The park seems completely desolate. If it weren't for my headlights, I'm not sure I'd be able to see such detail.

I try to zero in on the phone booth, but it's too far. All I can tell is that it looks misplaced—both in time and in location. Who would put a phone booth on the edge of a park, facing the water, rather than closer to the lot? I picture Peyton inside the booth, crouched on the concrete, telling Darwin how scared she felt.

But why would she ask him to come get her here? Was she not thinking straight? Or maybe the phone booth has a clue—something she wanted him to find.

I check the Jane site again. It's still down. There are no new messages in my inbox. Meanwhile, I have five missed calls from Garret, plus a bunch of texts.

I stare out into the darkness, flashing back to a conversation I had with Dr. Mary in the healing garden at the hospital. The purpose of the garden is to provide a stress-free space, but I couldn't have felt more anxious, biting my lips, scratching my palms.

246 laurie faria stolarz

"It's pretty here, isn't it?" Dr. Mary said. "Tranquil, meditative . . ."

Torturous. The flower petals reminded me of switchblades. The thorns looked like barbed wire.

"I don't belong here," I told her.

She reached out to touch a bloodred rose. "You feel the need to be punished. We need to explore why that is, why you're so angry at yourself." As if it were a mystery.

"My aunt is angry with me too."

"What makes you say that?"

"Because I feel it."

"Do you think it's possible that what you perceive as your aunt's anger is really just your own? Because, maybe, deep down, you feel unworthy of being loved?"

I eyed a flower, tempted to pluck it from the ground. Its stem reminded me of a dart. *How would it feel, punctured through my heart?*

Still in the car, I take a deep breath, able to smell the fireplace at the yacht club; the scent has melted over my skin and combed through my hair. I look out at the park. The swing set reminds me of the one back in elementary school. My mom and I had a game where I called out degrees of salsa spice for how high I wanted her to push me (mild, medium, jalapeño, hot . . .). Sometimes she'd swing with me too. We'd sit side by side, pumping our legs, trying to go at the same rate.

Time to turn back? Logic asks.

I venture outside. The cool fall air chills the back of my neck. The overgrown grass, wet from the drizzle, brushes against my ankles, makes my skin itch. The closer I get to the phone booth, the more lit up the area becomes. Overhead lights shine over the harbor, where there's a smattering of boats. I have an extra flashlight, clipped to my key ring (industrial-strength despite its mini size). But I keep it off, hoping to remain invisible.

The wind rustles a loose chain on the swing set. The seats have all been damaged: knifelike slits through the rubbery texture. I continue past them, keeping focused on the phone booth. It's steel gray,

with a foldable door and a bashed-in base, where the safety glass was broken.

I unfold the door and go inside, unable to spot any broken glass on the floor. Could Peyton have been trapped in here? Did she kick the booth open? I peer outside, toward the cement platform, but I don't see any broken glass there either.

The phone receiver hangs slightly crooked on the hook. I pick it up and hold it to my ear, wondering if Peyton might've used it to call someone. She had a cell phone—it's what she must've used to log on to Jane—but she also had bad cell reception, at least according to Darwin.

I fish inside my pocket for a quarter and drop it into the slot, checking to see if the phone actually works.

An automated voice (an operator's recording) comes on right away: *To complete your call, please deposit fifty-five cents. Please deposit fifty-five cents for your local three-minute call. To complete your ca—*

I hang up and continue to look around, searching for some sign or clue. I poke my finger into the change return and take out a handful of coins: ninety-five cents. I leave them on the counter just as the phone starts ringing: a blaring tone that makes my insides jump.

I let it ring, unsure what to do. Pick it up? Or continue to look around?

Nine rings.

Ten . . .

It doesn't seem to stop. At sixteen rings, I grab the phone receiver and place it up to my ear.

"*Hello?*" says a tiny female voice.

I peer outside, into the darkness.

"Can you hear me?" the girl asks.

A clamoring noise sounds—like metal on metal—somewhere in the park. Is someone else here? Does the person see me? Or was it just the wind?

"*Hello?*" the voice continues. "Are you there? Can you help me?"

A question strikes me like a match. Could it seriously be *Peyton*?

"Who's *this*?" she asks.

"Is this Peyton?"

"Is this . . . ? *Terra?*"

"Where *are* you?" I search the pay phone for a number, but it's been peeled off; there's sticker residue above the keypad.

"I can't believe you came." Her voice is riddled with tears. "I'm so sorry, and I'm so grateful."

"Don't apologize. Just tell me where you are."

"How did you even find me? Is Darwin with you? Did you talk to him?"

"Wait, do you have access to a phone?" Obviously, she must. "Are you calling from your cell phone? Did you also call for help?"

"Hold on, is Darwin there? Can I talk to him?"

"No. I'm alone."

"So, he didn't come? There's a pay phone where I am, but it only dials one number."

"Wait, *what*? How is that possible?"

"He took me, Terra. Just like I said he would, just like I always feared."

"Where are you now?"

"A junkyard, like the book page he left in my mailbox."

"In Pineport?"

"Yes." Her voice quivers. "It's not far from the phone booth."

I look back toward the street, unable to see much. The street-lamps seemed dimmed. One of them is broken. Still, I continue to search—by the slide, the swings, the bouncy toys, the parking lot, but I don't see anything. "Is the guy there with you?"

"No. He's been gone for a while."

"Tell me where you are, exactly—*where* in the junkyard."

"I don't think I'm going to get out this time."

"You will," I insist. "Just tell me how to get to you."

"Are you facing the pay phone? Look to the left of the harbor. Do you see a sign in the distance that says Smitherton's Salvage?"

It takes me a second to spot it. The sign stands tall, lit up with a spotlight. "Yes. I see it."

"If you drive to the salvage yard, park on the street—somewhere he won't spot your car. Then come on foot. You'll see a brick wall that's painted white. Go to the right of it—to the seventh or eighth section of chain-link fencing. One of those sections is curled up at the bottom. He made me crawl through it."

"And then?"

"Look for a bus."

"A *what*?"

"Hurry. I'm inside the bus. The junkyard is closed. I'm pretty sure it's been closed for days now, but still there's tons of stuff here—old cars, piles of building supplies . . . The bus is somewhere, but it's not exactly visible."

I grab my cell and turn it on. Twenty-five percent charged.

"Please, Terra," she says, her voice breaking over the words.

I close my eyes, trying to get a grip, my mind flashing back to the night of the fire, my bedroom on Bailey Road.

"I have to go," she says.

"Peyton, *wait*."

The phone clicks off.

I hang up and press Detective Marshall's number. It goes straight to voice mail. I leave her a message, choking out the words: "The girl I told you about . . . Peyton, from the chat site . . . She's been taken again. Please, can you call me back? I'm at Harborview Park in Pineport, Maine. This is Terra."

I end the call and dial 9-1-1, stepping out of the booth, desperate for some air. At the same moment, a rustling noise comes from somewhere in the darkness.

I grab the wasp spray in my pocket. Did the sound come from behind the slide? Or over by the fence?

Was it the snapping of twigs?

Or the swishing of a jacket?

Maybe it was a swirl of wind through the fallen leaves.

It's stopped now. My heart has too. I look back down at my phone screen. It's turned black again. How far is my car? Thirty yards at most. I hurry in that direction, one step at a time, through the park, propelled by Peyton's cries.

48

Back in the car, I lock my door, start the engine, and set my nav for the salvage yard. As I pull out of the parking lot, I try dialing 9-1-1 again, my pulse racing, my fingers trembling. The call connects as I turn onto the main road.

The operator picks up: "Nine-one-one. What is your emergency?"

"A friend," I blurt. "She's been taken. She's being held against her will."

"Can you tell me your name?"

"It's Terra," I say, avoiding my last name in case she's already heard it, in case she wouldn't take me seriously.

"Okay, Terra, can you tell me who your friend is?"

"It's Peyton," I say, but I'm not sure she hears it.

The navigation voice speaks over mine, tells me to turn left, onto a dark, narrow road.

"Her name is Peyton," I repeat, louder this time. "I'm not sure of her last name, but it might be Bright. Or it could be McNally. She says she's trapped inside a bus, in a salvage yard."

The navigation directs me down a dead-end road. The street-lights are even sparser here. It's started drizzling again. I click on my windshield wipers; they swoosh back and forth, making streaks across the glass and producing a scratching-scraping sound that grates inside my ear.

"*Hello?*" I ask.

Why isn't she talking?

I check the screen. It's gone black. The call got dropped. I have no signal. The nav has stopped working too.

How long were we connected? Was she able to trace the call, ping my location?

It seems I'm in the right place. A white brick building faces me, at the front of the property, just like Peyton said. The salvage yard sign stands tall and bright, though everything else looks dark.

I cut my engine and switch off the headlights. A chain-link fence surrounds the junkyard, as do a few spotlights—four or five, maybe.

I get out, locking the car behind me, keeping the wasp spray clenched in my hand. I move to the fence. A giant heap of scrap materials sits beyond it. Behind the yard is a wooded lot, what Stacey at the yacht club must've been referring to when she mentioned the conservation land.

I try my best to focus, looking for a bus—a school bus, a city bus . . . But what if it isn't a bus at all? What if Peyton is somehow mistaken?

I follow the fence to the right, counting up the sections. When I get to the ninth one, I see the place where the metal has been curled up. I take a moment to peer all around—behind me and over both shoulders—before checking my phone again.

Still no signal.

Twenty-one percent charged.

I take a photo of the junkyard sign and text it to Garret and Detective Marshall, along with a message that tells them I'm here. The text will go through eventually; there must be a hot spot somewhere.

My pulse races as I squat down and crawl through the hole in the fence. I imagine Peyton having done the same. How did that happen? Where did she get taken from? Or did she come here on her own?

Once on the other side, I click on my key ring flashlight and shine it over heaps of wood, scrap metal, tires, and bumpers. I move in deeper, passing smaller sections of junk: collections of things like hubcaps and car seats.

Peyton mentioned the bus wasn't exactly visible, meaning she'd been alert when she first arrived. Had she come to meet someone? Or had she been scouting out the area, looking for clues related to the page she got in her mailbox?

It's eerily quiet. There's only the clattering of wind chimes somewhere in the distance. I creep past a pile of car doors, still unable to spot a bus. Where is it? I continue to follow the fence, moving toward the back side of the salvage yard. I hold my flashlight high, able to see the wooded area that borders the yard.

Who owns this place? Does the person know about the wide, gaping hole in the fence section? Peyton said the junkyard's been closed, but for how long? And when is the owner coming back?

I shine my light over a mound of old bricks, five feet high. Behind them, I find two stacks of compressed cars, piled like multi-layered sandwiches. I aim my flashlight between the layers, spotting a golden-yellow color.

I edge closer, noticing a gap in the mangled metal, where two thick, black horizontal stripes stick out from the heap, making it clear.

It's a yellow school bus.

I scurry to get to the other side of it, to see if the folding doors are there, just as something crashes—a loud clank, like metal on metal, somewhere behind me.

I check my phone again, startled to find it's working. Eighteen percent charged.

I open up the keypad and dial 9-1-1. At the same moment, my phone vibrates with a call. Detective Marshall's name flashes across the screen.

I pick it up.

"Terra, hi. I got your message. That twenty-two-year-old woman you were talking about from Pineport, Maine . . . I couldn't find any missing-persons cases that matched her description with that location."

"Are you sure?"

"Definitely sure. We reviewed the chat logs. We also saw the photo you spoke about—the book page about junkyards that Paylee22 had sent . . . Long story short: It seems someone's playing games with you, which isn't so uncommon on chat sites of this nature."

"Wait, *what*?" My skin flashes hot.

"It's true," she continues. "Sometimes people suffering from one trauma will actually hide behind another, more fictitious one. That way they can get the attention they crave while still protecting their identity and the details of their trauma."

"*What?*" I repeat. What does all of this mean?

"The site *is* called Jane Anonymous, after all."

"But Peyton wouldn't do that."

"We *did* find a case that matched some of what Peyton reported to you: the shed, for example. The victim escaped after a handful of days. The authorities found the shed only weeks later, and yes, it'd been dismantled. The victim fit the profile too: a twenty-two-year-old female student taking classes at a community college . . . The victim reported that a white male, late twenties, dressed as a police officer approached her in the parking lot of an abandoned school and forced her into his car. But that crime happened a year and a half ago, not eight months. It also happened in North Carolina, obviously nowhere near Maine . . . or Chicago as Peyton first reported."

"So maybe she was lying about the location?"

"Or maybe she was using the details from this woman's case—passing them off as her own, that is."

"Might there be a connection to *my* case? Could the guy who took me be the same one from North Carolina?"

"Terra . . ." There's dismissal in her voice; it threads a needle through my heart.

"Are they still looking for the guy that took her?" I ask.

"That case is now closed."

"Why?"

"These things are complicated."

"Looking for someone after the victim has resurfaced alive, you mean?"

"The victim is now dead."

My eyes press shut.

"There was an accident," she explained. "It happened a few months after she got back from being missing."

I look out toward the woods, searching for a focal point, knowing I'm supposed to be concentrating on my breath. *Inhale, exhale. Just. Breathe.*

"Terra?"

"Yes. I'm here."

"Bottom line: This Peyton person obviously hasn't been completely honest with you."

"But I knew that already." How guarded she was being . . .

"Hold on," she says. "You knew this Peyton person was lying to you, misrepresenting herself, and you still involved me? Is that true?"

"I knew she was misrepresenting herself about *some* things, but not all of them."

"Are you listening to yourself? Do you know how valuable my time is? The time I spend tracking down false leads is time I could be spending helping someone else."

"I'm sorry for wasting your time."

"Please, just let us do our job. You have a job too. Finish school, move forward with your life, develop *real* relationships *with* real people rather than this online anonymous stuff."

I gaze back at the bus, still able to hear Peyton's cries inside my head, drowning out my thoughts.

"*Terra?* Are you hearing what I'm telling you?"

"Did you read the story about the water well?"

"Not yet. I've been so focused on the chat logs and this other case in North Carolina. But if I promise to read it, will you do something for me?"

"What?" I ask. How much time have I wasted?

"Get yourself home. Do you want me to have a car sent?"

"No. I'll be fine."

"Are you sure? It's no trouble."

"I'll be fine," I repeat. "I'm coming home now."

"Your aunt will be happy to hear that. Call me again if you need anything, okay?"

I hang up and shine my flashlight over the door to the bus. It's folded partway open. To the side of it, collected in a stack, is firewood. Why would it be here? I venture a little closer, able to hear something. The sound of a zipper, plus the shifting of leaves against the ground.

I take another step just as the lights go out—all of them, leaving me in the dark. I click off my flashlight too, and stand, frozen, flashing back to the darkness in the well, able to hear a high-pitched laugh that chills my bones.

I begin to back away, my limbs trembling, my lungs cinching. I try my best not to let out a wheeze, peeking down at my phone. I wake up the screen. Fifteen percent charged. I dial 9-1-1. The screen goes black. At first, I think it's dialing, but nothing happens. The number reappears on the screen. I press it again.

"Well, hello there," says a male voice, cutting through the darkness, making my entire body quake.

For just a moment, I tell myself it's the 9-1-1 operator. But I know it isn't. The voice isn't coming from my phone. It's coming from somewhere behind me.

I press my eyes shut. Could this just be my imagination—a horrible story my brain has conjured up to let me know that I really shouldn't be here?

A warm breath smokes against my face. It carries a sticky-sweet scent, like barbecue sauce. I bite my lip to keep from crying out, trying not to even blink.

His voice pokes through the darkness once again. "It's good to see you."

Can he?

See me?

Might he be talking to someone else?

"You know it isn't safe to be walking alone by yourself at night, don't you?" he asks. "Never mind in a salvage yard that isn't even open to the public."

I clench my teeth, feeling as though I might seriously combust. I position my finger over the spray trigger and listen for his breath, trying to gauge where he is—over to my right, at least two feet away. I hold the spray bottle outward.

But he grabs my arm and twists it behind my back. The cell phone jumps from my grip. I hear it knock against something hard.

Did it get through to Emergency? I didn't hear an operator.

I start to turn away and reach into my other pocket, but he grabs that arm too, pressing both wrists together, pinning them at the base of my spine. A loud, popping sound spouts from my shoulder. Still, I try to get away, using my legs, kicking outward, still unable to see.

"So much fight." His voice is at my neck; it sends shivers down my back.

Something damp and heavy blankets my face. A cold, wet cloth is stuffed into my mouth.

"I admire that so much," he whispers into my ear. "Such a strong character you are."

I sidestep, just as I learned in self-defense, so he can't get a secure footing, then bend at the waist to snap my head back, wanting to knock him down.

But he's grabbing my neck. His fingers press into my throat.

Did I even move?

Am I still bent forward?

Something hard and heavy compresses the crown of my head. I picture a helmet and do my best to duck. But somehow, I end up facing upward, lying on my back.

Is that the sky? I think it is. I see the moon. The darkness lightens. The moon morphs into a fiery white star that grows bigger with every breath as heat engulfs my skin, as smoke fills my lungs, and as my consciousness goes up in flames.

49

A phone rings, rousing me awake. I open my eyes. A fuzzy film clouds my vision. I blink hard. My head feels spinny. My eyelids are heavy; I go to rub them, but I'm unable to move my hand. It's pinned in place.

I open my eyes wider, able to see: pale yellow walls, something black and boxy . . . I roll forward to sit up. A vinyl seat is angled across from me. Its side is busted open. Cotton stuffing leaks out, onto the floor.

What is this?

Around my wrist.

A zip tie. I'm attached to a metal handrail, about four feet long, that runs parallel to the floor. My other hand is free.

Where is my cell phone? I reach into my pocket, but my cell isn't there. It's not in the pocket of my jeans either.

That's when I remember. It'd jumped from my grip and landed on the ground. I try my other pocket, searching for my spray, my keys, my flashlight . . .

Empty.

My heart pounds.

A camping lantern casts a soft glow over the space. Piles of junk block the windows: mounds of steel, what appears to be the front end of a car . . .

I'm inside the bus.

Where is Peyton? I shout out her name.

Meanwhile, a phone continues to ring. The sound is coming from somewhere behind me. I swivel to look, spotting a pay phone propped against the back of the driver's seat. The phone looks like the one at the park: a big rectangular box, black with silver accents.

I scoot forward on the ground to try to reach it with my free hand, sliding my zip-tied wrist all the way to the right side of the railing.

The receiver remains just a few inches out of reach. I tug on the zip tie. The hard plastic digs into my skin, bites at my wristbone. A cracking sound rips from my shoulder.

I inch out a little more, extending my fingers, holding my breath. Finally, I'm able to knock the receiver off the hook. I snatch it from the floor and place it up to my ear. "Hello?" I answer.

"Hello, Terra." A male voice. The same one from outside?

"Who is this?"

"Not *who, where*. Isn't that the question you should be asking? That is, if you want to find Peyton."

"Okay, *where*?"

"Peyton's in a safe place—for now, anyway. If you look carefully, you'll see that she left you a note."

I search around, spotting writing on the wall, behind the handrail. There's a message scribbled in marker:

Dear Terra,
I'm so sorry I lied, but please don't give up on me. Your friendship is
so much more than I deserve, but I need it now more than ever.
Love always,
Peyton

P.S. You'll always be like a sister to me.

"Where is she?" I ask.

"Did you find your coins?"

What coins?

"At the park," he says. "The coins in the change return. I hope you took them. You can use those coins to make a phone call or to make a wish, whichever you prefer."

"Who is this?"

"What is it you want more than anything else in the world?" he asks.

"To find Peyton." I continue to look around, searching for something I can use to free myself from the rail.

The interior of the bus has been tagged with initials and insignias of all types: stars, quotations, numbers, drawings. They're all painted across the seats, along the ceiling, and over the walls.

"*Be* honest," he says. "I know your character, Terra. You can't fool me."

"What do *you* think I want?"

"*No, no, no,*" he sings. "It's not that easy. You have to work a little too."

It's only then that it hits me. I struggle to reach a little farther, to push down the lever that hangs up the phone—tearing the skin on my thumb in the process. I just need another inch.

A mix of blood and sweat helps to lubricate my thumb. I use that lubrication to wrench harder and reach farther.

My skin rips more.

The knuckle pops.

But I'm able to touch the lever. I hold it down for three full seconds before reaching for the keypad.

I dial 9-1-1.

The call goes through.

I hear a ring.

"Hello?" someone answers. A female voice.

Blood rushes inside my ears. "Is this 9-1-1?"

"It is," she says. "What is your emergency?"

"I'm at Smitherton's Salvage. I'm trapped inside an abandoned bus."

"Smitherton's Salvage," she repeats. "Okay, let me check. Hold on just a second. That's in Pineport, Maine, correct?"

"Yes," I burst. "I'm trapped—secured to a railing."

"Can you tell me your name?"

"It's Terra Smith. I'm from Dayton, Massachusetts."

"Okay, Terra. Can you tell me more about this bus?"

"It's in the salvage yard, surrounded by junk—car parts, scrap materials. It's hard to even see the bus."

"How about the interior of the bus? Is there writing on the walls—phrases, quotes, pictures, including a ghost on the ceiling?"

I look up, spotting the ghost; it's about four feet tall. How does she know? Did Peyton call? Is help already on the way?

"Do some of the pictures look like illustrations?" she asks. "Like they belong on the pages of storybooks, rather than on the interior walls of a school bus?"

Wait, *what*? My skin turns to ice.

"Does the junk outside the bus trap you in, barricading the windows and the doors?" she asks.

"It does," I say.

"And are you speaking on a pay phone that doesn't really work?"

I look at the phone, feeling my heart steel.

"Terra? Are you still there?"

"I am." I nod.

"And are you speaking on a pay phone?"

"How do you know that?"

"The same way I know that you're pretty screwed." The person laughs.

My stomach twists. Bile shoots up into my mouth.

"What do you wish for?" she asks.

A thirsting wheeze escapes from my throat. *This can't be happening. I must be dreaming.*

"What do you want more than anything else in the world?" she asks.

I look toward the emergency door, on the other end of the bus. Is it barricaded too? I tug on the zip tie once more, wincing at the burning-cutting sensation. My entire wrist is weeping with blood.

"*Helloooo?*" she says. "Why aren't you answering? Has a cat got your tongue?"

I shake my head, flashing back to the voice of the guy who took me . . . that night in my room as he hovered over my bed. "Who is this?"

"It's Clara, silly. Don't you remember me? My name means *light*. Do you know what *your* name means?"

My name?

"I go to the Fox Run School," she says before I can attempt an answer. "Do you want to hear about the party I got invited to? It's for Sarabeth's twelfth birthday."

My eyes slam shut. My head starts pounding.

"Just drop three coins into the well and make your wish. Sound good? Just be careful what you wish for because it might very well come true."

I take a deep breath. "Where *is* the well?"

"It doesn't exist, remember? It's all in your head—the well, the book, escaping, me . . . They're all just stories you've made up to elicit attention. Don't get me wrong; I like stories too—love them, actually, which is how I knew you'd love this bus with all its words and characters. It's candy for a storyteller, don't you think?" She laughs again.

I hang up. And pull at the zip tie—*hard*—again and again.

No go.

I try some more, grunting, screaming, crying, seething.

The phone rings again.

I pick it up. My voice tremors over the words, "What do you want?"

"What do *I* wish for, you mean?" a male voice asks. "I thought you'd never ask. To continue playing the role of a hunter, your external antagonist."

External?

"Do you want to play too?"

The phone clicks.

My insides shake.

With trembling fingers, I hang up again and try calling 9-1-1 once more. This time, it just rings and rings. I press zero for the operator.

Nothing happens.

No one answers.

I gaze up at the ghost on the ceiling, then at the group of blue people drawn on one of the windows. Silver words are scribbled just beneath the people like storybook pages, like the water-well book.

Like the girl on the phone said . . .

These words and pictures are the pieces to yet another story— one I'm supposed to make up? One that's already going on? One that will lead me to Peyton?

I'm not really sure.

And I have no choice but to find out.

50

I continue tugging with my wrist, trying to get the zip tie to break, wrenching the fastened part against the metal railing.

Nothing works.

Even my thumb . . . I move it inward to make my wrist smaller, but I still need another few millimeters to pry my hand out.

I look around for something fine and sharp, like a needle or a pin, to jam into the lock. But there isn't anything, at least not that I can see. I check my sweatshirt zipper, but it's too wide, way too thick. What else can I use?

I peer back at the phone, wondering how hard it would be to take it apart. Freshman year at Emo, Charley disassembled one, inspired by a dystopian story involving a phone that could call different time periods. But what if I need the phone? If it rings again or I can get it to call out?

The message from Peyton, scrawled across the wall, glares at me. Where is she now? And what does she mean by not being deserving of my friendship? Is it because she lied to protect her privacy?

Or something more?

What if it wasn't even her on the phone?

I continue to pull on the zip tie, assuming the guy who took me before is the same person who's taken me now, because he knows so much—about me, about the water-well story . . . Unless he learned it from the chat site. Did he? Could he have read the water-well entries somehow, even though I made them locked? Is that why the Jane Anonymous website has been shut down? Because it got compromised?

Is he the same person who took Peyton before too? What would be the odds of that—of both of us ending up on the Jane Anonymous website, both victims of the same person? How did I even learn about the chat site to begin with?

A poster at work.

Did the guy who took me put it there? Was he lurking in the library? Did he leave those books on the return rack?

I grab the phone receiver and pull the whole unit toward me. Red and yellow wires snake out the back. They feed into a drilled hole in the floor, proving this . . .

Here.

Now.

Taking Peyton, taking me . . .

It'd all been planned, all been rigged: the phone, the bus, this salvage yard . . .

There are bolts keeping the phone together, but I have no means of unscrewing them. So, now what?

Sitting with my back against the wall, I focus on the blue people spray-painted above the windows—two women, eight children. Who are they? What do they represent? Floating above their heads are the words *It's your turn. Tell me a story.*

It reminds me of something Dr. Mary told me once: "If you don't like the story you've been telling yourself, then make a new one. Instead of being the girl who lost her parents, be the survivor of a fire."

"But what if I don't want to be the survivor?"

"Then start smaller. Be the niece of a woman who loves her. Be the girl who's almost finished high school. Be the artist whose creations are interesting and unique."

"My aunt doesn't love me."

"That's just another story. An unhealthy one. Why not try to rewrite it?"

I bite my lip as tears streak down my face, only able to tell one story—that of a stupid girl who's been abducted once again.

51

I continue trying to break the zip tie, tugging with my wrist, tearing through the layers of skin. A blister bursts over my wristbone. Blood and sweat seep into my palm. I press on my thumb knuckle as hard as I can to get it to move inward, to make the width of my hand smaller. But doing so only makes the throbbing worse. A burning sensation radiates to my shoulder.

This isn't working. I need to try something else.

I bite the plastic, chewing the locking part: the tiny, raised nub. I get my teeth around it and mash, grind, pull, gnaw, desperate to break through it.

The plastic has a salty flavor, or maybe that's just my skin, or the metallic taste of my blood. I tell myself a story: *This isn't a zip tie. It's the wax candy I used to buy at the corner store when I was little . . . the tiny bottles that were filled with pretty sugar water the colors of Easter eggs. If I just chew a little longer, a big burst of blueberry liquid will come gushing into my mouth, the latch will come unlocked, and I'll be able to break free.*

My jaw aches from all its work. My tongue does too; it feels torn up and tired.

A tired tongue.

A mouthful of plastic.

Teeth that clank together but miraculously never chip. I almost wish they would. Pain in exchange for release. Instead, a piece of the plastic breaks free, at last. But it isn't the right piece—not part of the lock; it's part of the slack.

Eventually, I sink down to the floor with my cheek pressed against the hard, bumpy surface, and I tell myself stories inspired by the images all around me: first about the blue family that moved across the country because of a job change, then about the orange bunny who started classes at a new school; and the briefcase-carrying green man, who lost his job and hasn't told his family.

I tell myself these stories in between tugging some more, despite my raw and torn-up skin, and stopping for bites, even though my gums have started to bleed.

How long have I been here?

A few hours at most?

I know because it's still dark. There's no light peeping in through the gaps of junk outside the windows. And there *must* be gaps. At least a few. How else would I have been able to tell that the bus was a bus? I was likely brought in through the folding doors. Though, those same doors appear to be barricaded now too. Still, I'm sure it hasn't been a full day. My mouth hasn't gone completely dry. My stomach isn't rumbling. There's no point in screaming yet. I need to save my voice until morning, when people might be around.

The salvage yard will eventually open. How many days has it already been closed? How long was Peyton here?

And how about Garret?

I told him I was in Pineport. Did he ever get the text with the picture of the salvage yard sign? Did Detective Marshall get it too? Though, she didn't mention it when I spoke to her on the phone . . .

I study the walls, searching for clues. In the window, above the lantern, someone's drawn two stick-figure people squatted behind a sofa. A word bubble blows out from one of the figures' mouths; in it are the words *You tell me your secret, and I'll tell you mine.* It's the same line of dialogue as in the water-well book—when William first met Clara . . .

Below that drawing is another one—a campfire scene. A stick-figure girl stands over the fire. Surrounding her are tall evergreen trees. It's labeled *Climax Scene*.

Another picture shows the same girl huddled up in a corner with a word bubble that says, *Please, Terra, don't give up on me.* I blink hard. Am I imagining the words? Is the stick-figure girl supposed to be Peyton?

Is she in the woods now?

Is she by a campfire?

The phone rings again, making my insides jump. I scurry across the floor to answer it, moving a little too fast, reaching a little too far. The thumb of the zip-tied hand dislocates. My fingers won't move, and I let out a catlike whine.

Still, I stretch with my other hand to grab the receiver.

Someone's crying on the other end of the phone—a female voice.

"Peyton?"

The phone clicks off.

I slide back, across the floor. My hand continues to throb; the wrist pulsates. I bite at the zip tie again, finally managing to mangle the locking-fastening piece. At the same moment, an idea hits.

I reach up the back of my shirt and fumble with the hook of my bra. It takes several tries before I'm able to get it unfastened. I un-loop the strap from my untied hand and pull part of the bra out the neck of my T-shirt. The underwire forms a solid tunnel. I bite the fabric open—one quick tear—and pull the underwire out.

It's hard and thin, long and narrow. Exactly what I need. I press the end into the latch, and jiggle it up and down, back and forth.

At last, something in the zip tie releases.

The lock loosens.

I feel a *click*.

The residual piece of slack is able to move. I slip it free and pull my hand out, my heart clenched. My pulse races.

I grab the lantern and trample down the center aisle to the emergency door at the back of the bus. I try the latch, surprised when it moves, shocked when the handle gives. The door swings open, and I step outside.

52

Using the lantern to light my way, I climb out the emergency door at the back of the bus, stepping on a pile of wooden planks—slowly, carefully. But my foot slips, propelling a plank upward. The plank clanks down, freezing me in place.

I hold my breath and count to ten before moving again, hopping down onto a clear patch of ground. The ringing starts again—the pay phone, from inside the bus. I look through the door, half tempted to go back and answer it so he doesn't know I've managed to break free. But I maneuver around a collection of hubcaps instead.

It's still dark. The air smokes out my mouth in one long, puffy swirl, making me feel exposed. The lantern does too, but I keep it low, by my knee.

A stack of tires stands to my right. I go to avoid it, smacking into something—*hard*. A workbench. Its steel leg meets my shin, and I hold back a wail, biting into my fist. Did the collision make a sound? All I can hear is the hammering of my heart; it penetrates my ears. I can feel it pulsing beneath my skin.

Is the phone still ringing?

Are those crickets chirping?

I begin counting again—up to twenty—scooting around the tires, following a meandering path as I make my way to the fence.

My teeth chatter—a mix of fear and cold. I look back toward the bus, unable to even see it now. It's too dark. I'm too far.

The tinkling of wind chimes cuts my nerves like a knife. I picture the chimes like sharp metal blades hanging from a hook somewhere close by. If only I had one in my hand. I scan the piles of debris for a weapon: broken bricks, a mountain of bicycle tires, a collection of fixtures (sink faucets, shower nozzles, door handles), and a heap of pipes, as though for plumbing. Most of the pipes appear long and cumbersome. Still, I go to grab one when I notice something better—a metal stake like the kind for camping. It's smaller (about eight inches), easier to conceal, and has a pronounced point. I slip it into my pocket and continue toward the fence.

I count the steps to get there—thirty-six. It appears to be at least ten feet tall—too high to climb. Where was the panel that had been curled up at the bottom? On the other side of the yard. Do I even want to look for it? What other choice do I have?

I take a step back, trying to get a perspective. A tugging sensation tightens my chest, cinches my ribs. Meanwhile, the stench of decay is all around me, like something died. I can practically taste it in my mouth; it crawls to the back of my tongue, pokes a hole in my throat, and I let out a gag—a loud retching sound. I peer all around me, checking and rechecking to see if anyone heard—if anyone's here.

I can't really tell. I don't really know. I take another step back to reassess the fence.

And that's when I notice.

The panel to the left looks slightly different—a whole lot wider. Two posts stand between it and the next panel (the one directly in front of me).

My gaze travels upward, and I spot a latch.

This must be a gate.

A chain lingers like a snake on the ground. Is it to secure the panels closed? Did someone unlock it?

I move closer, spotting the glimmer of a fire in the bordering woods. I blink hard, assuming I must be seeing things, that the flames are inside my head.

But still they remain. The embers float up toward the sky, time-traveling me back to Bailey Road. A flurry of lights shines behind my eyes.

With jittering fingers, I pull the latch upward and draw the gate open, just enough to allow me to slip through.

Now what? Save myself, as I did in the house fire? Or try to find Peyton? What would my parents want? How would they advise me? I take a deep breath. Inside my head is a high-pitched blare.

The flames in the woods lap in the wind. Sparks snap up into the air. But still, it appears to be a contained fire, as though for camping, exactly like the image inside the bus.

What are the odds that I was meant to escape? That this is part of the hunt? Why else would the gate be unlocked? Why would the emergency door to the bus not have been welded shut? Why wasn't a chain, rather than a zip tie, used to secure me to the handrail?

What if I'm supposed to hunt for Peyton?

While someone else is hunting for me?

NOW

53

Beyond the gate, I find a parting in the trees where there appears to be a trail. I follow it, keeping focused on the campfire, which looks to be about thirty yards away. Branches reach out and scratch my legs. Something long and viny gets tangled in my hair. I keep moving forward on a dirt path, listening for any approaching sounds.

I can smell the fire from here, like smoked meat and burning pine needles. I can hear it too: the crackling of sticks, the snapping of twigs.

When I near the end of the path, I tuck myself behind a thick, leafy bush and peer out the side, making sure the coast is clear. I can make out part of the flame. Boulders are positioned around it as though for seating. I swipe a handful of branches from in front of my eyes.

The fire is in full view now, about eight feet away. Beyond it, I spot something. My nerves steel as I look closer. Someone's sitting on the ground, with their back toward me and their knees bent upward. The person is wearing a robe of sorts. The hood is drawn over the head, but dark wisps of hair lap out the sides.

"Peyton?" I call; my voice shakes.

Did the person's hand just flinch?

Did they let out a moan?

I inch forward. The fire is only a couple of feet away now, but it looks contained. It *is* contained, I remind myself. There's no possible way it could ignite these woods.

The slack of the robe ripples in the breeze. "Peyton?" I repeat, standing just behind the figure now.

The glow of the lantern casts over the side of the face: dark skin, a pointed chin. I move around to the front, finally able to see.

A blank face. No eyes. Colorless lips.

A mannequin.

I step back, and peer all around, eager for an explanation, noticing something else. About ten feet from the fire, stuck between two of the boulders . . . I go to check it out, positioning the lantern beside it; the object has a flat, rectangular shape like an old album or book.

I pick it up.

My stomach churns.

I know what it is without even having to look—the weight, the texture, the size and width . . .

The Forest Girl and the Wishy Water Well.

It looks exactly the same, with its frayed ends and dirty, beaten corners. I open up to the middle as dirt sprinkles out. I can smell the dirt too—on the pages, the musty scent.

"Hello, Terra." His voice sends shivers all over my skin.

Wearing dark clothes and a black ski mask, he emerges from between a couple of trees. His shoes have some sort of protective plastic covering them, secured at the ankles. What is it for? To hide his treads?

"Well done on surviving the plot twist. I imagine you saw my red herring." He nods to the mannequin. "Have you come for the climax?"

My fingers tremor, and I drop the book.

"Has a cat got your tongue?" He sticks out his tongue—the same red dart, through the hole in his mask—and waggles it back and forth as he did that night. "I see you found my book too."

As he comes closer, I recognize his eyes—the pale blue color, the hooded lids . . .

"I'd expect no less of my starring character."

I swallow hard—a mouthful of bile.

"You never told me what you thought of my story." He runs his gloved hand over the cover of the water-well book.

I retreat two steps.

"Going so soon? Not yet." He smiles. "Please, have a seat. Did you like the William doll I left for you?"

Left for me? Is he talking about the troll doll inside the well? Or the ceramic garden gnome on the back deck?

"How about the cuddly blanket?" he asks. "I was more than generous with my gifts, don't you think? Leaving the lid open during the rain . . . Giving you moments of light . . . I even threw you a bone."

A sparerib bone.

My body chills.

"I wanted you to have a fighting chance," he continues. "So we could continue our story."

"Where's Peyton?" I ask him.

He scratches his head as though in thought.

"Is she even real? Was it Peyton who called me?"

"Are you implying that it could've been someone else?" He smirks. "An actor, for instance, playing the role of Peyton? Perhaps one had used one of the many high-tech voice-changers on the market. Did you know some of the more sophisticated models can completely alter pitch, tone, and volume of a voice?"

"Is that the case?"

He reaches into his pocket. There's something in there. A gun? A knife? More of the stuff that put me out? "I used to love story time as a kid," he says. "I lived for it—*literally*. Stories were my passion: reading them, role-playing them, writing fan fiction . . . But you were the same way, isn't that right?"

The same way?

"The possibilities are endless. Put a character in a hole and see how she behaves. Does she fight for what she wants by climbing out? What obstacles lie in her wake? Limited light, lack of tools, hunger, thirst, pure fatigue . . . And let's not forget the heroine's backstory too. What lurks in her past? How reliable is she as a result? What motivates her to act? To make things even more interesting, give the character a magical tool—something that gives her a superpower."

A superpower. "Like the power of invisibility," I say, his identity becoming clear.

"Exactly." He removes his glove, revealing his hand. On his fourth finger is the mood ring I won in Dr. Beckett's class.

"Charley."

"Miss me?"

It's been years since I've seen him. He's taller now. His voice is deeper. But his eyes look the same—bold, piercing, icy blue. After he left Emo, his number no longer worked, and I didn't know where he lived. When I asked Ms. Melita what'd happened to him, she said she wasn't at liberty to discuss other students, then added that smallish places like Emo couldn't provide the resources that larger institutions could. I assumed that meant Charley needed something more. But how much more? What kind of "more"? And would he be coming back after he got it?

"I've missed *you*," he says. "Our time in the quiet room, escaping into plotlines . . ."

"Charley," I repeat, feeling the ground beneath me tilt.

"I hated leaving Emo so abruptly, not having the chance to say goodbye."

"Why *did* you?"

"I started over at a new place, one with more rules, less freedom . . . But now I'm back." He grins. "And do you want to know why?"

"Why?" I ask.

"Because you're the perfect heroine: an unreliable narrator, motivated by the guilt she feels for surviving a fire that took her parents, not to mention the guilt she feels about *other* things, a secret she shared. *Remember . . . ? You tell me your secret, and I'll tell you mine . . .*"

I *do* remember.

Freshman year, in the quiet room, not long before Charley

disappeared for good, I wagered a deal: if I told him my biggest secret, he'd have to tell me his. Charley agreed. And so we tucked ourselves behind the corduroy sofa—the one with the cigarette burn holes in the fabric—and I confided something I'd never shared with anyone. In retrospect, I'm not even sure why I made the deal in the first place. Because I simply *had* to know his backstory? Because I wanted to bring us closer? Or because on some subconscious level, I needed to reveal a truth about myself to someone whose own truth was, quite possibly, even more unspeakable than mine?

With brittle words and a face as burning as the hottest flame, I dredged the secret from the vault inside my gut, the place where I've always felt sick, and spewed it into the air. And when I was done, I opened my eyes, bracing myself for a look of repulsion. But instead, his face puzzled, and he didn't utter a sound.

"Say something," I told him, my voice riddled with tears.

"I didn't hear you."

Had I not spoken the words aloud?

He slipped the mood ring onto my finger. "This will make it easier."

Oddly enough it did. The ring made me feel invisible, so I was able to confess again: "I started the fire, the one that burned down my house, that killed my parents." The words, out loud, made my head spin. The air in the room spun too, making it harder to breathe, to catch my breath. I let out a gasp as tears ran down my face. When I opened my eyes, I saw that Charley's face showed neither repulsion nor surprise.

"It was an accident," I told him, suddenly realizing that I'd been rocking back and forth, that a spittle of drool hung off my lower lip. "It'd been so cold in my room. I'd gotten up and gone downstairs. The wood-burning stove was still on. But that was normal. The house was old, and it didn't have a good heating system. I'd been allowed to feed wood into the stove ever since I'd turned thirteen, with a clear set of rules."

Charley patted my hand. It wouldn't stop trembling. My lungs felt like they were collapsing.

"It'll be okay," he said.

I shook my head. *It wouldn't ever be okay.* More tears came. Charley handed me a tissue, but his face remained expressionless, as if my secret weren't enough, as if somehow his was even more horrific than mine.

I slipped the ring off my finger and slid it onto his. "Your turn now."

Charley took a deep breath and started to utter something: the words *sister, stolen money,* and *wilderness community.* "I told myself it would all be okay, that nothing bad would happen," he said. "But when I woke up . . ."

"*What?*" I asked.

"It was all my fault."

"Wait, slow down, what was?"

He didn't answer. He just stood up. His upper lip quivered, and there were splotches all over his neck. "Tomorrow," he said, leaving me with the burn marks.

"*Terra?*" His voice snaps me back to present day. He removes the mood ring from his finger once more—like déjà vu—and sets it down on a rock. "Take it. It'll help you disappear. *Remember?*"

"I don't understand. We were *friends,*" I say, though after sharing my secret all those years ago and not hearing his in return, it felt as if I'd been violated somehow, as if something inside me had died.

"More than friends. You were like a sister to me."

"So, then why are you doing this?"

"Role-playing, creating stories, constructing my own reality? It's what I've always done. Nothing much has changed, except that I've started using real players as inspiration for my work. I've also been writing my stories down." He puts his glove back on. "The water-well book was my first attempt at seeing a project all the way through. Now, I want to write *your* story, with you as my main character, taking creative liberties as I see fit, twisting plots and altering storylines as needed."

I shake my head. I still don't get it.

"I'm already writing the story," he continues. "You're already starring in it. You got out of the hole, only to face a plot twist: You were captured again. Now what?"

I take a step back, doing my best to search the area: the grouping of trees he appeared from, the mannequin, the heap of dirt a few feet from the fire . . . But no matter where I look, the answer sinks in.

The truth becomes clear.

The Peyton I knew doesn't exist, never existed.

"It seems you're having a hard time focusing, am I right? Would you prefer to talk about a different story? One about salvage yards, perhaps? Or a story about a family living off the grid in the middle of the woods, free from greed and possessions? We should all get unplugged, don't you think? Spend some time in nature, away from all things materialistic."

His words jog my memory, because I've heard them before—on the chat site.

"Are you Darwin12?" I ask him.

"You're such a skillful storyteller." His smile widens. "Able to detect unnatural dialogue when you hear it. Just another reason you make a worthy heroine."

"I don't understand," I tell him again. "Why not just befriend me again? Why take me from my aunt's house? Why put me in a hole?"

"For play," he says as though the answer is simple. "Like old times, like we used to do. Now, take the ring. Use it for its power of invisibility. The ring made me disappear, didn't it? And then I used it to make *you* disappear."

I grip the lantern. It has a heavy base; the batteries must be inside it. A thick plastic dome surrounds two vertical lights. I imagine smashing him with it—at least ten pounds of metal, plastic, and glass coming down on the crown of his head.

"So, now that you've caught me again?" I ask.

"Let's continue our story."

"How does it end?"

"We'll have to keep going to see. I'll resume the role of the villain who enjoys the hunt, and you'll continue to be my prey. Who will win?"

"Except I don't want to be hunted. I don't want to play."

"Deep down you do. You saw the Jane Anonymous poster. The message spoke to you—the part about going from a victim to a victor."

"You put that poster in the library." And lured me here by creating Peyton.

"You logged on that very night. It took virtually nothing to engage you. Now, what do you say? I'll give you two minutes."

I grip the stake, trying to hold it all together despite my desire to lash out. "Two minutes?"

"If you agree to play, you might get your way. Then you'll be free, free, free for eternity. Do we have ourselves a deal?"

"What do you mean? What kind of deal?"

"You got away once. Then you got away twice. If you get away a third time, I'll have to play nice. If you use the ring to escape into the night, the heroine will win, and I will do what's right."

"What's right?"

"Our story will be done, and the heroine will have won."

"And if I don't escape?"

"Then continues our fun and the villain has won. We'll run away together and spin our tales forever and ever. *Tick tock, tick tock.* Run, run away or you'll have to stay. The villain of this story really loves to play." He sits down on a boulder.

It's only then I nab the ring and slide it onto my finger.

"Two minutes," he reminds me, covering his eyes with his hands. He begins to count, like a game of hide-and-seek.

I grip the stake in my pocket, suspecting he's watching me from the spaces between his fingers. I can't lash out now. And so, I turn away and run for my life.

54

I grapple through the woods, swiping branches and brush from in front of my eyes, desperate to get back to the fence, wanting to find my car.

But the brush is way too thick. I'm not on the same trail. The branches scratch my skin. One of them pokes my eye. I rub it, trying to absorb the pain, hoping to ease the blur.

The lantern's still on; I can't see without it. Still, I'm tempted to let it go. It's too heavy, way too cumbersome. Plus, it gives me away.

I struggle through a grove of berry bushes, sure the two-minute mark has already passed. His first instinct will be to go for my car. I squat down, where I am, behind some bushes, click the lantern off, and wait to hear him approaching, hoping he'll continue past me.

It doesn't take long. The sound of his body swishes among the trees. His soft grunt makes my insides shiver.

Is he a few yards away?

On the other side of these trees?

I hold my breath, telling myself it's all a big game, just another role-play with Charley. The metal stake is gripped in my hand.

"*Come out, come out, wherever you are,*" he sings. "*My hero couldn't have gone too far.*"

I inch out, unable to see a thing. He isn't using a flashlight or lantern. So how is he looking for me? Night vision goggles? Does he have them?

I count to ten inside my head, wondering how concealed I am. Is he able to see any part of me—my shoes, my clothes, the outline of my hair?

"*Terra* . . ." His voice sounds so close, just a couple of feet away. It's followed by the cracking of broken twigs, the scuffling of dirt, and the crinkling of the plastic covering over his shoes.

I picture his step and listen for his breath, able to hear his deep inhalation: the sucking of air up his nostrils. He sounds right at my side now. I clamp my eyes shut as if that will make a difference.

And maybe it does.

Because everything goes quiet.

Even the crickets stop chirping.

Where is he now?

I start to stand up. My knee joint clicks. The sound shatters the silence, echoes inside my brain.

"Well, well, well," he says, freezing me in place.

I drop back to the ground.

"*Look what we have here? A sweet little victim who's oh-so-near? Does this really mean what I think it might? We'll spin our tales every day and every nigh—*"

I cut him off, stabbing into the darkness, plunging outward with the stake, imagining the cloth dummy from self-defense class. So many nights I spent stabbing Rummy. And kicking sandbags.

And dodging punches.

And ducking from high kicks . . .

Finally, there was a payoff. He lets out a grunt.

I stand up and click the lantern on. I've stabbed him in the gut, through his T-shirt. He's got a pair of binoculars strapped around his head, over the mask: night vision goggles.

He goes to reach into his pocket. But before he can, I strike out with the lantern. The base clonks against the side of his head. His hands fly up to his face, and he turns to the side.

With both hands gripped on the handle, I imagine the lantern like a baseball bat and slice through the air before he's able to rebound, knocking his forehead. He lets out a wail and stumbles back.

How far did the stake go in—three inches? Four?

He motions to remove it, and I kick him—*hard*—aiming for his groin. He goes down on his knees, still trying to pluck the stake free.

I kick him once more—this time, in the chest; the heel of my boot meets his ribs. The base of the lantern smashes against his face as I pummel him once more. He falls back, rolls onto his side.

His eyes appear closed. I can't tell if he's breathing.

I scooch to the ground, remembering *his* backstory—one that was ever changing, thanks to a reality he said was all too grim, way too dark. *You don't want to know* was all he'd ever said of it.

"Charley?" I call out. With one hand on the stake, I use the other to remove the goggles, to lift the mask and expose his face.

Thin lips.

A square jaw.

High, pronounced cheekbones.

A flash of dark curly hair, just like I remember.

With trembling fingers, I lift his eyelid, able to see the steel-blue color of his eyes: the shade I haven't been able to paint.

I start to pull my hand away, but he grabs me—*hard*. His gloved hand wraps around my wrist. Still gripping the stake with my other hand, I drive the blade deeper into his gut.

His eyes bulge. His mouth parts open. The grip on my wrist loosens, and I'm able to get up, to back away.

His chest doesn't move. I don't think he's breathing. I look toward his pocket, tempted to see what's inside it, but I grab the lantern instead and move back through the woods, desperate to get away.

NOW

55

I trample through the woods on a dirt-lined trail, using the lantern to guide the way. Sticks break somewhere behind me.

I picture Charley running to catch me.

Was his chest truly still? Could he have been holding his breath? Did he only pretend to be hurt? To prolong the chase? To continue the story?

Finally, I reach the chain-link fence. My hand is still throbbing. What did Charley have in his pocket? Could he use it on me still? Has he already gotten up?

If only I'd thought to take his night vision goggles. It's so dark, despite the lantern. I'm barely able to make out more than a couple of feet in front of me.

I stop a moment—to catch my breath, to listen for him approaching. It's quiet again; there's just the hooting of an owl. I snatch a rock from the ground, just in case, and continue to follow the fence around to the front of the salvage yard, and up to the street, to where I parked the car.

There's a spare key hidden beneath the bumper—my dad's old trick. I go to retrieve it, scooting down, and searching frantically beneath the lip.

My hands won't stop shaking.

My eyes won't stop tearing.

Where is it?

On the other side of the bumper?

I stand to check, suddenly noticing my tire has been slashed. I move around the car to check the others. The two front tires have been slashed as well.

The road is completely desolate. I begin in the direction of where I came, still anxious about Charley, still wondering where he is—if he's come to. I quicken my pace, my shin aching from where I hit it.

What time is it?

Where should I go?

Finally, I get to the end of the street. Streetlamps shine over a post office, a convenience store, and the town bank. All of them are closed. Antique-style houses sit back from the road, farther down the street. All the lights inside them are off. No one's awake.

A clock on the front of the bank reads just after one. Is it even correct?

I start to cross the street, to head toward the houses, just as a dark truck turns onto the road, making a screeching sound like a wounded animal.

I stop short.

The driver does too. Headlights shine directly into my eyes. I wave my arms, desperate for help.

The door flings open. A guy gets out—tall, medium build. It takes me a moment to recognize who it is.

The sight of Garret is almost too much to take in. I drop the rock and feel a huge release inside my chest.

Garret says something, but it's all too much to process. His phone is in his hand. I grab it, turn it on, and dial 9-1-1.

"Please come," I tell the operator. "I think someone might be dead."

I think I'm going to be sick.

I half think Peyton is still alive, still for real.

"How can she not be?" I ask aloud, looking down at the mood ring. What if Peyton has one too? What if she used it to disappear?

Garret doesn't respond. At least I don't think he does. Instead, he drapes something warm and heavy over my shoulders. It takes me a beat to realize it's his sweatshirt.

The operator asks me questions, but I can't answer now.

I don't want to talk.

I just want to sit on the side of the road and watch the flames go out one by one. And so that's what I do—until I can no longer smell smoke, until I can finally breathe free.

NOW

56

Six weeks later.

In my room.

I stand at my easel, painting a new self-portrait: an assignment given by Cecelia Bridges, the therapist Aunt Dessa recommended. I've been seeing her twice a week for a few weeks now. Our sessions are work; I'm not going to lie. But I haven't even minded because I've been able to communicate through my art, which Cecelia encourages, and for now that feels more telling than words.

My canvas has been prepped in solid matte black. But my intention is to create lightness. I've chosen two main colors to do that: gold and white (iridescent eggshell, to be exact). In the end, my piece will glow.

I start at the very bottom and paint the strong roots of a hearty tree: roots that extend far beyond the canvas. I imagine they're more than a hundred feet long, burrowed beneath the soil and made up of the generations before me, those whose influences have helped raise me up.

I paint hands in the roots—palms that lift; fingers that stretch, leaving their prints in the trunk; and wrists that bend just enough to allow lessons to seep in, truth to unwind, and stories to flow. I specifically paint my parents' hands, picturing my mom's bony fingers and my dad's crooked thumb. I also add my aunt's swollen knuckles and the burn mark on my palm.

A survivor's hands.

With able fingers.

Strong wrists.

And a network of rooted souls.

The branches of my tree extend upward like arms reaching for the sun. I shade muscles into the arms: well-worked biceps capable of helping me up a twenty-foot chain and taut quadriceps for scaling the driest of dirt walls.

The brain is a muscle too, at least that's what I believe. I paint mine purple, perched on a nest of letters that spell out the words *work in progress*—because that's what I am, with my paper heart and my phantom scars.

I paint the heart red, smudged with my thumbprint, scattered about the ear-shaped leaves. You have to look closely to see the heart; otherwise, the prints look like flowers: bunches of them blooming like roses, sprinkled about the tree limbs—a heart in pieces like petals.

Plus, tiny tree buds that spell out the word *trust*.

And fallen twigs with shadows that resemble old vices. Extinguishers, knives, starry doorknobs, and bottles of maple syrup . . . None of these vices is gone completely. I'm human, so sometimes I creep back into the darkness to find them, but I do so far less, preferring to get my power elsewhere. My art—the paint; my canvases; every marker, pencil, and brush—has become my home, the one place where I can truly express who I am. And so, I spend time here, whenever I can, basking in its natural glow.

57

After the dust has somewhat settled from the Storm of Peyton and its dirty aftermath, Aunt Dessa sits me down on the living room sofa and takes my hands, just like after I got back from the well. "I'm sorry," she says.

I bite my lip, not quite sure what the apology is for. Because I got taken again? Because she didn't believe me the first time it happened?

"There's something I want to give you." She reaches into her pocket and pulls out a long tan box. She snaps the cover open, revealing a gold necklace.

"What's that?"

She lifts it out, letting the pendant charms dangle into her palm. The necklace is just like hers, except with the initials *M* and *T*.

"Years ago, when I couldn't find your mom's necklace in the debris, I hired someone to search for it." she says. "Unfortunately, he wasn't able to locate all of it, but he did manage to salvage the M for Maeve. I had a jeweler refurbish it and create a T for Terra. Then I chose a chain just like mine and your mom's." She hands it to me.

I hold the necklace up, my pulse racing. The ropy links glisten in the light.

"You don't have to wear it," she says. "I just thought—"

"I *want* to wear it." I fasten the clasp around my neck.

"Once upon a time, your mother never took that off. Neither of us did.",

"And I won't either." I hold the *M* over my heart. "Thank you."

Tears well up in her eyes. "I'm sorry it took so long for me to get to this place."

"What do you mean?"

"There's something you should know—the reason your mom and I grew apart . . . It was my fault."

"*What* was?"

"Your mother's attack . . . I've always blamed myself for it. I was supposed to be watching her at that party. But I'd gone off with a boy." She grabs a pillow and hugs it into her middle the way Mom used to do. "I didn't even drive her home that night. She ended up running out, bolting from the party. Some guy—a stranger, someone whose identity we were never able to figure out—spotted her walking along the side of the road with torn clothes and crying. He gave her a ride, no questions asked. Even *he* was better than I was."

If I didn't know better, I'd say it was my mother on the sofa, only inches from me now, all rolled up like a hedgehog, unable to look me in the eyes.

"You shouldn't blame yourself," I tell her. "It wasn't your fault."

Aunt Dessa snuggles the pillow tighter. "Everyone felt it was, including your grandparents. Including me. Your mother and I grew distant after it happened. Then, flash-forward twenty years, and all of that happened to you after the sorority party . . . I wanted to make it up to my sister somehow, to do things right and protect you the way I should've protected her. But then when I thought it was a lie, I couldn't really handle it—couldn't relate to someone who would make up something so horrific. In my mind, you simply *had* to be sick."

"And what about after the fire? Why didn't you want to protect me then?" The questions form a lump in my throat.

"By taking you in, I felt I *was* protecting you, at least on some level. It's complicated." She sighs. "But when my sister died, so did the possibility that she and I would one day be close again. It really has nothing to do with you."

For the past several years, I've felt it had *everything* to do with me. After the fire, investigators were able to determine how the initial spark had started. They tried to ask me questions: if I'd noticed the stove was on prior to going to bed that night; if my parents had ever forgotten to close the stove door; if there had been a rug, rather than a flame-protective pad, in front of the hearth . . . But I couldn't answer a single question. Because the breath in my lungs had ceased. And I dissolved to a pile of dust. My knees gave way, and I collapsed to the floor, trying to process what the news of the fire meant: that I'd made a mistake, that I hadn't followed my parents' rules.

And that my mistake had caused the flames.

And that my mistake had caused the flames.

And that my mistake had caused the flames.

My aunt was there too, with the fire marshal. But after that day, neither of us would ever speak a word about the fire's origins. "Just tell people it was an electrical thing," was the last thing she'd said about it, which somehow made things worse. More shameful. Far more horrific.

"*Terra?*" Aunt Dessa asks. She's still balled up on the sofa, still snuggling a pillow close. "I'm sorry if I projected any of my sister stuff onto you. And I'm especially sorry if that made me seem distant."

It actually makes her more human . . . knowing she's been battling guilt, like me, that she's had a shame-labeled vault locked up inside her too.

"Now that I know you were telling the truth about being taken," she continues, "and that I chose not to believe you, I'm left blaming myself again. I'm so sorry—for *everything:* the silence, the mistrust, the clearing out of your room . . . I know that isn't nearly good enough, but right now, apologies and promises to do better are all I have to offer. I hope you'll accept."

"I do." I nod.

Aunt Dessa reaches out to take my hand again. For just a moment, as I look down at our fingers clasped together, I imagine it's my mom's hand—her fragile grip, her chewed-up nails, her freckled skin . . .

"No matter how difficult our pasts have been, or how much shame we carry as a result, we all deserve to allow ourselves to be loved." She squeezes my hand tighter. "That should've always been the number-one rule on our survival list."

I open my mouth, wanting to ask how she even knows about the list, but I stop myself from speaking because I'd prefer to believe the message was channeled by my mom somehow, that Mom's here with me, holding my hand, answering my questions.

"I'd like it if we could talk about my mother more."

"I'd like that too." She curls back into her pillow. "I'm sorry I haven't been more open to that."

I place the initial *M* up to my lips. "None of us is perfect."

"Especially not me."

"So, we have to forgive ourselves for the choices we'd no longer make."

"That's a really nice idea, but an unbelievably hard lesson."

"I'm still learning it too," I say.

Still adding light to my painting.

Still boldening the trust.

Still working on my paper heart.

58

I haven't been on the chat site since the night of the salvage yard, mostly because it reminds me of Peyton, and I really, really miss her.

Sometimes I'll wake up in the middle of the night, feeling that oh-so-familiar tightness in my chest. My pulse will race, and I'll work so hard at trying to catch my breath, thinking about things like Story Land and maple syrup packets. My gut instinct will be to log on to Jane—to seek Peyton out. But not half a second later, I'll remember. She won't be on. Because she doesn't exist.

The site is still active, and I miss it too . . . the other members, "hearing" and reading their stories. So many nights (and so many long, endless days), just knowing that people were on and that I could chat whenever I wanted made me feel a little less alone.

So now, six weeks later, I grab my laptop, wondering if people on the site will comment about how long I've been away. After the Peyton/Darwin incident, the Jane Anonymous administrators sent out messages warning members about the potential for online danger and catfishing. Those messages had followed news reports about the disappearance of Charley Mullins, the twenty-one-year-old man who abducted twenty-two-year-old Clara Peyton Adelman from Ashby, North Carolina, a year and a half prior and put her in a shed.

The same man who also abducted me.

Previous news articles regarding Clara's disappearance stated that she'd been taken by a man who'd been posing as a police officer. Investigators found DNA (aside from Clara's) among the shed debris, but they weren't able to link it to anyone relevant until what happened behind the salvage yard. Charley's DNA was discovered in a pool of blood made by the stab wound; only, by the time the police arrived on the scene, he'd already fled, leaving the mannequin behind, but managing to take the storybook with him.

The Forest Girl and the Wishy Water Well.

No one was able to find it.

Recent news reports didn't leak my name, but they *did* detail how Charley had sought me out on a chat site for trauma victims, "under the guise of a twenty-two-year-old fellow survivor of abduction." They also mentioned the first time I was taken—from my bed, in the middle of the night—acknowledging that it'd actually happened. The fact that they were admitting it felt empowering at first; at last people would know I hadn't made the story up. But after that initial spark, the power on their words went out. I no longer felt they mattered.

What matters to me now is that Charley is still out there—still capable of taking someone else, still not getting the treatment that he needs. Charley Mullins: the boy who loved storytelling even more than I did, who used to help me escape the inferno inside my head with magical rings and twisty plots; whose own backstory was always too unspeakable to share . . .

It breaks my heart to know it's him.

NightTerra has entered the chat room.

JA Admin: Welcome, NightTerra. Remember the rules: no judgments, no swearing, no inappropriate remarks. We here at Jane Anonymous make every effort to ensure a safe space for honesty and support, but, unfortunately, we live in a world where complete safety isn't always possible.

Please alert us to any member's comments that make you uncomfortable or that you feel should be reviewed.

TulipPrincess: NightTerra!!! Long time no chat.

LuluLeopard: How are you???

NightTerra: I'm ok, and you guys?

LuluLeopard: We all heard about #Peyton

RainyDayFever: Word travels fast around here.

TulipPrincess: Speculation also doesn't hurt.

TulipPrincess: So, just to be clear, that guy they're talking about on the news . . . The storyteller . . .

TulipPrincess: That's def him, right? The guy who posed as Peyton and Darwin . . .

TulipPrincess: They said he was active on a chat site. It sounded like this one . . . created by a woman who'd been abducted herself . . . Everyone's saying it is.

NightTerra: Yes. Same guy.

TulipPrincess: Plus, the story, what they're saying . . . It kind of went along with your story, what you went through.

LuluLeopard: But they didn't mention a well.

NightTerra: Turns out it wasn't a well. It was an old mining pit for coal. It took them a while to find it.

TulipPrincess: Have you been back there?

NightTerra: Not yet. Maybe someday.

LuluLeopard: Chills. I can't even imagine.

LuluLeopard: Seriously . . . Knowing that guy was on here posing has kept me awake at night.

RainyDayFever: Me too. I almost didn't come back on here.

TulipPrincess: I could never stay away. You guys have helped me get through so much crap.

TulipPrincess: I'm not sure I would've made it these last few months if not.

TulipPrincess: I'm moving out, btw. For real. It's happening.

LuluLeopard: Wait, you didn't tell me this!!!

TulipPrincess: Yep. My grandma said I can come live with her, as long as I enroll in school, which is kind of what I want to do anyway. So . . . I'm going.

TulipPrincess: !!!

TulipPrincess: San Diego, here I come!

LuluLeopard: How does your mom feel about it?

TulipPrincess: Honestly? She seems happy for me.

NightTerra: That's great!

RainyDayFever: Yay, Tulip!!!

LuluLeopard: So happy for you!!!

TulipPrincess: Thanx. But getting back to you, NightTerra . . .

TulipPrincess: That guy is on the loose now, right? How are you doing with that?

NightTerra: I'm ok.

TulipPrincess: Better than ok. Sounds like you're super brave.

NightTerra: I'm ok in this moment, but you know how that goes. These things change. One moment ok . . .

RainyDayFever: The next in a fetal position, eating a carton of doughnuts. #Confessions #WhatIDidLastNight

TulipPrincess: Lol!

RainyDayFever: Is anyone else craving doughnuts right now?

NightTerra: I just have to take each moment as it comes.

TulipPrincess: #SoWise

NightTerra: #JustWords #NotEasy

NightTerra: But thank you guys for being here and believing my story. It's made all the difference. #Truth

TulipPrincess: #Love

LuluLeopard: #Trust

RainyDayFever: #Doughnuts !!!

NightTerra: Thank you guys again. Talk to you soon.

TulipPrincess: Later, NightTerra!

LuluLeopard: Sending a virtual hug.

RainyDayFever: Sending virtual doughnuts. Lol!

NightTerra has left the chat room. There are currently 4 people in the chat room.

59

I've learned some things.

Like that people will "love" you when it's popular to "love" you. They'll be right there beside you when you're a star on the news for doing something heroic. Escaping from an abductor is heroic, so they'll love you for that. Bonus points if you were abducted twice—and if those same people didn't believe you the first time it happened.

They'll shower you with "love," apologizing for turning their backs before, and offer to bring you lunch / take you shopping / buy you coffee / listen to your story. They'll tell you how brave they think you are—brave and heroic and sparkling and strong—and call you their best friend, and thank god for your safety.

"Love" like theirs can feel both comforting and intoxicating. But it isn't real. And it doesn't last.

I've learned that real love comes from those who stick around regardless of what's popular. They don't necessarily have to be with you in your own personal hell, but they can still sit beside you and offer a sweatshirt for your tears.

After the incident at the salvage yard, when police asked me questions and made me go over all the details, Garret was there, by my side, holding my hand and reminding me to breathe.

He's also been there every day since. I've learned that love like his—that comes from true friendship—is super rare and well worth the risk.

A few weeks following my escape from the bus, when Detective Marshall had me come to the station to discuss a few more things, Garret insisted on being there too. And when the detective gave voice to what I'd been fearing, Garret held tight around my shoulder and reminded me I wasn't alone.

Detective Marshall pushed a photo of Charley toward me, across the table. His gray-blue eyes angled slightly upward. His grin looked somewhat shy, not too wide; there was just a peek of teeth. It was a kind face, one I used to look forward to seeing, one that helped to reassure me. But now, it's left me with so many questions. Like, why me? Why now? Was it truly our history of telling stories together that drew him here, after all these years?

And what about *Summer's Story*? Was there a specific reason he wanted me to watch the show? Do clues to *his* backstory lie somewhere hidden in the plot? The theme of broken spirits? Of abandonment? Of abuse? And what about the setting of a camp commune? Was it similar to the setting of the book in "Peyton's" captivity quarters—if such a book exists? Or the camp Charley had mentioned all those years ago in the quiet room?

"Terra?" Detective Marshall's voice. "It's possible he'll come looking for you again, wanting to finish your story. The problem is we don't know when. It seems he's pretty new to this type of 'storytelling,' involving victims. But he's getting better. He left DNA at the scene of his first crime. He knew better than to leave it at the second. The third time, in the salvage yard, he was overly confident. It'll take him a bit to recover from that."

The salvage yard, where he'd been working part-time, off-the-books, for the past eight months.

"What was his connection to the victim from North Carolina?" I ask.

"Clara. It seems he knew her, at least briefly. They'd been in a playwriting class together at a local community college, months prior to her abduction. People say Clara was a bit of a loner, never quite fit in. We know she lived and worked on her family's animal farm, that she'd lost a sibling—her brother—due to health issues."

"Were the issues related to his heart? Was his name Max?"

Detective Marshall jots the questions down, promising to check. But I'm not even sure the answers matter. The details are close enough.

"Clara enjoyed going on hikes," she added. "She was on a hike when she got taken, having detoured from her route to explore an old abandoned one-room school."

"A one-room school, just like the storybook. Did Clara also work at a yacht club?"

"She'd worked part-time at a local bed-and-breakfast. It seems Charley likes his stories inspired by real life but not limited by them. He takes artistic license, which makes studying his fairy tale—your version of it, that is—all the more complicated. We haven't yet been able to uncover the actual storybook." She sighed. "Further complicating is the fact that Clara died in a hiking accident—also like in the storybook—just months after her return from the shed, so we can't exactly ask her questions."

"Any chance there was foul play?"

"Nothing that was noted, but I'm not ruling it out. We just want you to be alert, aware, and to call us for anything."

I pushed the photo of Charley away, no longer wanting to look. "He said he won't come for me; that if I got away the third time, my story would have ended, the heroine—I—would've won."

"He may change his mind and want to add another twist."

"Or maybe he'll leave me alone."

"He's still out there. You and Clara might not actually be his first crimes. We've been looking at cases where the victim resurfaced, alive, after a matter of days."

"How many cases fit that profile?" Garret asked.

"At least four."

"And have those families been contacted?"

"They have." She nodded. "It's going to take some time. I'm just glad we now know what we're dealing with here. I'm sorry it's been such a long process."

Garret gave my forearm a squeeze as though reading my mind. Her apology didn't make up for the six previous months of being shunned by everyone I knew, the eight weeks I'd spent on the mental health floor of the hospital, or the time that was wasted not searching for clues.

"We'll have cars circling your house to keep an eye on things," she said. "There will also be an unmarked car parked on your street overnight."

Overnight? For how many nights? Did it even matter? Could I really count on them?

"Just promise me one thing," she said, her eyes narrowing. "You'll leave the investigative work to us, okay?"

Part of me wanted to ask where she thought we'd be if I'd never gone to look for Peyton. Would investigators have ever connected the two crimes? Would they have identified Charley and realized they had a serial abductor on their hands?

"And you can call me for anything." She gave me yet another card.

I still have a stack of them by my bed. Maybe one day I'll use them in my art. For now, they're just another reminder to listen to my gut, regardless of what others say: rule number five.

And speaking of my parents' rules . . . I'm grateful for them. They've given me a sense of safety and helped me to keep my parents close. But they haven't always worked, which, I think, brings me to one of the biggest lessons of all: There are no guarantees. No absolutes or foolproof plans. But, as RainyDayFever would say, at least there's ice cream and doughnuts.

60

I've asked Garret to take me to the site of my childhood house on Bailey Road. It's no longer a heap of concrete and dust. Fresh grass has been planted where I used to do somersaults. A new house sits on the lot, painted bright blue with white accents.

We sit out front in Garret's truck for several minutes, as I take it all in: the basketball hoop in the driveway, the wreath of oyster shells hanging on the front door, and the field hockey sticks propped up against a fence.

"People live here," I say, stating the obvious. I'd heard the land had been sold, but I still half expected to find remnants of the fire.

I gaze across the street. The stained-glass sun is still there, in Mrs. Wilder's front window. What would the scene look like now, through one of its rays?

"A lot different?" Garret asks as if responding to my thoughts.

"Different good. The house looks happy."

"It does," he says, pointing out sets of children's handprints cast into a patch of cement on the walkway.

"Life goes on," I say. Wanting to share something else from my old life, I pull the doorknob from my bag. "This is from my bedroom, from back when I lived here. I salvaged it from the debris."

"That's actually kind of cool."

"On the night the house burned, my father wanted me to open

my bedroom door. I'm not sure why—to save himself or to save me. But I never did, because I burned myself in the process." I hold out my hand to show him where the knob lines up with my palm.

Garret runs his thumb over the phantom scar. "So, the knob represents survival, I'm assuming."

I blink hard, taken aback by the word. "Why would you think that?"

"What else *would* I think? This knob survived the fire, and so did you."

"But my parents didn't. The knob has always represented what I did wrong—what I should've done differently."

"What *could* you have done differently?"

"Forced the door open, for starters."

"The door might've saved your life. Did you ever consider that?"

One of the firefighters had said the same, especially when I described the smoke coming through the grain. But I hadn't wanted to listen, because his words didn't change what'd already happened, what I already felt I'd done.

"There's something else," I tell him, hearing the wobble of my voice. "Before the fire started, I'd gone downstairs to feed a log into the wood-burning stove. I thought I'd closed the stove door. But obviously I hadn't."

"You don't know that for sure."

"Why else would the fire have started?"

"A stray ember, a dirty stove, an antiquated system . . . Maybe something got clogged in the flue. Maybe someone had poked at the fire after you'd gone back to bed. The point is you won't ever know the answer. But you have to be able to move forward without letting the question haunt you."

I look away, sucking back tears. His words feel years late.

"I told you about my grandfather," he continues, "about how he was a vet, taking on cases no one else would touch. He wasn't able to save every animal, but he did his best with what he knew."

"Did I do mine?" I peek up into his face.

"You're here, aren't you?"

I look back at the house, no longer able to recognize a single shred of what used to be. "For years, I've wondered what I could do to make it up to my parents somehow."

"Who says you need to make anything up? Just go on living. Do the things you've always dreamed of. That's what your parents would want. That's what any good parent wants for their kid—just for them to be happy."

"You really think so?"

Garret reaches into his back seat and grabs yet another of his sweatshirts. He uses the cuff to wipe my cheek. The fabric smells like soap. I want to blanket it over me, and so that's what I do, allowing myself to lean my back against his chest. Garret wraps his arms around my shoulders.

It feels so good—opening up, letting myself get close. Part of me wants so much more, but this is about all I can handle right now as I work to smolder the very last of my burning flames.

61

It's not until after Garret drops me off that I notice the unmarked car parked across the street from my house. The officer gives me a subtle wave. I wave back before unlocking the door, pausing only to grab the mail and go inside.

Aunt Dessa isn't home yet. I lock up behind me and set the new house alarm, then put my things down on the table in the entryway, including Garret's sweatshirt. I start to thumb through the stack of mail, hoping to find something from one of the art schools I contacted.

I pause at a large manila envelope. My name and address are written across the front in black all caps. There's no return address. The postage stamp shows it was mailed from Mexico City.

I tell myself it must be junk, despite the handwritten lettering. I tear the flap open and pull out what's inside. A booklet of some sort. A letter is attached to the front cover:

Dearest Terra (whose name means earth),

First and foremost, I'm sorry for not playing fair all those years ago in the quiet room with our secrets game. How I wish I still had a magical ring that could time-travel me back because I would do things a lot differently.

*If you still have interest in knowing my secret, you may be pleased
to learn one of my future story ideas, that of a young boy who lives
in a wilderness community with twenty-one members he calls his
kindred family. One day, having seen where the elders hide the
community's stash of money, the boy becomes overpowered by that
evil villain Greed. When the elders discover a sum of money is
missing from the stash, they blame the boy's blood-sister who'd
already garnered herself quite a reputation for mischief-making.
Fearful for himself, the boy does not correct the elders' error. When
he wakes up the following day, he discovers his sister is no longer
there. Three strikes out, is all Chief Elder has to say by way of an
explanation. The kindred family has no room for liars and thieves.
The boy must live the rest of his life haunted by the mystery of
what happened to his blood-sister and the part he played in her
absence. His days will be consumed with stories he makes up to
fill in the blanks. These stories torment him, so much so that he
resorts to living in a fantasy world, one that protects him from his
thoughts.*

*Dearest Terra, how I would love to know what you think of this
woeful tale. But unfortunately, I'll have to imagine your response
as our story has come to an end. You, my brave heroine, managed to
climb out of a hole, face the villain, and still run free, having learned
a lesson. Well done. However, I must confess, though it would have
defied the archetype of hero, I'm sad, in this case, the villain didn't
win because it means we'll no longer be spinning tales together. I'll
miss that probably more than you'll ever know.*

*The one consolation is that now that I know the ending of our story
I can write about it. In the meantime, I thought you might like to
have this one for your shelves.*

Your friend forever,
C

My heart breaks as I imagine a younger Charley living with the guilt of a lie he told, a secret he kept, and a truth he might never know.

It's no wonder we found each other.

It's no surprise we got lost in each other either.

I pull his letter from the booklet, revealing a picture of William, the troll-like character from the Wishy Water Well. I flip through the booklet pages. It isn't an illustrated copy, but it seems the story's all here: *The Forest Girl and the Wishy Water Well.*

My insides crawl.

I recheck the door. Locked. Bolted.

The house alarm has been set.

I take a deep breath and count to twenty, trying to piece together what all of this means. Obviously, I'm the heroine. Obviously, Charley, the villain, has fled to Mexico (or so he'd like me to believe). And perhaps, a little less obviously, he isn't going to come hunting for me again. Our story has ended.

I'm safe.

For now.

At the very least.

Epilogue

The Forest Girl and the Wishy Water Well

Once upon a time, there was a girl named Clara who lived on a farm, and every morning before school, Clara tended to her animals. She fed the chickens and cows fresh corn and grain. She gave the pigs and goats table scraps from breakfast. The pigs, especially, loved cereal and eggs. The goats favored the pumpernickel bread.

Before she left for school, Clara sang cock-a-doodle ditties with Rudy, the rooster. She also played fetch with her farm dog, Mugford. Clara loved her animals, and they loved her just as much.

When it was time for Clara's lessons, she grabbed her bag and walked three blocks to the Fox Run School. She sat in a classroom with fifteen other children of varying ages. One day, a group of girls pushed their desks together, toward the back of the room. Clara noticed that all the girls wore the same sparkling gold headbands. They also held matching red envelopes. Clara remained at the front of the room, looking on to see what was inside the envelopes.

"What could it be?" asked Meredith, tearing her envelope

open. Inside it was a card. The words *You're Invited* were printed across the top. "What fun!" said Meredith. "I can hardly wait!"

All the girls in Mrs. Tuttle's class were invited to Sarabeth's twelfth birthday party—all except Clara.

Later, at recess, Clara remained hopeful that she too would get an invitation. While the group of girls played hopscotch and jump rope, Clara stood on the sidelines, awaiting a turn, but no turn ever came. When the bell rang, indicating the end of recess, all the other children rushed back inside the school, but Clara remained outside, drawing farm animals on a boulder with a piece of chalk, doubtful that anyone would notice her absence.

As the hour ticked by, the sun drifted behind a cloud and the air became chilled, forming gooseflesh over her arms. Clara began to weep, saddened that no one inside the schoolhouse had come out to look for her.

"Don't be sad," a squeaky voice announced. "It's better out here."

"Who's talking?" Clara asked. She looked all around.

There was no one else in the schoolyard—unless one counted the butterflies, the bumblebees, and the chalk-drawn animals. Was it possible the voice had come from one of them?

"Good guess," the squeaky voice said as though reading her mind. "But try again."

Clara hopped off the rock and peeked just behind it. There, she saw a tiny orange man wearing a green-and-white-striped suit, a black top hat, and a pair of shiny black shoes.

The man was truly tiny, no taller than a sand pail, and no wider than its shovel. Clara scooted down to get a better look. The tiny man's eyes were his biggest feature, taking up most of his scrunched face. He extended his hand for a shake. Clara gripped it between her thumb and index finger.

"And who are you?" she asked.

"My name is William. I'm the minder of the Wishy Water Well." The tiny orange man gave his long white beard a mighty tug.

"Well, hello there, William. It's nice to meet you. My name is Clara."

"Clara . . . what a beautiful name. Did you know that it means *light*?"

"Why, no. I didn't. You must be very smart."

"I am." The tiny man giggled. "But I didn't get my smarts from going to schoolhouses like this one. I've learned all I need to know from life's experiences, and I've certainly had a lot of them. You probably would never guess this, but I'm one hundred twenty-two years old."

"You're lying to me now," Clara said. "No one is that old."

"You'll learn soon enough. I'm not like other people."

"Well, I suppose not," Clara said, noting his tiny shoes the size of shelled peanuts and his even tinier nose, like an ice scream sprinkle. "How did you get to be so old?"

"It's a long story—a very, very long one, indeed—but I'd be happy to share it. Let's you and I make a deal. You tell me your secret, and I'll tell you mine."

"My secret?"

"Yes, the reason you were so sad just now. If you tell me that, I'll reveal how I got to be this ripe old age. Do we have ourselves a deal?"

"Yes, I believe we do." Clara's face brightened. "I was sad just now because I wasn't invited to Sarabeth's twelfth birthday party, and all the other schoolgirls were."

"Good grief. I can't believe such a thing! It's such a pity, and I'll bet that party would have been so much fun." William balled up his fists and kicked a rock in frustration.

"I just feel so excluded sometimes," Clara said.

"No doubt you do, dear girl-whose-name-means-*light*. But if you let me, I think I might be able to help."

"How?" Clara asked, desperate to know. "Oh, but wait. Weren't you going to tell me your secret? How did you get to be such a ripe old age?"

"All in good time, my dear oh dear. First, let us take a walk." William led Clara away from the Fox Run School into the wooded area behind it. They walked and walked for several minutes, along a path bordered by willow trees and butterfly bushes. Eventually, William stopped at a log. He set a kerchief down and crawled on top of it so as not to dirty his handsome striped pants. The pair sat facing one another, surrounded by flowering cherry blossoms and lilac bushes. Pretty yellow finches flew above their heads, eager to feast on a patch of wild lavender.

"So, let me tell you all about the Wishy Water Well," William said.

Clara squealed with delight. "I'd love to know all about it."

"It's a magical place indeed," said William. "If you drop three coins into the well, you will be granted your wish. You can have anything your heart desires."

Clara clasped her hands together at the mere idea of such a wondrous well. "Anything at all?"

"Of course," said William. "How do you suppose I got to be such a dear old man?"

"Where is this well?" asked Clara. "Can anyone use it?"

"Anyone who finds it can use it," William said. "But finding it isn't an easy feat. The forest keeps the well nicely hidden to protect it from those with ill intentions."

"What kind of ill intentions?"

"Well, unfortunately, I'm sure you can imagine . . . not everyone desires a well-intentioned return. People can be quite selfish and sly. For example, there was once a stickly woman who no longer wanted to care for her ailing husband. She wished him gone so that she could have what she believed would be a more fanciful life."

"How awful." Clara gasped.

"Yes, it was indeed. But still the stickly woman dropped her three coins into the well and made that woeful wish. That very night, her husband passed in his sleep, and the stickly woman danced around the bedroom with delight."

"Oh, my goodness. How dreadful," Clara said.

William smirked, raising one eyebrow upward. "Yes and no. You see, just because the stickly woman's husband's body had been ailing doesn't mean his mind had been ailing too. You see, he too had visited the well, days before, unbeknownst to his wife. Despite pain, muscle weakness, and a very high fever, he made the trek to the woods to search for the well, following directions he'd found in his wife's recipe book. When at long last he found the magical well, he tossed in his coins and made his wish."

"What was his wish?" Clara asked.

"Eternal life."

Clara frowned. "But he died soon after. Isn't that what you said?"

"Fear not." William smiled. "The ailing man indeed got his wish. He died and was reborn into the charming gent you see before your eyes."

"You?" Clara gasped.

"That's right. Shortly after I was laid in my casket, I awoke to find I'd shrunken in size. No one else was around, but a contract lay at my feet, explaining that because my wish had counteracted my wife's, I'd be given eternal life, but it would come with a price."

"What kind of price?"

"I was to become the minder of the wondrous Wishy Water Well, which to me was far more of a privilege than a price."

"Wow," Clara said. "That's quite an honor. And what do you do as a minder?"

"I collect the wishful coins and manage the overall operations of the well."

"That sounds so mystical."

"As I said, it's a privilege. Now, what do you say we take a hike out to find this wondrous well. I heartily think we've jibber-jabbered here enough. Wouldn't you like to have your wish, what you so desire?"

"Oh, I really, really would."

"Well, then, shall we?" William extended his tiny hand to Clara to help her off the log, then led her farther into the enchanting wood to find the wondrous water well.

Along the way, they passed through a grove of flowering cherry blossoms, as well as an alcove of blooming crab apple trees.

"It's deliciously beautiful here," Clara said.

"Indeed, it is," William agreed, "one of the most enchanting places on Earth."

They continued their trek, following a winding creek and circling a frog pond. They also picked bunches of lilacs, tasted the sweetest of wild raspberries, and danced over water-tumbled stepping-stones. Eventually, they came to a cluster of berry bushes.

William turned to face Clara; a wide grin crossed his scrunched-up face. "Here it is, oh, girl-whose-name-means-*light*. Welcome to the wondrous Wishy Water Well."

Clara looked all around—behind the tiny man, toward the bushes, and beneath the shrubs—unable to see any hint of a water well. "But where is it?" Her face scrunched up too.

"Come," William said, leading her a little farther. He parted the bushes, exposing the redbrick walls of the well.

Clara came closer and ran her fingers over the tracks of cement—slowly, carefully—as though touching a sacred altar.

"Have you never seen a water well?" William asked curiously.

"I have," Clara said. "But this one is magical."

"Indeed, it is," he chirped. "Now, are you ready to make your wish?"

Clara reached deep into her pocket and pulled out three shiny silver coins. "And nothing bad will happen once I make my wish, right?"

"Whatever do you mean?"

"I mean, are there any negative consequences?"

William scratched his head, considering the question a moment. "There are indeed consequences to any thought or action, wouldn't you agree?"

"I suppose," Clara said. "But what does that mean as far as wishes and wells?"

William grinned. "You're a very smart girl—too smart, in fact, for that Fox Run School. There is most certainly a consequence, but it's a small price, if you ask me, for achieving what you so desire."

"And what is that price?" Clara asked.

"For every wish the well grants, you shall lose one day of your life."

"Oh my," Clara said, clasping over her mouth.

"But think of it this way," William said. "How long do you plan to live? Seventy years? Eighty? Maybe even over a hundred. Subtract one day from whatever that number is— one less day to have your most desired wish granted."

"You do have a point." Clara peeked inside the well, surprised to find that it didn't look magical at all. It was just a long, dark tunnel that burrowed down at least twenty feet. "But there are no coins down there," Clara said.

"Because I've collected them all. That's my job, remember?"

"Oh yes, that's right." She smiled.

"So, do we have a deal?"

"We do." She clasped her hands together in joyful anticipation.

"Very well, then," William said. "Whenever you're ready, just close your eyes, make your wish, and toss the coins into the well."

Clara clenched the coins in her palm. "Shall I say my wish out loud?"

"Don't you know the rule of wishing wells?" William teased. "You're not allowed to tell anyone your wish, lest you risk it not coming true."

"Very well, then." Clara closed her eyes and said her wish inside her head. *I want to get invited to Sarabeth's twelfth birthday party,* she thought. After that, Clara tossed her coins into the Wishy Water Well.

The following day at the Fox Run School, Clara found a bright red envelope sitting on her desk. With it was a sparkling gold headband, just like the kind that Sarabeth and the other girls wore.

"How pretty," Clara said, peering out the window, where the group of girls was playing a game of hopscotch. Clara tore the envelope open, elated to have received an invitation to Sarabeth's birthday party at long last. "I can hardly believe it!" she exclaimed, beyond grateful for William's help.

That Saturday afternoon, Clara enjoyed herself at Sarabeth's party. The group of girls played lots of games, including Memory Match, hide-and-seek, and Pin the Tail on the Garden Gnome. They drank pink lemonade from curly straws, ate barbecued spareribs with sweet and sour sauce, followed by chocolate cake with fresh strawberries and vanilla ice cream. Sarabeth made a wish and blew out her candles, and the girls watched in awe as the smoke tendrils spun into pinwheels and floated up toward the clouds.

"Thank you so much for inviting me," Clara told Sarabeth when it was time to go home.

"You're most welcome. I'm dreadfully sorry your invitation wasn't delivered with the others. It had gotten lost at the bottom of my bag."

Clara hid her surprise with a cheerful grin, but deep down she wondered if Sarabeth had been telling the truth about the invitation. Had it truly gotten lost? Had she not needed William's help, after all? Still, she didn't let it bother her much. She simply went about the rest of her day, at home, on the farm.

The following afternoon, after Clara had finished feeding her animals, she took a hike to the rambling river, reminiscing about her time in the woods with William . . . seeing the pretty cherry blossoms and tasting the sweet wild raspberries.

As if by fate, William appeared at the river, sitting on a log, on his kerchief of a blanket. "Why, hello," he said. "I was just going to come looking for you."

"How delightful," Clara said. "And *I* was just about to say that it's funny meeting you here."

"Not so funny at all, in fact." William leered. "You see, today is a very important day for you, oh dear Clara, whose name means *light*."

"More important than yesterday or the day before that?" Clara asked.

"Well, every day is important, indeed," William said. "But, yes, I'd say that today holds a bit more weight."

"And why is that?" Clara smiled.

"Come and I'll show you." He popped up from his seat

and led Clara to the edge of Spider Hill, where one could see all of the villages and valleys beneath.

"It's breathtaking," Clara said, taking care to stay at least a foot from the edge. "But I still don't understand. Why is today more important than tomorrow or yesterday?"

"Because today is the day that you are going to die. You were fated to die tomorrow, but recall that because you made your wish at the wondrous Wishy Water Well, you lose one day. That means today is it."

Clara could not believe what William was saying. "That doesn't make any sense. I'm not ill. How would I ever die? That's the most absurd thing I've ever heard."

"I promise you," said William, "I would never joke about death. Recall that I nearly died of illness myself."

"Then how shall I die? Tell me that."

"I shall show you now."

And so it was: the tiny orange man with the green-and-white-striped suit and the scrunched-up face inhaled a deep and powerful breath, then blew it out: a wind so fierce it knocked poor Clara over the side of Spider Hill.

Down.

Down.

Down.

Down Clara fell, because she made a wish at the magical water well.

Acknowledgments

Many, many thanks to the talented team at Wednesday Books (Cathy Turiano, Beatrice Jason, Sara Goodman, Melanie Sanders, Brant Janeway, Sarah Bonamino, Anna Gorovoy, DJ DeSmyter, Alexis Neuville). It's been such a pleasure working with all of you. A special thanks to my editor, Tiffany Shelton, for her critical questions and insightful perspective, and to Kerri Resnick for designing a stunning cover.

Thanks to my agent, Kathy Green, for always being there to provide literary guidance (as well as for when I want to chat about reality TV).

A special thanks to friends and family members who read pieces and/or drafts of *The Last Secret You'll Ever Keep*, and/or who indulged me in conversations related to its characters and plot strands: Shawn, Ed, Julianna, Emily, Kathy, Susan, Shari, Cat, Sara, and Robin. I'm forever grateful for your time, feedback, and generous support.

Thanks to all the teachers, librarians, bloggers, vloggers, book club members, and readers who read and shared *Jane Anonymous,* the companion novel to *The Last Secret You'll Ever Keep*. I really appreciate the role you play in promoting reading, authors, and a sense of literary community.

And, last, huge thanks go to my readers, who continue to support me by reading my work and sharing it with others, who reach out with kindness, gratitude, and (so often) perfectly timed words of encouragement and support. I've loved being on this journey with you.